Friends Who Move Couches

Almost a Memoir

A novel by

CJ Zahner

Author of:
The Suicide Gene
Dream Wide Awake
Project Dream

This is a work of fiction. The names, characters, places, programs, projects, and incidents are either a product of the author's imagination or are used fictitiously, and any resemblance to actual persons living or dead, business establishments, events, locales is entirely coincidental.

Friends Who Move Couches
COPYRIGHT© 2020 CJ Zahner

For information contact Cyndie Zahner
www.cyndiezahner.com

Published 2020
Printed in the United States of America
Print ISBN: 978-1-7332391-1-0
First Printing, 2020
www.cjzahner.com

Dedication

For Jeff,
who held me every day for eleven months when I cried over friendship. But for that beautiful October day in 1981, I could be Nikki Grey.

For the relentless support of my daughters **Jessie and Jilly** (who have my back, always) and my son **Zak** (who golfs off rooftops).

For **Layla Grace** who, in month twelve, whisked me out of self-pity and thrust me into the world of grandparenting.

And for my **friends who move bodies:**
Carol, Carolyn, Cyndi, Debbe, Heather, Jan, Karen, Laura, Linda, LeAnn, Mary, Nancy, Rana, Robin, Rosanne, Roselle, Teresa, and, yes, Jody and Val.

I love you all.

Chapter 1 The mistake

"We get nudged back onto our life's intended path, no matter which way we turn." - CJ Zahner in a moment of inept optimism.

Two of the three women who have helped me hold my head above water for the past twenty years lounge on either side of me like two pin-pricked swimmies.

Neither of them realizes I'm sinking.

"Brittany is too good for Jax," one says.

My gaze fixes on the ground beneath six weeping arborvitaes that stretch their withering brown branches in every direction of one corner of my back yard. Inside my head, I stop hearing Jody's and Ellie's frivolous chatter about good girls who like bad boys and swear at myself for planting the can't-see-you barrier between me and the neighbor who has turned my life upside-down.

I hate her. I love her. She's ruined my life—and my yard.

Unlike the tailored suburban yards that line my street, mine busts at the seams with kinks. A swarm of sneaker imprints laughs at me from that large mucky patch of mud, which is sandwiched between the dying arborvitaes and my crystal-clear pool. There, a sludge so deep we've lost shoes in it usurps sun—to no drying avail.

My friends sit oblivious to my distraction.

They sip wine, Jody and Ellie, engrossed in a deeply-philosophical conversation about *Vanderpump Rules*. When

once we discussed careers and politics, now we argue reality TV and detergents.

I sigh.

Our life goals have plummeted.

"I'll say this," Jody asserts. "She has a mind of her own."

In post-college, pre-nuptial days, we vowed to change the world. But marriages, pregnancies, and seven kids removed us from the corporate world and catapulted us into play dates, health-club kiddie classes, and heavy drink on the last day of every school year.

This last vice is where we are now. All of us are a little tipsy, but none of us is slurring our words—yet. The afternoon is early. We have three hours before the kids leave academics behind and rambunctiously arrive home to spend every hour of the entire summer threatening our sanity.

"Reah said she was in the Miss America pageant," Ellie says. They've blathered on to *The Bachelorette*. "That goes against every grain of my being."

"Used to," I chirp. Mainly so they remember it's my wine they're drinking. Up until now, I've been removed from their conversation.

"What do you mean used to?" Ellie straightens in her seat.

"You took your ten-year-old for a pedicure yesterday," I remind her. "That almost makes you a stage mom."

"Okay, Mrs. Better-than-me, didn't you just buy pom-poms for Gianna?"

"She's eleven. You can't enroll an eleven-year-old in basketball when she wants to play with dolls and hammer out cheers."

"You promised. You said if we had girls, they'd play basketball and run track and do anything but cheerlead." Ellie states the truth. I had promised.

"Yeah, well, I said a lot of things before I was forced to tote three screaming kids into a store to pick up tampons and pain meds. An excursion like that thrusts life into proper perspective."

"They're in middle, high school, and college now. You should be over that."

"I suffer PTSD from those trips."

"Not to mention your kids' damage," Ellie quips.

Jody will chime in now. She is our voice of reason.

"Our lives aren't so bad," she says.

Predictability comes with aged friendship. And just like I know Jody, I know Ellie. She'll counter.

"She made the conscious choice to quit and be a stay-at-home-and-drink mommy." Ellie gulps down wine and makes a thirst-quenching hissing sound as if that dig was her best yet. And it could be.

"I work," I counter.

"Part-time doesn't count. Plus, you're done for the summer."

True. I have summers off. I work two days a week during the school year in the personnel department at the Fairview School District administration building. The job bores me as much as sorting a laundry basket of baby socks.

The week I quit my challenging, full-time, real-world job I took my oldest child, Delanie, to a Mommy and Me class at the YMCA. I'd spent three years wearied by working-mom guilt, wishing I could sign up for that class. Then when I left corporate America behind and enrolled, seven of us mothers and eight children lined up, held hands, broke into a middle-ear shattering *Ring Around the Rosy*, and I thought, "Oh my God, what have I done?"

I turn toward Ellie. "I deluded myself into thinking stay-at-home moms had it all."

Our children grew like wisteria, fast and clingy, their idiosyncrasies as showy as a mud-caked communion dress—which, of course, Delanie wore down the center aisle of Our Lady of Peace Church one bright May afternoon. How four years later she signed up for cheerleading I blame on her father's side of the family. They knit, sew, you know, do all that domestic stuff like cook.

Now her little sister sports pom-poms, too—bright pink and white ones—with sparkles.

I must also admit, mention rather, I have a son—a high-spirited boy. He drove his friends around the neighborhood in his father's Jeep when he was fifteen. Teed up—from the rooftop of our house—and knocked a golf ball into the bay window of the house across the street at thirteen. And tossed a stone through the front window of a bus in grade school.

Neighbors refer to him as go-home Hux.

Huxley is the mischievous nucleus of my future nursing-home selectors. He rounds out my loud, lively, bullying threesome. Together they represent the type of kids I don't want my kids to hang around with. Kids—I never say this out loud—who inevitably are going to disappoint their parents. No doctor, no lawyer, no CEO.

How do I know? I see the signs. I, myself, experienced the same fall from dream.

Raised in a small town and educated in both a high school and college that bragged of scant student numbers, for years I was led to believe I had a special purpose in life. When I realized I was as plain and dull as unbuttered white toast, I shifted my dreams to my children.

God, in His infinite wisdom, allowed my husband to earn a great living, so I could dedicate my time to raising our kids. I expected my due through parental praise. Isn't that what every classical book like, I don't know, the *Grapes of Wrath,* was really about? Contributing our small part to enhance history? Learn from our mistakes and make life better for the next generation?

Somewhere between the tampon run and the stained communion dress, I realized my kids' places in the world were as infinitesimally small as mine.

I shifted my goals.

Instead of recording dreams in a diary hidden upstairs in the bed stand, I scribbled hopes in chalk on the sidewalk below a Freudian slip—Mother Hubbard has no cupboard. I stopped fantasizing that my kids wouldn't bully others, miss curfew, or drink before they blew out twenty-one candles, and refocused on getting them through high school without getting pregnant and through college without being arrested.

A report card with changed grades, a week's suspension for a drinking binge on the beach, and two trips to the District Justice later, I abandoned those hopes and, after a mysterious leak in the pool, which the kids knew nothing about, I secretly painted more realistic expectations on my basement wall with a brush and waterproof sealant that disappeared into the cement blocks, so I couldn't be held accountable.

Several cliff-hangers later, even the unseen cellar goals seemed lofty.

"Remember how badly you wanted kids?" Ellie interrupts my thoughts. "More than Jody and me. You insisted on raising them yourself, though you earned enough to hire that slutty little slip of a girl Reah hired—what's her name?"

"Ashley Schlabach and she's not slutty. She's a very nice girl," Jody defends, because she's tired of women disparaging her twenty-something next-door neighbor who's movie-star pretty.

"Right Shlutty Schlabach—she's a great nanny. You just don't want her lurking around your husband or son or any other guy over the age of—twelve."

I ignore the Ashley innuendos. I'm not pedaling as fast today. My mind lingers on the how-badly-I-wanted-kids accusation.

"Guilty. I wanted to quit and raise my kids myself." I'm not saying this for Ellie's benefit. I'm reminding myself— that I'm drinking my wine. "I didn't think it would be so lonely."

"Lonely? Are you kidding? You have a million friends. You're never home."

"I like being busy."

"You've signed up for every activity within a fifty-mile radius."

"I have not."

"Really? What have you said no to lately?"

"Golf."

"That's because you stink at it. You throw a golf club father than you hit a ball."

I screw up my lips and sigh. I'm the worst golfer I know. My husband loves it. He signed us up for private lessons. I feign headaches, cramps, or appendicitis on lesson days.

"Plus, you hate golf because of Mark," she adds. "We all secretly hate our husbands' first loves. Doesn't count. Name something else."

"Well." I think about this. Try to garner a defense. I'm signed up to work at the neighborhood kids party with Reah, participate in a running clinic with my friend Carol, a beach-glass class with college-friend Karen, a walking club on Tuesday and Thursday with high-school girlfriends Mary and Carolyn. I can't recall a single invitation I've turned down other than the golf lessons.

"I'm not in the book club," I say, sarcastically.

This is a sore spot between Ellie and me because Ellie remains in the neighborhood book club that I no longer receive emails and invites for.

Her face goes blank. That was a shot to the chest. Ellie feels guilty for staying in the club without me, but it's not her fault I was ousted. I'd written my own ending. Immediately, my Catholic guilt rides in. I backpedal. "But you're right. I'm in over my head. Too much to do. My life is out of control." "Mine too." She bites. I've thrown her a shovel, and she's digging her way out of the mucky book-club dilemma. "When did life become so complicated? My kids are going to drive me to drink," she says. "Wait, they've already done that."

She pours more wine into her glass, and we drown ourselves in the whose-kid-is-worse comradery we stoke every year on our annual last-day-of-school wine parley.

"Your kids? The next time Hux knocks a ball through Mr. Gorney's window, I'm jumping off a cliff." Replacing one of Mr. Gorney's windows due to Hux's wild swing of a club is not a will-it-happen question. It's a when question. He's inherited my golf skills. "I'm not sure if it will be the girls or Hux who kill me."

I gulp down wine.

"Our kids are fine and our lives aren't bad," the grounded, not-out-on-a-ledge Jody contends.

Jody works part-time for a consulting firm. She teaches teachers how to teach. She's a brilliant, tiny soul who never raises her voice. She stands a hair above five feet, has short brown hair, never wears makeup, and tips the scale at one hundred pounds. She's perfect in every way. People love her. How I am lucky enough to call her my friend is beyond me.

I've been blessed throughout my life with many friendships. But friends are like diamonds, you're not sure if they're precious until you look deep inside them.

Jody is a gem. One-of-a-kind.

Suddenly, I realize I'm staring at those dying arborvitaes again. I force myself to sever my locked leer and refocus on the moment. Oddly, what hits me first are the little lines surrounding Jody's eyes. The same lines I saw in this morning's mirror. I glance at Ellie. They're on her, too. "Not bad compared to a root canal without Novocain," I respond half-consciously.

"Well, think of it this way," positive Jody says. "You could be Brittany marrying Jax, or you could be Lisa Vanderpump."

And with that, a ray of hope surfaces. I snap out of my stupor and take a breath, marvel at how low even Jody has fallen. Ellie has somehow sucked her into our entangled reality-TV web.

If ten years ago, someone told me Jody Cancilla would watch reality TV, I would have said Hillary Clinton was more likely to be Monica Lewinski's matron of honor. Jody had so much common sense she made Dr. Phil look like a bald Charles Manson.

"Lisa Vanderpump," Ellie yells. "Are you kidding? She has it all."

"She's suffering post-traumatic stress," Jody asserts. Her life evaluating skills have resurfaced.

"From what?" Ellie's appalled. "Todd's hair implants?"

"Todd did not have implants." I can't believe Jody is debating this.

"He did so." I expect this arguing from Ellie, however. "They transplanted hair from Giggy."

Now Jody leans and laughs hysterically. Tears streak her face. I laugh because I love when grounded Jody loses it over one of our hideously stupid remarks. It's as if she's human.

"Careful. Lisa's a dog lover," she finally manages.

"Well, something has her Spanx in a knot," Ellie counters.

"Nikki," Jody says, drawing me back into the conversation. She may have noticed my arborvitae stare. "Are your kids around when you watch *Vanderpump Rules*? I'm starting to feel guilty about watching that show."

Jody always shepherds me back. Ever since my epilepsy diagnosis, she watches me like a guard on a jewel. She's my keeper.

"Yes, they're around."

If I were at a table sipping wine with anyone other than Jody and Ellie, I would have lied. "Oh my God, no," I'd say. "Expose my children to such lewdness? Never."

It's nice having flawed friends you don't have to lie to.

"Me, too." She inches forward in her chair, spreads both forearms onto the table, and folds her fingers together. I'm pretty sure she's drunk. She's the lightweight drinker of the crew. "I feel like it's bad parenting."

"Reah says they hear worse in high school," I say. "Where is she, by the way?"

"Probably pouting over your new car." Ellie has a way of pointing out our gang's most inner secrets. "You know how she is."

"Really? My car?"

"Don't let her bother you. She'll get over it. She always does." Jody pats my arm to grab my attention. "And I'm serious. Do you feel guilty that our kids hear the f-word all the time on reality TV? How do you think that will affect them?"

"Who the fuck cares?" We hear footsteps, and in walks Val. The dynamics of our little afternoon brood-fest is about to change.

Val is a new friend—as in we have only known her seven years. She lives two streets over. She's not in the book club. Val hasn't read a book since she discovered crib notes.

She enters through the side gate carrying a bag—which is never good.

"Whatcha got there?" My curiosity springs first.

She dashes toward us as if she's evacuating a crime scene, but this is normal moves-like-an-ostrich Val. Even when she sits, her arms flail and her knees rock. Attention deficit at its finest.

"You'll be happy to know I confiscated this little gem from a stray bookbag in Deidra's room."

We all stand. We know it can't be good. Deidra is Val's clone. Karma is a nasty evil. Val extracts a pipe and a bag of marijuana from the knapsack. "Want to have some fun?"

"What's this?" The screen door to my house squeaks open, and out struts Everett. He's carrying a sheet of white notebook paper.

"I swear you two lease a car together." Ellie is referring to Val and Everett, who enter within minutes of each other at every social event they grace their presence with.

Though they aren't related by blood, I call Evy and Val the suburban twins. They were born on the same gloomy day in the turbulent 1970s. Both stand at five feet nine inches with dirty-blond hair; Evy's is cut close to his head, Val's, straight to her shoulders. Evy serves as our group's conscience. Val inspires our fun.

Ellie plops back down into her chair. "If Everett wasn't gay, I'd swear you two were having an affair."

Everett doesn't hear her. He's on a mission. He makes a beeline for me and shoves the paper in my face.

"Darling, what could this possibly be?"

"My happy list," I say with the enthusiasm of a toad.

"Your what?" Everett swoops a hand on the side of his face as if he doesn't know I've been depressed for years.

"My happy list. Ellie said I should keep one when I'm feeling blue. Write down the good things I have in my life."

His glance goes to Ellie. Then back to me. He rips the paper in half.

"Never let that shrew talk you into feeling better about yourself. You're as low and sad as the rest of us. Don't go digging yourself out of a hole on the last day of school. We need you and that great big your-pee-will-turn-blue cesspool you own." He picks up the bottle of wine in the middle of the patio table, turns it to read the label. "Or at least we need your wine. This is a forty-dollar bottle, girl."

He grabs a stemmed glass, pours, swirls, and drinks.

I wait designedly, then I say, "Janice Everglade dropped it off last weekend."

Janice Everglade's house sports a marriage-is-between-a-man-and-a-woman banner.

He spits the entire contents of his mouth over the table. Red wine spritzes all three of our shirts. I stand and shake my arms. Ellie squeals. Jody laughs.

"I was kidding, you nitwit," I holler.

"Oh, well then." He pours again, drinks, and takes a seat under the sunny edge of our table's umbrella.

"You ruined my shirt." Ellie tosses her poker-straight, black hair over her shoulders and inspects herself. "My favorite one."

"Oh, darling, the dime store has a ton of them. Maybe you should consider one size up when you replace it." Evy says this to ruffle Ellie's weight-consciousness. She's tiny. Sometimes Val and I feel like giants next to Jody and Ellie.

Ellie shrieks but no one pays attention to her because our eyes are glued to Val. She stuffs the pipe and lights up.

"When is Marky coming home?" Val inhales deeply.

Our afternoon picnic has turned into a free-for-all.

"He works late tonight, and you know he hates when you call him Marky."

"Shouldn't you be asking when Delanie gets home?" Jody adds a pinch of logic into our last-day-of-school ballyhoo.

"She's right. The kids will be home soon." Everett scoots forward in his chair. "Let's hurry."

And just like that, Val infects us.

An hour later, we are stoned. This is a first for the last day of school. Up until this year, we'd stuck to wine. But today our parenting skills have fallen so far below sea-level we can't see land. We giggle as if Val had pulled the fire alarm at the wastewater treatment plant—a Huxley inspired thought—and we're secretly reaping the benefits of a canceled tour.

When we finish the marijuana, we resort back to our wine. My stomach turns. My head aches. But everything is so hysterically funny that I laugh until I can barely breathe.

I don't realize I'm not feeling well. I toss one arm around Ellie and the other around Jody and tug them close.

"I love you guys. But where is Reah? I wish she were here."

Life is never good when I become sentimental or contemplative. I squeeze my mouth into a pout and release the stronghold I have on the two of them. My bracelet gets tangled in the lace of Ellie's shirt. We try to dislodge it carefully but can't. Val leans over and rips us apart. My bangle breaks. Ellie's shirt rips.

"That was uncalled for," Ellie scolds, but she's laughing. Black streaks cascade down her cheeks.

I dab the corner of one eye and examine my finger: black.

"Do I look like her?" I ask Jody. "Raccoon faced?"

"Darling, you do. You truly do," Everett interrupts, then I feel Jody's hand on my shoulder.

"Are you feeling okay?" Jody's peculiar expression makes me laugh so hard I snort.

"She's pouting because Reah has dissed her," Ellie says.

"Why has Reah dissed me?"

"Your new car," she reminds me.

"It's not your new car." Evy wiggles annoyedly, facing his backside to Ellie. "Reah's been jealous of you for years."

"Why?" I ask.

"You've got that whole Reese Witherspoon thing going on."

"I have what?"

"Look in the mirror. Blonde hair, blue eyes, wide mouth, charmingly senseless. You're a skinny Reese Witherspoon. Reah hates it. She'd give thirty years of her life to change places with you."

"I have a wide mouth?" I place my hands on both sides of my face.

"That's all you got from that?" Evy shakes his head.

"No." I drop my hands in my lap. "I'm trying not to feel bad because Reah dissed me."

"Girl," Everett whines. "You rely on friends like ticks on deer. When are you going to stand on your own? You don't need anyone. Not me, Ellie, and for sure you don't need two-faced Reah. You're lignum vitae."

"I'm what?"

Instantaneously, everyone roars. Val bursts into a spitting laugh. Wine spritzes across the table out her mouth and nose.

"That had to sting." Evy grimaces.

"Where did you come up with lignum vitae?" Val's eyebrows arch. Her mouth rounds. She looks like a cartoon character.

All I can do is laugh.

"It's wood, you ninny." Evy pours more wine in his glass. "The hardest wood in the world."

"Crossword puzzle?" Jody asks.

"You know it, girl." Evy can do a crossword puzzle faster than Ellie can spill a secret. That's lightning fast.

"Name a softwood," I say. "If I were wood, I'd be soft."

Evy strokes his chin, pondering.

Ellie's hand shoots up, and she blurts out the answer proudly, like a student to a teacher. "She's pine."

"Basswood is softer," he responds. "It's like you, Ellie, soft and pliable. Easily bent."

She lowers her hand. "What's that supposed to mean?"

"It means you're a Chamaeleo Calyptratus, darling, a Furcifer Pardalis, a Rieppeleon Brevicaudatus—oh wait, that's your husband."

Now we all snort wine out our noses.

"Is he calling me a chameleon?" Ellie asks Val, and all of us use our outdoor laughs, try to hoot the loudest to prove we understand Evy, who is much smarter than us.

"Nikki," Jody shouts above our peals. "Are you sure you're feeling okay?"

"I'm good," I say, even though I'm fairly certain I'm not. "You worry too much. I haven't had a stare-away in years—since the new medication."

The din quiets.

"That you weaned yourself off a year ago," she rebukes.

"Has it been that long?" I pretend not to remember.

Jody keeps my medical records. She's like a medical alert necklace that goes off on its own.

"What time is it?" I change the subject. "You guys told your kids to come here after school, right? To swim?"

"No," Val replies. "To eat pizza and smoke weed. That's the only reason my kids will show up."

This reminds me we must rid ourselves of every last particle of the pot before the kids arrive. "We have to smoke everything. Destroy the evidence."

"Calm yourself down, darling. It's long gone. We smoked the last of it a half-hour ago." Everett uncorks another bottle of wine. "Tossed everything in the trash."

An unusual quiet hits us. Evy wrinkles his nose and sniffs. We all glance at the corner of the yard at the same time as if we've had an epiphany when, really, we just smelled dope. The trash bin sits below a faint grey cloud of smoke. My golden retriever, Furgy, slices our quiet in half with a shrieking bark.

Jody, the culprit, sinks into her shoulders.

"You weasel," Everett says. He hasn't a care in the world about my smoking trash or the smell of marijuana permeating the neighborhood. He thinks only of the waste. "I said I'd finish that for you."

"You'd had enough. We all did. Ellie's face is black, Nikki's is as white as an egg, and your pupils are grossly dilated," Jody tells him.

She's right on all counts. Ellie's raccoon face has cemented on her skin, I don't feel well, and Evy's green eyes look like two plump olives with gigantic pits.

I break into another unbecoming, belly-jiggling laugh. Furgy barks more aggressively. But not at the trash. She's woofing at me. I try to pat her head, but she's jumping around uncontrollably.

"Nikki, you look awful," Jody adds.

"Of course, she does." Val tips her glass in the air. "Her kids are spending the next twelve weeks with her. Marky's never home. She's a washed-up CFO who can't balance her checking account."

"Stop calling him Marky, and I can balance my checkbook," I say, fanning myself. "I just don't have the time."

I laugh, fan faster. The sun is so blazing hot I start sweating. The insane dog keeps barking. She's an inch from my ankle. If she wasn't the best dog in the world, I'd think she was about to bite me.

No one else pays her any mind.

"Maybe you should hydrate." Jody waves a hand to Everett. "Did you say you were getting chips? Grab water for Nikki."

"You're right. I'm famished," he realizes and scurries toward the house.

Ellie, Val, and I holler requests. "Chips." "Popcorn." "Pickles."

Jody, Val, and I glance at Ellie.

"Pickles?" Jody asks.

We bust into minutes of senseless, irrepressible laughter. When the slam of the screen door collects our attention, and we spot Everett holding water in one hand, pickles in the other, and struggling to balance a mound of chips in an armlock in between, we snort and cry and gasp for air.

He drops the bags on the table and hands Ellie the pickle jar.

"I know you're not pregnant because you're a horrible bitch today," he says. "Must be stomach acid from unkindness spurring your craving."

Our throng becomes so loud that our voices are echoing like an old auditorium microphone that's seen better days. The echo intensifies, as does my sense of smell.

What's that odd aroma? Not the garbage fire we are all ignoring, something else. Popcorn? I thrust a hand toward the bag, but Val grabs it first. I moan. I'm having trouble finding my voice, my fingers. Laughing is all I can manage.

Suddenly, Jody stands. Ellie points to my forehead. Val grabs the glass from Evy and pitches water in my face.

I'm laughing when I go down. My right arm stiffens first. I slide from the chair onto the ground knowing full well that the seizure has begun, that my kids will smell the smoldering marijuana, that Marky will never leave work to meet me at the hospital, Reah will be sorry she missed my seizure, and that smoking that marijuana is the worst parental slip-up I have made to date.

But for some reason, I don't give a damn.

Chapter 2 The hospital

"Cherish every moment spent with family throughout your life, but if you want to be happy, find yourself some good girlfriends." – CJ Zahner's thoughts as she sprawled out on an emergency-room floor while Carolyn and Vicki fought to save her life.

I open my eyes. Singing angels dance across the sky. One grips my arm, and a long translucent thread guides us toward a blinding light in the heavens.

I focus, try to see my Maker. Faint shadows grow like flowers blooming. The echo of the angel's soft singing dissipates to humming then whirring then—wait, what is that? I'm not in heaven?

My vision clears and the room around me materializes. A dangling IV, stained-white ceiling, and buzzing fluorescent light stare down at me. I smell a nauseating antiseptic that resembles embalming fluid and hear a gruff voice that sounds remotely like what I believe the angel of gloom might sound like, hot and nasally. A doctor's voice.

Oh, for God's sake, I'm not even in hell. I'm alive.

Whoopty freakin'doo.

I snap my eyes shut, disappointed in God's decision to spare Mark from single parenthood, a plight I've sworn for years he could not handle.

My memory of the back yard, the wine, and—oh, dear Lord—the marijuana aroma swirling around the medics' heads hits me in flashes. I remember people arriving. Faint voices.

"Mom? Were you smoking dope?" It's Delanie, home from her part-time summer job, and Gianna, home from school. "Mommy, Mommy, don't die." "Shut up, Gianna. Stop crying. Mom's not sick. She's stoned."

I block the rest from seeping into my memory and pray inside my head.

Bless me, Father, for I have sinned. Forgive me. Take me. Now. Quick.

A voice responds but not God's. Evy's. He's talking to the nasal-sounding doctor.

"You can't expect her to wake up in this room. The drapes are orange, for God's sake. Do you want her to have another seizure?"

Though my eyes are shut, I can feel their presence, too many people hovering around my bed. Normally, I'd crave the company, but right now I want solitude. I tighten my eyes, wishing them away so I can die in peace.

"Nikki, are you awake?" Jody, of course. She never misses a beat.

I keep still. Not a twitch.

"I know you're awake," she says, a slight snigger in her pitch.

I pinch my eyelids as tight as I can, screw up my lips, and sigh.

"Open up," she instructs, and I do because only Jody knows what's best for me. I've listened to her for years.

"Did they do a blood test?" I whisper. At first, no one else notices I'm awake.

She nods. Raises her eyebrows.

"For who? You or me?"

"You." She laughs.

"She's awake," Evy announces, and suddenly people lunge toward my bed as if I had flat-lined.

"Why me?" I whine out loud because now everyone knows I'm not dead, and if there is one thing I like more than having lots of friends, it's having lots of friends who feel sorry for me. "Couldn't you, for once, take the heat for Val's blunder?"

"You were a willing participant." Val leans her face over mine. "Fortunately, you have a good friend like me who delivers medical marijuana to you because you're no longer tolerating your epilepsy medication."

She winks. A hitch in conversation allows me to look directly into her eyes, then Evy's, Ellie's, Jody's, and finally, into Doctor Death's.

Is Val throwing me a rope? I don't know if medical marijuana is even legal in Pennsylvania, but I grab on to that twine and dangle.

"Thank God," I say. "It could have been worse."

"Not much." Now Ellie leans over me. "But your face is almost back to its normal pallid white."

This is a dig. Ellie is a sun goddess. Her sprayed-on tan makes Lindsay Lohan look like an albino.

"Why did you stop the medication?" The doctor ignores our glib chat, raises his iPad to his potbelly. He taps a stylus pen to its screen, drops his chin, and peeks over the top of his frame-less glasses.

The room holds its breath while I struggle to fabricate a response. Should I tell the truth? The medication makes me loopy? Lethargic? Fat? Or should I lie? What lie would be excuse enough for a doctor not to scold an epilepsy patient for stopping her medication?

I can't think of a good reason, so words rush over my lips before I can suck them back in. "I have a stress fracture."

"Here we go." Evy jabs an elbow into one hand and slips the palm of the other under his chin. "Go ahead, darling, tell him how many ounces you've gained in the past two weeks since you've run yourself out of your sneakers."

"Leave her alone." Val shoves him. "Just because you eat 3000 calories a day and still wiggle your skinny butt into those jeans doesn't mean the rest of us can."

"Oh, c'mon," he tells her. "You shove tapioca pudding in your mouth like Ellie shoves Ismile."

Another dig. He's cleverly killed three squirrels with one arrow. Ellie whitens her teeth and Val eats pudding more than I squeeze into running garb.

Life heats up whenever the suburban twins argue. Then it quickly simmers down when the queen of sage officiates.

"Quiet." Jody sets a hand on Val's arm before Val can counter. "This is about Nikki."

The doctor adjusts his glasses. Breathes heavily. His breath is hot. I feel the burn of it reach across my bed, past my friends.

"A stress fracture?" Little balls of spit punctuate his words.

I'm in too far now. I have to admit my hypothesis.

"I think running staves off epilepsy."

Evy, Val, Ellie, and Jody stare Doctor Death in the eye as if this is his fifteen seconds of fame. I'm not sure if they believe running prevents seizures, or if they think I'm crazy, but their gazes are glued to him as if he's announcing Best Picture at the Academy Awards.

Doctor Death pauses, contemplates. He's unsure how to respond. He knows exercise helps but doesn't cure epilepsy. I've set him up. It's Faye Dunaway and Warren Beatty all over again. He shoves his glasses up his nose, once more. The rest of us shrink into a clumpy wordless audience, waiting for the MC to announce the wrong best story.

"There's no proven correlation between exercise and seizure prevention." We hang on every word, five slipping tight-rope walkers held together by one hand. "However, running typically reduces stress levels in people, and stress is known to cause seizures. Have you been under extreme stress lately?"

"Yes. Yes, she has." Evy lets go first. "She has this neighbor who used to be a friend—God knows why they were friends—but this terrible neighbor friend? She's rounded up the entire neighborhood and kicked her out of book club. Horrendous."

Thunderstruck, the doctor stares at Evy.

Evy misreads this as his cue to continue. "And her husband? He is never there for her. Look around. Where is he? Working."

"Wait," Val interjects. "Has anyone bothered to call Marky?"

"I called him," Jody says. "He should be here soon."

"Also?" Evy gazes once over each shoulder as if he's about to reveal who Courtney Kardashian's ex is sleeping with. "She has the worst three kids in the neighborhood." He fans a palm out against his mouth and whispers, "Mass murder-ish."

The doctor remains so still we don't know if he is baffled or having a focal seizure himself.

"Has anyone told him about her sister?" Ellie steps apprehensively toward Doctor Death. "Her only sibling, Barb, has early-onset Alzheimer's. She lives at South Hills nursing home."

"She's at Manchester, you ninny," Evy corrects her, then turns to me. "See? See what I mean? You can't trust Ellie. I bet she called Reah and told her you wet your pants."

"I did not." Now Ellie shoves him. "I called and said she'd had a seizure—a real one. Not a stare-away."

"They're called partial seizures, Ellie. Nikki has temporal lobe epilepsy." Evy puts one hand on his hip and waves his other hand in my face. "I do not know how you can still be friends with Ellie. You have a million friends, darling, more than all of us put together. Why do you put up with her?"

"Temporal lobe epilepsy can—" Doctor Death tries to interject, but Ellie and Evy talk over him.

"Put up with me? What are you talking about?"

"Your nasty-ass comments."

"I wasn't being nasty," Ellie retorts.

"Sure, you were. You thrive on insult. Learned your nasty affronts from Natasha. You're her puppet, you and Reah, and your other book-club cronies."

"I'm not—"

"Stop." For once, Jody raises her voice. "This is about Nikki, not you guys."

Bewilderedly, Doctor Death raises a hand and asks everyone to leave.

Evy takes three steps toward the door and jams his skinny butt into the only chair in the room.

"Nice move," I say. This is the first I've smiled since my train wreck.

"Thank you, darling. I'm finished now. Not another word." Evy imitates zipping his lips.

Val, with great emotion, and Ellie, with glimmering annoyance, make apologies for leaving and kiss me goodbye. Parental duties beckon them. Jody leans against the window ledge and sends me mixed signals. She crosses her arms and smiles.

"Well, Ms. Grey." The room finally awards Doctor Death the attention his nine years of medical school, residency, and internship deserve. "Your records indicate that several years ago you had an allergic reaction to Tegretol. You've also tried…"

He trails off, repeating the same information I've gotten for twenty years. I stare but don't listen. His voice transforms into a noisy wah-wahing—the old Peanut's adult's thing. "Wah-wah, wah-wah-wah," says the teacher. "Yes, ma'am," says Charlie Brown.

My mind blocks his words and wanders off with all the imposing questions this little episode evokes. How will I get to my activities, drive the kids around? What about the fall when I go back to work? Hopefully, the stress fracture will mend by then, and I can walk there. It's less than two miles. But I can't ask friends to drive me everywhere else. How do I get to the health club? Yoga? My Saturday morning run on the peninsula once my foot mends?

Most of my friends live miles away, and Natasha's venom has infected those who live close by. Lots of neighbors aren't speaking to me because of her, and I don't dare bother those who are with menial requests for rides. They'll hate me.

How will I go grocery shopping? Take Gianna to cheerleading practice? The questions run on like that old cartoon song that never ends.

I sigh dramatically.

Oh my God, this is worse than the book-club debacle.

"Are you listening, Ms. Grey?"

"Oh, yes."

I gaze at Jody, and when I'm sure he isn't looking, I feel the edges of my lips curve upward. I pantomime, "Wah-wah-wah."

Jody understands. Her smile widens, but she makes no sound. That simple little twinkle in her eye is sweet comfort, loyal comradery, the reason this seizure is tragic for me.

I am a girl's girl at heart. I love Mark, don't get me wrong, but when there is an explosion, and my world comes crashing down around me, I don't run to him. I run toward the coffee shop with my girlfriends—and Evy. We each grab a caffeine-loaded cup of our favorite drink reconstruction. We draw plans on little brown napkins, wipe the dust from each other's faces, and carry on.

Life is simple. Surround yourself with friends, and you've got it licked.

I refocus. I know what's coming. What Doctor Death is politely skirting is that this epilepsy will prevent me from spending time with my friends. He's about to shrink my independence, reduce me to a fool begging for rides.

The wah-wah-wah sounds on until his last sentence jerks me back into the room.

"We had to suspend your driver's license."

Yes, I know. Six months. Thank God school is out because now I can't pull my weight in the neighborhood carpool. I'm already on neighbor lady's voodoo-pricking list. Not driving will lure me onto every other neighbor's don't-make-eye-contact, she'll-ask-for-a-ride dodge.

I glance at Jody. She frowns, shrugs. Of all my friends, Jody knows there is nothing worse that can happen to me in life than not being able to drive.

Most people believe it's petty of me. But the suspension doesn't simply confine me to my home. The loss of my license paralyzes me, penalizing me for something I can't control. This sentence is a fate worse than death because now I must rely on others, and I am the sort who likes to stay one up on my friends. One favor in front of them in line.

Even though I'm scads of favors in front of Ellie and Reah, I don't want to ask for a single favor in return. They'll stop coming over, calling, liking me. They'll become friends with the neighbor lady, my nemesis. The person I can only admit hating because if I tell the truth—that I still love her—everyone will take me out back in my yard and stone me.

When Doctor Death leaves the room, I muster the courage to utter the arborvitae-inspirer's name for the first time in months.

"Natasha will love this."

Jody doesn't argue. Ellie would. Reah would. Val would say, "Screw Natty Lou." That's what she calls her.

"I did not just hear that name." That's what Evy says. "How can you let that woman's name cross your lips? You can't possibly still care about what she thinks."

But I do care. I miss Natasha. And more than her, I miss Reah, whom she's stolen from me. Yet now I can't try to make amends with Natasha because she'll think I'm doing it for a ride.

Evy reads my mind. "You don't need her." He leans forward in his seat, back straight, hands in lap, two little feet nudged tightly beneath him. He's a rooster with his feathers ruffled. "I'll slap you silly if you mention her again. I'll slap you until my hand is imprinted on your cheek for a week."

A nurse has propped the big, heavy door open and stands in the doorway, disbelief stuck on her face.

"He doesn't mean it," I assure her, and she strolls toward me, arcing widely around Evy. She steps to my bedside, raises a little plastic cup, and taps two pills into my hand without saying a word.

"My sleeping pills?"

"They're for the epilepsy."

"Sleeping pills," I counter. I've done this before.

I gulp them down with dust-flavored water from a Styrofoam cup that's been sitting on my overbed table for who knows how long. I pick up the ugly mustard-colored water pitcher and pour more stale water into the cup. Drink again. Then I sit back and wait for my eyelids to become heavy.

One thing I've learned over the years about epilepsy is the medication will make me sleep, which right now doesn't seem bad. Maybe I can sleep my health, friend, and family problems away.

Mark comes with a dozen roses—nice, he made it— right as I'm dozing off. Evy gets up to leave. He kisses me goodbye and whispers something about friends then repeats some quote by Stephen somebody, but I'm drifting away. Jody closes the book she's reading and steps toward me.

My gaze falls to the novel in her hand, one I recommended, *The Secret History*. Ironically, it's about a bunch of friends who murder another friend, and oddly, seven words of that 503-page book spring to mind. They appear over and over in my head as I begin losing consciousness.

Like elevator music in the background, Doctor Death enters and informs Mark that EEGs, MRIs, and blah-blah-blah brain scans are scheduled for tomorrow, Friday morning. Jody sneaks away. A nurse sets a vase on the window ledge. But I'm not paying attention. I'm floating off, dreaming.

I'm a child at school, standing at a chalkboard. I'm being punished for a lesson unlearned. A lesson the nun says is critical before moving to the next grade.

"Write down what you need to learn," she says nastily from beneath her black habit. "Fifty times."

I stand at the blackboard in my little blue-plaid skirt, black loafers, and cross tie. I pick up white chalk with shaky fingers and begin writing *The Secret History* sentence that has overpowered me.

Our own selves make us most unhappy. Our own selves make us most unhappy. Our own selves make us most unhappy.

Suddenly, the quote by Steven Daniels that Evy was referring to slaps me like a flyswatter. *A good friend will help you move a couch, but a true friend will help you move a body.*

I grab an eraser and expunge the words I've written. The chalkboard coughs up white dust then I fill every inch of its space with what I need:

Friends who move bodies, friends who move bodies, friends who move bodies.

Chapter 3 The card

"Why do you want to hang around people who don't want to hang around you?" Jeff to CJ, when a neighbor left them off a baseball game invite.

Our past haunts each of us.

This thought overpowers me on Friday morning as I lie in my hospital bed. Loneliness has taunted me since childhood. Solitude torments me as viciously as any physical ailment could.

People don't understand this about me. They believe I'm petty because I hurt over what they perceive to be a frivolous neighborhood spat, but it is so much more than that. It's a scraping emotional pain that began years ago.

Hundreds of patients suffer in rooms above, below, and around me. Who's to judge which one of us hurts more?

Mark slumps in a corner chair, unaware of my anguish. His flowers fall loosely over the edges of a hospital vase, instantly reminding me of my backyard arborvitae problem. *Will I never get that woman out of my mind?*

I don't remember much of last night. I slept through most of the evening and middle-of-the-night hours. Reah did visit, but I couldn't get my eyes open. My running friends crept in quietly, left cards and chocolate on the windowsill. My high school girlfriends stopped by. Vaguely, I remember them mentioning they dropped off dinner at home for Mark and the kids.

Mark thanked them, and when everyone was gone, he sat beneath the wall clock, opened his computer, and worked until at least 1 a.m. He was gone by 3, still missing at 5, but now snores unattractively in a big bulky chair that has magically appeared beside my bed.

I glance above him. 7:15. My tests begin at 9. Until then I can have no food, only water, which is good because the IV adds calories to my body that I would prefer to spend on a hamburger and fries.

Somewhere between Mark's friend—our family doctor—showing up to mark the marijuana as medicinal, and Mark's 3 a.m. disappearing act, I recall a whispered phone conversation he had with his boss saying his weekend trip was off.

Thank God.

I'd forgotten about the San Diego conference. There'd be hell to pay for his missing that. He's a great husband but a hopeless workaholic. A patent attorney, dull and boring. My mother always said dull and boring was good.

I could go for a bit of the mundane now.

A nurse who resembles Kanye West arrives. Her expression is as distorted and bitter as his might be if Kimmy lost best dressed at the Oscars—to Taylor Swift. She unhooks my IV tube with a vengeance, yanks out the needle, rips the tape off my arm, and leans back to toss the remains in the garbage.

That's when I see it. The card. It's wide open on the ledge, its signature laughing at me.

"Excuse me," I say. "Could you please hand me that?"

Her gaze follows mine to the windowsill. She lifts a pastel-colored card.

"This?"

"Yes."

She hands it to me, and my chin hits my chest. I wiggle into a sitting position in bed. "I don't believe it."

"You're awake." Mark sits up, and the nurse exits, propping the door open behind her.

"Please tell me somebody delivered this, and that bitch didn't show up here last night."

"Well, good morning to you, too."

"Sorry, good morning. Was she here?"

"Not for long," he says. "She left when I ignored her."

Say what you will about good old Mark, but he has my back, always.

"I can't believe she had the nerve."

"You're not going to like this." Apprehension washes across his face.

"Like what?" I toss the covers aside, dangle my feet while Mark props elbows on knees, folds his hands together, and drops his chin on top of interlocked fingers. This is his signature brace-yourself warning.

"What?" I repeat.

"She came with Reah."

Oh. My. God. I lose my breath. This can't be happening. Isn't it bad enough I just had a seizure? I jump to the floor, bare feet to cold tile.

"No." I suck air in and exhale forcefully. "You did not just tell me that."

My friend Reah visits with my ex-friend Natasha? Whom I introduced her to? Who now loathes me?

Grade school memories spring from my hippocampus. I'm in homeroom. Reah enters. I'm sitting in my normal seat, thinking she's coming to sit in front of me where she has sat all year. Instead, she makes a beeline for Mary Ellen Lamont, bypassing me. Later, she tells me she's "convincing" Mary Ellen that I'm not a nerd. That I'm cool like her, Reah.

This is where my neighborhood, friends, book club, and loneliness has led me—back to a grade-school mentality.

Friendship, or lack thereof, cripples me every time. I never learn.

With my cheeks burning, I blurt out, "We have to move. I can't take it anymore. We have to get out of the neighborhood. Maybe out of Fairview."

"Move?"

"Yes. Move."

"And what? Transfer Gianna to another school?"

I hate it when Mark is logical. Our differing logic skills mar our marriage. He wallows in common sense. I flounder in oblivion.

But I'm not completely deranged. "Okay," I concede. "Just out of the neighborhood, so they aren't flaunting their look-who-I'm-hanging-around parties in my face."

"What do you care who they hang around with?"

"Natasha and Sam cut us out of their lives, Mark. Now Natasha is warming up to Reah. Stealing Kevin and Reah from us. Don't you care? Not even remotely?"

"No. I don't. And listen to yourself." He sighs. "Why do you want to hang around with people who don't want to hang around with you? You spent years pacifying Reah. Trying to keep her in your life. Why?"

"Because I grew up with her, and I don't want to lose her friendship because Natasha doesn't like me."

"My God, it's high school all over again."

"Yes, it is, Mark. It's the same friend struggles I had in grade school, high school, college. Some twenty years later nothing has changed. I still want Reah in my life. So shoot me. I'm a girl's girl."

"You have more friends than anyone I know."

"Then why do I feel alone? It's not as if I can talk to you about anything."

There, I said it. Now he'll make me apologize for dragging him into my delusional world, as he calls it.

In other words, I've reasoned in my mind that this obsession with the book club? It's not a Nikki thing. It's a girl thing.

So, today, Monday morning, I allow myself to disregard the epilepsy and mull over the plain and simple unpardonable nature of women—like Reah hanging out with Natasha. Stabbing me in the back.

I had alleviated the hurt and bitterness of my neighborhood ostracism by staying busy. Ellie had been right. I never said no. I accepted so many invites—running, walking, hiking, tennis—that I exercised my way into a stress fracture.

What the heck will I do now that I can't run or drive? I've been sentenced to sit in a cell that is located right beside people I'm trying to forget.

So being recently sprung from the hospital, I tango around my kitchen, busying myself with fruitless tasks. I resist the temptation to gaze out the window toward Natasha's house, but only because Mark is home. As soon as he leaves, I'm getting the binoculars.

Before then, I pack lunches.

Dr. Felt, Mark's golf friend, kept me in the hospital an extra day because my EEG showed lesions, which, confusingly, can be a sign of temporal lobe epilepsy.

Or was it the other way around? I don't recall. I don't care, and my lack of knowledge and concern is why red crawls up Mark's neck and spreads across his face this morning.

"You're impossible. You never listen." He wiggles his tie closer to his throat. He's so annoyed that his jugular juts above his collar like a Twizzler out the top of a bag. "Not to me, the doctor, no one."

"Yes, I do."

His frustration with me bleeds into his fingers, and he can't right his tie. He rips it apart and begins tying all over.

I take the tie from his hands and make a perfect knot. He wiggles the top, but this time his knot is where he wants it to be.

"Take the damn medication."

Mark's worried I might make him a single parent.

"Take your lunch," I reply.

For once, I've slapped tuna and Miracle Whip on bread for him. I wrap the sandwich in waxed paper and drop it inside a brown bag along with a candy bar, apple, and napkin. I roll the top of the bag and shove it at his chest. "Here."

"You didn't have to do that. Pack my lunch."

"I know. Think of it as a peace offering." I step toward him and wrap my arms around his waist. "I couldn't live without you, Mark. We do need to spend more time together. I'll try to do better."

Last night's heart-to-heart chat inspired this comment. Mark said I need to forget the neighbors and pay more attention to him, the kids—I pat Furgy—and the dog.

"I want to be a good wife and mother. I love you."

Mark doesn't respond, but he tugs me close and plants a long, warm kiss on the top of my head.

"I'll do better," I reaffirm, more for me than him. But before he goes out the door, I'm tempted to peek out the back window toward Natasha's.

"Bye," I holler, then I sit and sip coffee, waiting for the rumble of the engine to rush by the kitchen window and the click of tires over pavers to cease as his car hits the street.

What takes him so long, I don't know. He revs up the engine, and my obsession with Natasha grows.

We did everything together for years, then somehow the friendship soured.

I think about the play dates between Gianna and Natasha's daughter, Kate. The shopping sprees. Running Benadryl through the back yards when the kids were sick.

Cooking dinners for each other when our parents passed away. Spending time together at Christmas.

I wallow in the past until I realize I'm not sure if Mark left. I stand and peek down the driveway. He's gone. I limp to the back window.

Will this dang stress fracture never heal, so I can run? I glance outside and—O. M. G. Like the miracle of Fatima, a phenomenon has descended from the sky and hovers behind my arborvitae.

I hobble to my back door and step outside. There is a shed so big and brown and beautiful that I can't believe my eyes. The neighbors who moved in last March have built a monstrosity of a shed on the other side of my property line, just behind the dying arborvitaes.

I can't believe my eyes. Not an inch of Natasha's house is visible.

I realize I've got my cell phone in my hand, and I'm dialing Jody.

"Did you say you were stopping by this morning?"

"I'm turning into your driveway now. Are you okay?" Jody's there to check on me. I've been home a whopping twelve hours.

"Yes. I'm great. Come out back."

"What are you up to?" She hears the anxiousness in my voice.

I don't answer. I rush to the driveway and wave my hand, motioning for her to come quick.

"I'm not going to hell," I tell her when she steps beside me. "Neither is Evy. Or Val."

"Why do you say that?" She chuckles.

"Because God has a sense of humor."

I take her by the hand and lead her to my back yard. Then I point to the biggest, towering Taj Mahal shed that has ever been built on an 80- by 185-foot lot.

Immediately, Jody bends in laughter.

"God, in His infinite wisdom." I pause for effect. "Has swooped down and built an ark to protect me from the floodwaters."

"Oh my God." Her hand flies to cover her mouth. "When did that go up?"

"Over the weekend. Looks like I'm not going to need the medication after all." I point a flat hand toward the shed. "Viola, all my problems solved."

"I'm not sure about that but not seeing Natasha wandering around her back yard will help."

Jody walks toward the shed, and our laughing spell heightens. We are still howling a few minutes later when the neighbor comes out with stain or paint or some sort of shed decoration.

"Good morning," I holler over the fence, and Jody pushes me toward the house because she can't stop laughing.

"Morning," he says, but he's preoccupied and pays no mind to us rushing away. We hurry inside and Jody runs faster than I've ever seen her run, darting toward the kitchen's back window.

"This is great. She won't be able to see you at all, and you won't be able to see her."

We giggle and toss comments back and forth, then I pour coffee into two mugs. She sits down, composes herself, and proceeds to fire twenty-five questions at me as if she's a home health-care worker.

Oh, Jody, Jody, Jody, I love and abhor you all in one.

When I've answered everything and satiated her nurturing appetite, she stands. "Just make sure you rest. I'll be at the grade school for a talk this morning, but I'm stopping for groceries afterward. Anything I can get you?"

"No, Mark and I stopped on the way home from the hospital last night."

"When do you go to the doctor?"

"Not for a few days."

"I can take you if you want."

"Mark is taking me."

She wrinkles her nose and looks away. Mark isn't the most reliable ride. He's notoriously late and doesn't show at all if he has too much work.

"I'll see you tomorrow." She hugs me goodbye tightly, which I translate as she's worried about me.

After she leaves, I hurry upstairs to Gianna's room and gaze out her window. I can't see Natasha's house.

Could I from Delanie's?

I listen. Hear the rush of water against the tub. She's showering.

I tiptoe into her room, but I can't see anything from her window, either.

I drag a desk chair across the floor and stand on its seat. Nothing. I step onto the top of the flimsy desk we bought Delanie when she was five. I go up on tiptoes. A cracking sound emanates from beneath my feet. I hold my breath. No more sounds. I peek out the top corner of Delanie's window, and I can see Natasha through her double-paned kitchen doors. She's sitting at her kitchen table. Someone's with her. Who?

I extend my toes until I'm stretching tendons, and my stress fracture twinges. The woman has dark hair. Is Reah there, having coffee?

"Mom."

Delanie's voice jolts me. I jump, knock myself off balance, and do a little dance to right my feet. The desk cracks again, only this time, the top bends in the middle. Luckily, her bed sits close to her desk, and I plunge safely into soft, cushy blankets.

We both look at the desk, its surface is bent into a v.

"Sorry," I whine.

"You are pathetic. I knew you wouldn't be able to stand not snooping on Natasha."

"What?" I react. "You have cobwebs in the corner."

"You planted those arborvitaes to block Natasha's house, and now that you can't see her, it's killing you."

"Well—" I have no defense.

She grabs her coat and purse and stomps away.

"You're pathetic. I'm not coming home from school next summer. I'm finding a job there."

This is the worst thing she can say. I didn't want her to go away to school, even seventy minutes away. We have three perfectly good colleges near Fairview. Now Hux is following her to Slippery Rock in September—another battle lost.

I stand and compose myself as Gianna comes running in.

"Mom, did you wash my tights?"

Of course, I didn't wash her tights. I spent the last three Godforsaken days in the hospital, but I don't yell because I'm two kids down and one to go.

"I did," I lie. "They're in the dryer. I'll get them."

I nudge her out of Delanie's room, but she glances around me.

"What happened to the desk?"

"Mommy broke it dusting cobwebs."

When it comes to my children, I'm just a big kid in mommy jeans. If one is mad at me, I coddle the other two. Just like when one of them is in trouble, the other two celebrate because Mom isn't yelling at them.

Gianna glances at the ceiling. She's no dummy. Right now, she could slap me across the face, and I'd apologize.

"Did you pack my mustard sandwich?"

Ugh.

Teachers think I abuse Gianna because she's lived on white bread and mustard for years.

"Yes," I say, but as soon as I fish her leotards out of the hamper and toss them in the dryer with three dryer sheets, I go to the kitchen, remove her sandwich from her lunch box, take out the turkey, slop mustard in its place, and rewrap it. I can't have two kids mad. This is my life. I'm a firefighter battling one relationship blaze after another. My parents are gone. My only sibling is losing her memory. My husband's never home, and the neighbors hate me. If I lose one more person in my life, I'll crumble.

Wait, I already crumbled.

When Reah honks—she's driving the girls to summer camp—and Gianna runs outside, Hux wakes up, throws clothes on, and comes running down the stairs. He storms out the door without a word. As usual, he's late.

Not one of the three of them thinks to ask how I'm feeling. Seems they've forgotten Mom spent the weekend in the hospital.

Someday I'll write a book about my life. I'll call it *Don't Mind Me, I Came with the House.*

Chapter 5 The list

"Friends Who Move Couches? Is that another thriller?" Jeff asked when he heard the name of CJ Zahner's next novel.

"It's paradoxical in more ways than one, darling."

"What do you mean in more ways than one?" I shake my head.

"The Taj Mahal is a grave. Built to house the body of a woman who died in childbirth. Perhaps this represents the death of your childish addiction to friendship."

I was excited to show Evy the shed, but he's annoyingly turned this miracle into a history lesson.

"She merely said it was a Taj Mahal of a shed." Val, who admittedly never scored more than a D on a history exam, chimes in.

"Yes. A philosopher lingers deep within us all. Her comment was Freudian."

"Big, Evy." Now I scold. "I simply meant it's big, Taj Mahal sized."

"You need to sit in on one of my lectures this summer, Naggy."

Evy's pet name for me is inspired by the initials of my full name, Nikki Anne Grey.

"Aren't you teaching paint by numbers?" Val asks.

"Oh my God, I teach two classes in the summer, philosophy and pottery. I swear I won't agree to return to this shallow planet unless I find a more palpable assembly."

He's speaking of reincarnation. Evy believes he's a scholar and Val, Ellie, and I are the sloths he's destined to save. He says we come back with him in different bodies every hundred years.

"Regardless," Jody turns the conversation. "She doesn't have to watch Natasha entertain the book club anymore."

"Ah, the dreadful book club," he counters. "I brought paper to lineate Naggy's friendship journey and show her she shouldn't waste time on Janice Everglade and her misled disciples."

We're sitting under a cloudy sky today. No umbrella. Our kids splash around in the pool. Years ago, frequenting the neighborhood playground with our children drew us together. Evy's twins, adopted, are two years behind Gianna and a year behind Olivia, Ellie's daughter. Jody's youngest, Becca, is six. She floats around in her swimmies while the other girls dote over her.

Evy opens a folder he's brought along. "I'll draw the list of good friends. Those who move bodies."

He hands me the paper. "You write down friends who stab you in the back, like Ellie, on your list."

"Why am I a bad friend?" Ellie squeals.

"Because your mouth runneth amok."

"Nikki, am I a good friend?"

"A very good friend," I say. I write Friends Who Move Couches on the top of my list and enter Natasha's name beside the number one.

Evy drops his pen and stares at me.

"What?" I react. "I'm not putting Ellie on the bad list."

He stands up, points a finger, and taps the top of my paper. "What does this mean? Friends who move couches?"

"That's the saying. Which kind of friend are you? A friend who moves a couch or a friend who moves a body?"

"My God, save them from themselves. The saying is 'A good friend will help you move, but a true friend will help you move a body.' No mention of couches. Has that seizure crashed your memory?"

"What? It's not friends who move couches?"

"No! No couches."

"Are you sure?"

"Positive!" He puts his hands on his hips, and I gaze down at my list.

I think for a bit.

"I like friends who move couches. It sounds better."

"I do, too," Val agrees.

He sighs, dramatically.

"Have it your way." He sits down and writes his name at the top of the friends-who-move-bodies good list. "Ellie belongs on the couch list."

I write Janice Everglade on line two, under Natasha Stewart. Then I can't think of anyone else, but Evy grabs the paper and writes down Reah and Ellie. Ellie gets mad, grabs Evy's body list, and marks a big x over his name.

We all stand and wrestle with the papers, shouting at each other, until we realize the girls are hanging on the side of the pool. Their hair is cemented to the top of their heads, and five pairs of beady eyes stare at us.

"What are you doing?" Leah, one of Evy's twins, makes us feel as if she's the parent, and we are the kids.

We stand wordlessly for a moment.

"Nothing," I finally say, then we grownups sit down slowly, shamed by a child.

We attempt to act like adults and compromise. Evy insists Reah go on the couches list, and I insist Ellie go on the body list. When we finish, I take the lists inside and place them in the rolltop desk, but Evy must sneak in at some point because when the kids get out of the pool and everyone goes home, I see Ellie is on both lists, penned with exclamation points.

I laugh, close the desk, and listen to my messages. Mark will be home late.

No kidding.

Carol, my running friend, called to check on me. Carolyn will stop by over the weekend. Laura will, too, when she gets back in town, and Hux is going to a graduation party with friends.

I'm alone in the house. Delanie has dropped Gianna off at dance rehearsal; her dance review is this weekend. Delanie will pick her up later but is dropping her at home and going out afterward.

She's dating that boy from high school again. The cad who broke up with her a week before her senior prom. What a parental fiasco that was. The boy's mother and I worked together, awkwardly, until the summer break saved us from each other.

Now Delanie's made amends with him, but I can't stop the grind of my stomach every time I hear that boy's name, Tyler. His mother transferred to another office in the fall, but we still ran into each other in the halls. It was never the same between us.

This is the one exception to women's forgiving rule. We can forgive and forget more than men unless someone hurts one of our offspring. Then our fangs come out, and we suck the life out of everyone around us.

When—if—I arrive at the pearly gates, I'll remind God he granted me my motherly instincts. If He hints I should have forgiven Tyler for hurting Delanie, I'll argue there were no proms back in his day. Proms are the chalice of a teenage girl's existence. Ripping it from her was Tyler's demise.

God can't give mothers these protective instincts and then penalize us for them. Can He?

I pour myself a glass of wine, despite the drowsiness I'm experiencing from the epilepsy medication, and I open a book to drown my thoughts. I fall asleep reading the first page then wake at dusk. I listen. There's no one home. But— what is that maddening noise? Something is clanging somewhere above me.

I sigh, find my spot in my book and reread the page I fell asleep reading. But I'm irritated that no one cares enough to come home and check on me, and I'm annoyed by the badgering clanging. After reading the same sentence fifteen times, I slam the book shut.

I stomp upstairs toward the sound. The noise is muffled, clattering above me. I yank the string in the hall, and a ladder drops from the ceiling. I'm halfway up the attic steps when the phone rings. I jump down, the ladder springs upward with a thud, and I hurry to find my phone, hoping one of my family members is calling.

"Ms. Grey?" My shoulders slump from disappointment. "Could you talk to your sister for us? She's concerned you forgot her shampoo."

OMG, my sister!

Not only have I forgotten to pick up her favorite shampoo and lotion, but I've forgotten her altogether.

"I was in the hospital. I'm sorry."

"I figured something happened. I hope you are okay?"

I look around the dark house. At least the nursing home cares.

"I'm fine. I won't be able to get there as often."

"The stress fracture?"

"No something else, but speaking of the fracture, could you make sure she gets out into the courtyard a few times a week? Walks around the perimeter? It does her good."

"No worries, two of your friends, Carol and Laura, take turns. They said they'll each come once a week and take her for a walk until you've healed. We checked. You listed them as people permitted to take her out."

"Yes, I did." This thrills me.

"They've been great. I'll let Barb know you'll fetch her shampoo when you can. She can use ours until then."

"Tell her I'll be in soon."

"Will do. See you then."

I hang up with a smile on my face. My running friends are wonderful. I'm blessed to have them in my life.

This is another epiphany.

"I need more friends like them," I say to the dark room then hurry to the desk and remove my friend lists.

I turn the overhead light on, and my world lights up. My epilepsy and neighborhood problems don't seem so bad with the lights on.

My life's not gloomy, I tell myself. All I need is to move the people from my couch list to my body list.

I decide to win back everybody—Reah, Natasha, my kids, Mark. I open my laptop and search John and Janice Everglade. The Everglades own half the city. Janice is the most powerful stay-at-home mom in Fairview. We aren't Facebook friends, but she hasn't blocked me.

I scan her posts for a few minutes and find she and John joined the couple's golf league that Mark mentioned.

I google the league. They need additional players.

I hate golf, but Mark loves it. I'll agree to golf with him. If I can befriend Janice, Reah and Natasha will beg me to come to their summer barbeques.

I sign on to my email and search my archived messages from old book clubs, find the books for the upcoming months, and write them down.

I google the books, but then realize Mark will suspect ulterior motives if I purchase several at once. So I search through drawers until I find my library card. I'll take out the books and let Janice know I'm still reading the novels even though I've been booted from the club.

Instead of books, I order a recumbent bike. Mark mentioned I've gained weight. I'll get back in shape, so he wants to come home to me.

And I'll allow Gianna to play with Amy Everglade, which up until now I've discouraged because the girl is such a bully.

I gaze long and hard at my lists. Evy's right. I don't need friends who move couches. I fall prey to their demands.

I scratch Reah and Natasha off the couch list then write their names along with Janice Everglade's on the body list.

I set my pen down.

"I just hope the body they move isn't mine."

Chapter 6 The bike

"What is in our driveway?" CJ asked her son,
Zak. "Jessie was running late and backed over the
garbage," he explained.

"Momma, can Amy Everglade come over and swim in our pool?"

Ten days later, I've done so much dancing I could shame the performers on *Dancing with the Stars.* Step by step, my plan falls into place. Like water into an ice cube tray.

"Sure she can."

I feel a bit like Abraham sacrificing his son, but I'm hoping God spares Gianna, too. After all, Gianna has two older siblings; she can be a bit of a bully herself. Maybe Amy Everglade needs a Gianna in her life.

Three hours after we call Amy, Natasha is standing at my front door. She hands me a dinner in a glass roasting pan.

"I should have done this sooner," she admits.

"How sweet of you," I whine, melodiously.

I'm sure she heard Amy is coming over this afternoon. She's hoping Gianna will invite her daughter, Kate.

"How are you feeling?"

I glance over my shoulder, praying Gianna doesn't come down the stairs. She'll want Kate to come, and I'm hoping Gianna can bond with Amy—alone.

"Pretty good. How about you?"

We converse for a few minutes, and Natasha gets her wish, Gianna prances down the stairs and begs me to allow Kate to come swimming.

"That would be great," I say because "not on your life" would confirm my pettiness.

"Thanks, I'm sure she'd love that. Is anyone else coming? I'll bake cookies."

For a moment, I hesitate and gaze straight into Natasha's eyes. It's as if we're playing a game of battleship. Searching for each other's destroyers. Sinking each other's ships.

You know Amy's coming.

Natasha's pettiness supersedes even Janice Everglades. Her eyelashes flutter. She's trying not to laugh.

"Yes, Amy Everglade."

"How nice; so it will be the three of them? I can pick up hamburgers and fries since, I'm sorry, you can't drive."

O. M. G.

"That won't be necessary. I'm making chicken nuggets."

I hope to God Hux hasn't ravished them.

"Just the cookies, then. What time?"

Ten minutes after never.

"Two-thirty. The pool is warm by then."

"You told Amy two," Gianna excitedly corrects.

"Did I?" I rub my hand down the back of her head then raise my eyes and smile at Natasha. "Two, then."

"She'll be over."

I try not to shut the door too hard.

Two hours later, Janice drops Amy off, and I'm still fuming because Kate, the third wheel, is coming, but I'm sweet as candy to Janice.

"Here's her bag with a change of clothes," she says. "I brought her bike, too. The girls might like to ride over to the library today for a book. The school library is open from two until six on Tuesdays all summer long."

"That's a great idea."

"And I know you can't drive—"

Bitch.

"Or walk."

Who mentioned my stress fracture to her?

"So I left her bike in the driveway."

"Perfect," I say, then relax my faking-bliss face when she leaves.

The doorbell rings a minute later. I put my happy face back on and open the door thinking it's Natasha dropping off her wheel, but I find Evy standing on my porch with both hands on his hips.

"Oh." I collapse my lips. "It's you."

"That was not who I think it was."

"Quiet." I grab his arm and wrench him inside. "Amy is upstairs with Gianna."

"Amy Everglade?"

"No, Amy Schumer. Yes, of course, Amy Everglade."

"When did Gianna start playing with Amy?" he whispers. "My girls call her D-Amy. Short for Damien, the bad seed."

"Whatever." I wave a hand. "I can't choose Gianna's friends. If she wants to hang around with the devil herself, I'll be the good little mother and let her."

"You are afraid of your own kids."

My shoulders drop, and my head sags to one side. "Is that why you're here? To criticize me?"

"No, I bought you a gift. I felt bad about flogging your ego. Think of it as an olive branch."

"A what?"

"Never mind. Just open it."

Mercifully, the phone rings. Whenever Evy surprises me with a gift, I get lectured for not understanding its underlying meaning.

"Hello."

"Mom," Hux hollers into the phone. "I forgot my lunch. Can you bring it?"

"Hang on, Evy." I hurry to the kitchen and see Hux's lunch bag with his turkey sandwich still sitting on the counter.

"If you'd get up earlier, you wouldn't be leaving stuff at home all the time."

"Just run it over, Mom. I only get a half-hour lunch."

"I can't drive."

"Oh, c'mon, it's six blocks. It's not like you're going to run someone over."

"I could, you know." I remove my keys from a hook in the kitchen and stomp toward the front door. "There are a lot of kids in this neighborhood."

"You're such a pansy. Have you ever done anything wrong in your entire life?"

"In case you forgot, I smoked dope the other day, Hux." What am I doing? Trying to impress my kid? I've lost more than my license. I've lost my mind.

"Yeah and that's what got you into this mess. It's not my fault you lost your license. Bring me my lunch. It will take less than three minutes."

He's right. This isn't his fault, and I am cowardly. I'm a law-abiding pansy. My idea of breaking the law is jaywalking. "Just because you break the law all the time—"

"You're such a prude," he interrupts.

"What did you call me? I'm your mother, for God's sake."

"Mom, you've driven to school thousands of times. What do you think is going to happen this one time?"

He's attempting to guilt me into this. I know. But it's working because I never do anything I'm not supposed to, and I'm sick and tired of the dull-and-boring Nikki I've aged into. That's probably Mark's annoyance with me, too. "There's no excitement in our life," he complains, relentlessly.

"Is that Hux's lunch? I can drop it off," Evy says.

Hux hears him. "There, if you're chicken shit, have Evy bring it."

"What?"

My blood boils. I head out the front door and hurry toward my SUV.

"You little shit." I'll be mortified later that I swore at one of my kids, but he's being such a spoiled brat right now I don't care. I pull my mouth away from the phone. "Evy, can you please keep an eye on the girls for a minute?" Then I holler into the phone again. "I'm getting you out of bed tomorrow at seven-thirty, you hear me?"

"You're not supposed to drive," Evy scolds as I get in the car and turn on the ignition.

"Seven-thirty? I start at eight-thirty. It takes less than ten minutes to walk here. I don't know why you won't let me take your car, anyway. It's not like you're driving it."

"Naggy," Evy hollers. "You're not allowed to drive."

"You wrecked my car, Hux. That's why your father had to buy me a new one."

I turn around and gaze out the back window because my old car didn't have a camera, and I forget my new one does. I step on the gas, giving it more than expected. I feel a jolting motion and hear a crunch.

My first thought is, my God, I've run over a kid.

I shove the car into park and run to the back. Evy beats me there.

"Oh, darling, please tell me that's D-Amy Everglade's bike and not Gianna's. It would be sweet justice in so many ways."

I glance at the mangled bike lodged beneath my back bumper.

The front door opens, and Amy Everglade lets out a scream that sends our dog, Furgy, scurrying out the door and down the street.

Evy opens the car door and grabs Hux's lunch.

"I'll drop this off and find the dog. You might want to call in the pit crew, Mario."

My plan to win more friends might not be working as well as once thought.

Chapter 7 The lesson

"What is wrong with your arms?" PGA & LPGA Pro Golfer Karen Bukowski asked CJ when she saw her holding a golf club.

"I've agreed to golf in the league and take private lessons to, one, get Mark to stop nagging me about riding over D-Amy's bike, and, two, to win Janice Everglade's friendship," I tell Jody three days later. She's agreed to drop me off at the driving range. "Thanks for picking me up. I don't dare drive."

Mark and I took golf lessons in a group last spring. I'd quit, much to his dismay. Now, he's ecstatic about my return to golf and has booked me private lessons. But today he has a morning meeting in Pittsburgh and can't take me, so Jody offered.

She wipes tears of laughter from her eyes. This is the first she's heard of me crushing D-Amy's bike.

"How upset was Janice?'

"She was so happy Amy stopped her tantrum she forgot all about the bike."

Amy threw a fit in our front yard that coaxed nine neighbors out of their houses and stirred the meter man to call 911. People thought someone ran over a child. Evy assured the ambulance driver and Fairview cop that he had unintentionally caused the blunder.

"Evy took the blame. He told them it was him, so I didn't get in trouble for driving. Although, for Pete's sake, I didn't even get out of my driveway."

"Evy told Janice he rode over the bike?"

"He did. When I told him I'd tell Janice the truth, he begged me to tell people he drove over the bike. 'I'll be the hero at the next LGBT meeting. Everyone hates her,' he said." I give Jody my best Evy impression.

"I don't know if this golf lesson is such a good idea, either."

"Why?"

"You hate to golf."

"Yes, but Mark loves it, and he has a man-crush on John Everglade, who not only owns half the businesses in town but is the best non-pro golfer at the Kahkwa Club. Maybe he'll calm down over my crushing D-Amy's bike. He was furious. He wants to be friends with John as much as I want to be friends with Janice, although he won't admit it."

"Do you really want to be friends with Janice Everglade?"

"Yes!"

"Why?'

"To get back at Reah and Natasha, of course."

"Of course." Jody shakes her head but smiles. "I love you, Nikki, but you never learn."

"I know. I'm my own nemesis. Why don't you take a golf lesson with me? You like golf."

"No, you're on your own. Although I mentioned to Archie you were taking a lesson, and he said Blake Anderson is the best."

"He's going to need to be the best if he wants to teach me how to golf."

"Is it an hour lesson? I can pick you up," Jody offers.

"No, Mark will. It's Friday. He's usually home early on Fridays."

Jody frowns. I read her eyes. She thinks Mark won't show. Jody's husband, like Jody, is punctual. When we go to dinner with them, they give us a half-hour leeway. They tell us dinner is at six-thirty if it's at seven, seven if it's at seven-thirty. Unfortunately, we've figured this out, so no matter what time they tell us, we're late.

Archie, Jody's husband, is a computer nerd who has some cockamamie dream of working in Silicon Valley, and now that both of Jody's parents have passed away, Jody has agreed to move. She has a sister in San Francisco.

"How's Archie's job search?" I hold my breath. I secretly wish bad luck to Archie. I don't want him to take Jody from me.

"Not great."

My hope shoots up. Maybe Jody won't leave. "What do you mean?"

"Well, Peggy (Jody's sister) is in San Francisco, but Archie can't find a job he wants there."

"That might not be good for you, but it's good for me."

"He's found one in Seattle that he wants."

"Seattle? You can't go to Seattle. It rains there. Twelve months a year."

"Believe me, I'm not thrilled about it. But I've kept him here for ten years."

"What about you?"

Jody loves her part-time job. Someday when her kids are raised, I'm sure she'll run that teach-the-teacher consulting firm.

"I can work in Seattle. My company has twice as many schools there."

My hope sinks. I hate losing people in my life, but the loss of anyone else could not compare to the loss of Jody. She's my rock.

"I have to go, Nikki. He's unhappy where he works now."

Archie is the type of guy who would stay if Jody asked him to. That's part of the reason she has to go. He's a great husband. I've always known they'd eventually leave Fairview.

"I know you do."

Friendships come and go in life, but I can't imagine not having Jody living down the street to drop in on, run to the grocery store with, get an opinion from, or calm me down when my kids work their way into binds. Jody is the glue that keeps Evy and Val and Ellie and me together. It used to be Reah, too. But now Natasha has shepherded Reah away from us.

There is such a difference between these two childhood friends of mine, Jody and Reah. Distance can't dim Jody and my friendship. Her leaving will be a grave inconvenience, but she'll only be a phone call away.

That's how I deal with the possibility of her moving, of her cutting a huge hole in my heart.

"It's a five-hour plane ride," she says.

"Five and a half," I correct.

She tosses me that sad little smile that means I love you, I'll miss you, but I'll never leave you totally. If you need me, I'll jump on a plane and be here in half a day.

That's the thing about true friendship. It never dies.

For the first time, I see Jody tear up. This is a startling switcheroo. I'm the crier. Jody's the soother. But I rise to the occasion.

"Seattle will become my new hiding place," I say. "When things go wrong, and, of course, they will in my life, I'll hop on over to rainy Seattle. Bring my biggest umbrella. Although, you know, I will have my new best friend Janice to take your place soon."

She laughs hard, forcing a few tears to streak down her face.

"Buy a big house. Janice and I will visit."

"She can't." Jody giggles.

"You don't want my new best friend coming with me?"

"She'll melt."

My mouth drops. Has Jody just told a joke?

"From the rain," she clarifies as if I didn't understand. She's so proud of herself she's baffled me into silence.

I bust out laughing. In the forty years I've known Jody, I can count on one hand how many times she's insulted someone. This is amazing. An early going-away present. We toss Janice Everglade jokes across the front seat for the remainder of the ride. We jab her house, her polished appearance, money, kids, extravagant trips, ugly artwork pieces. Nothing Janice owns is sacred.

The best of friendships has secrets. Secrets shared and secrets kept. You'll tell your inner fears to a true friend, yet if it's something detrimental to them, you'll keep it locked up in your heart forever. You sacrifice.

That's what Jody has done. I've wallowed in a "poor me, I'm losing Jody" sulk ever since she told me six months ago that Archie had his heart set on finding a job on the West Coast. Jody is grounded and tough. It never once occurred to me that she doesn't want to leave me.

I'm flighty. I'm petty, but I suddenly realize something good about myself. I am loyal and loving. The best friend Jody will ever have in her lifetime because no one—not a single human being—will ever say anything mean about Jody while I'm in the room.

That's something, isn't it? My loyalty?

So I set a padlock around my sorrow over her leaving me alone, and she deadbolts the chamber in her heart that hurts because she's leaving her best friend, and we take it all out on Janice Everglade. At her expense, we arrive at the driving range in better spirits. I start to wonder a bit if Jody secretly wants to pick me up, usurp as much time with me as she can before I leave.

"Keep your cell phone ringer on. If Mark is busy, can I call you?"

She flashes a warm smile. "You know you can. And Nikki?"

"Yeah?"

"Try to stay out of trouble."

"Hahaha," I sneer, and I get out of her car, ostentatiously flashing her my middle finger. She's laughing as she drives away.

When I turn around, the golf pro is staring at me with a little I-saw-that smirk. I smile back.

"Blake Anderson, right?"

"Right. Nikki Grey?"

"I am. I'm not sure what my husband paid for these golf lessons, but I'm quite sure it's not enough."

His eyes twinkle. "We'll see about that. Let's get started."

He shows me how to master the art of holding a golf club, saying how my fingers sit on the grip can help my swing tremendously. He bends my arms inward before realizing I'm double-jointed, then he teaches me how to compensate for that and helps me straighten my arms.

He shows me how to stand, position my torso, and lectures me about the importance of how far apart I place my feet.

Really? My feet matter?

Forty-five minutes of my hour lesson is spent on semantics. When I finally edge up onto my square of the driving range to hit a ball, I'm excited. He has successfully bored me into wanting to swing.

He was easy on the eye, this instructor. He walked beside me, carrying his little bucket of balls, looking more thrilled than me. I caught myself wondering if he was married, has kids, a real job. Or wait, was he gay? I couldn't decide. Mark said he was a pro at one of the golf clubs in town, but I didn't know what that meant. Was that a full-time thing?

Regardless, fifteen minutes before my lesson is up, I step onto a square rubber mat on a cement landing. The mat has two permanent tees on each of its sides.

"I think you want to face the other tee." He grins.

I glance at him, annoyedly. I wasn't planning on hitting off the left tee, my mind had simply wandered over to the old lady in the next stall. She was smacking the crap out of the ball.

"Right."

How stupid does he think I am?

The adorable smirk on his face widens, and I look away. I set a ball on the right tee—I'm right-handed—and stand back to take a stance, intentionally ignoring him.

My first two or three or twenty shots go nowhere. Eight times I miss the ball completely. My inability is embarrassing. The eighty-year-old lady beside me is knocking the names off the balls from her rubber square of the driving range, embarrassing me further. At least her direction faltered. She couldn't hit a ball down the middle to save her life. She was slicing? Splicing? I'm not sure of the correct term, but she had a wonder ball. You wondered where it was going.

Once, when I am about to swing, she hollers over to me, "Honey, you're tense. Relax a little."

At this, the smiling pro agrees. "You are tense."

He steps up behind me like they do in the movies. He leans close and sets his arms and hands over the top of mine. His chest rubbing against my back and shoulders is disconcerting and yet nice at the same time. While he blah blahs on, I think, gee, this is what it's like to spend time in another man's arms. Even if he is gay, it feels fine.

In twenty years, no one has been that close to me other than Mark and one homeless guy who roamed the streets downtown where I worked before the kids were born. Before my stretched, child-bearing hips began knocking lamps off end tables.

The homeless guy's name was Winky. He had one eye. I still had it going on back then.

So the smell of Blake the Pro's cologne as he breathes down the back of my neck seems up-front and personal. A little too sexy for an old married mom. I don't hear a word he says. At the end of his little speech, he manipulates my fingers into an extremely uncomfortable position on the grip of the club, and all I can remember of any instruction before I swing is that the little old lady told me to relax.

So I relax, swing the club, and it sails through the air— the club, not the ball. That's still perfectly perched on the tee.

Humility overpowers me, and I burst forward out of my little rubber stall and run for the club. The last thing I hear before the eighty-year-old lady's ball makes a line drive to my temple is Blake the Pro yelling, "Don't go after your club."

I regain consciousness and refuse the ambulance. Blake the Pro says he'll give me a ride home, but once we are riding in the car, he admits he lied. He's taking me to the hospital. Anger and delirium overpower me. I try to get out of the car at every red light, but I keep rolling down the window instead of opening the door.

Once we arrive at the emergency room, he does all the talking. He strolls into the room with me as if some of this was his fault.

I don't dare to admit I am a hopeless born loser.

We make glib chat in the sterile silver and white room while we wait for the doctor. I encourage him to go home several times, but he says he'll wait for Mark. Finally, an hour later, the door opens and in walks—you got it—Doctor Death.

"Well, hello again, Ms. Grey."

I look at Blake the Pro. The twinkle in his eye has re-sparked. Is he laughing inside?

"Do this often?" Blake the Pro's teeth are so straight and white that it strikes me. I may have found the perfect match for Evy.

Mark walks in and Blake the Pro apologizes but, oddly, stays. Maybe the look on Mark's face as he traipses through the door arouses Blake's curiosity.

Furious, irate, and enraged with me, Mark wanders off on a teeth-gritting tirade, ranting about some lunch opportunity with a client being rushed.

Embarrassedly, I counter, "Do you think I got hit in the head just to ruin your lunch?"

"You're always getting yourself into these fixes," he grumbles.

My mind whirls. I can't respond calmly. It's hard concentrating with Blake the Pro and Doctor Death listening. I become enraged. I progress to screaming.

"I'm not doing these things on purpose!"

Then, Doctor Death enters my ring of fire.

"You passed out," he doesn't yell, but his tone closes in on disgust. "I'm adding the time to your license suspension."

No, no, no. That will take me past Christmas.

"I took a blow to the head," I yell.

"Nikki, lower your voice," Mark chides.

"Doesn't matter." Doctor Death is a heartless bastard. "You lost consciousness."

I pick up a tall metal IV holder off the floor. Mark tries to pry it from my fingers, but this time my grip is firm. I step toward Doctor Death.

"How about you run for the door, I swing this with all my might and knock you on your ass. Let's see if you lose consciousness."

Clearly, I have more than just friend problems.

Chapter 8 The bus

"You rode all that way, got out of the car, then turned around and threw up in the back seat?" CJ asked Carolyn who, for once, threw up from drinking.

"You can't improve your Uber rating on a moment's notice, Mom. Get the Lyft app." Delanie is desperate to dissuade me from riding the bus. She, Gianna, and Mark say suburban housewives don't ride buses.

But I can't get an Uber driver to accept my car-ride request because my rider rating stinks, and Natasha's three nephews drive for Lyft. I refuse to download that app on my phone. So I'm set on riding the bus to the library today. I've googled how to take a bus, and I'm on our town's website searching for schedules.

"What the heck is a route number closet?" I ask.

"What?" Delanie jerks her hands out, palms up. "There's no such thing."

"Yes, there is. It says so right here." I read a sentence off the internet. "Begin by finding a route number closet."

She leans down, reads, then immediately straightens and yells at Hux. "Oh my God, see? I told you she couldn't do it." She walks away, grabs her purse, turns around, and crosses her arms.

"What?" I bawl.

Hux leans over my shoulders, reads the words, and bellies out a laugh. "You didn't read the whole sentence. It's a typo. 'Begin by finding a route number closet to your starting point.' It's supposed to be closest."

I lean in, look. I didn't read the whole sentence.

"Mom, stop. I'll take you to the library when I get home from work," Delanie pleads.

"I'm not waiting all day." I lure the conversation away from my bus ride. "Why can't I improve my Uber score?"

"You think raising it from a one to a two will help?"

"How did I get so low?"

"You can't throw up in an Uber and expect a good rating."

"But I paid for the cleaning. That should count for something. And how do you know so much about Uber?"

"We Uber all the time in college, Mom."

I know what that means. "Delanie, you aren't even twenty years old. You should not be drinking."

"God, you're such a—" She stops. She doesn't dare call me what she wants to call me. Not because she's nice but because she's futilely attempting to keep me from embarrassing her. She doesn't want people seeing her mother standing conspicuously at the bus stop, which sits on the corner entrance of our subdivision.

Gianna doesn't, either. "Don't embarrass me, Mom."

Then again, Hux thinks it's hilarious. "Are you going to wear your boot?"

I have a large grey boot for my stress fracture. The doctor said I should wear it if I walk long distances.

"I have to." Delanie and Gianna let out matching moans. "It's a half-mile walk from the bus stop to the library once I get to the bayfront."

"Oh my God," he wails. "This gets better and better. We have to get pictures."

"You're not helping, Hux," Delanie cries.

The three of them burst into a quarrel. Nostalgically, I listen. When did I become such an embarrassment to my children? Wasn't I changing their diapers yesterday? Reading them stories? Holding them when they were sick? Chasing the bad dreams away?

Standing there observing them reminds me of the time I watched Delanie through the glass elevators of our town's shopping mall. Last year, before she marched off to college, we passed each other in those side-by-side elevators in the middle of the mall. She traveled up. I traveled down. She frowned and turned her backside to me as soon as she saw me, but that's beside the point.

What I remember of that passing is the symbolism. Her life taking off. Mine winding down.

That moment in time is forever etched in my memory. I watched the elevator whisk her upward. I waved, hollered, and helplessly observed her rise above me, well aware the moment mirrored life. You want to teach your children everything you can, hoping to somehow make the journey ahead of them easier.

They never want to listen.

Yet today, listening to them talk about me as if I'm not in the room, I realize they've been watching me as much as I've watched them.

Clarity surrounds the moment. I see their individuality, uniqueness. Each has their own talents, futures, dreams, experiences ahead of them. I study them from my elevator, hoping and praying that they have a good journey upward as I helplessly drift downward. Move farther and farther away.

I love these three more than life itself. My heart swells with pride. We mothers have mixed emotions when our children grow. We have nurturing qualities men don't have. We're more understanding, compassionate. We hate yet love our children's new-found independence.

They carry on as if they hold my destiny in their hands. I watch them rise. She can do this, one says. She can't do that, another. She'll get lost. (Oh, how I love them.) She'll get hurt. (So sweet.) She won't know how to get off. (I will.) She's too dumb to find the right bus once she gets downtown. (Wait a minute.) She'll call her friends, and no one will be around. (Are you kidding me?) We'll have to pick her up. (You spoiled brats.)

I snap out of nostalgia with a vengeance. I'm only forty-five years old. I'm going down fighting.

"I'm right here. I can hear you," I rage. "And I'm not changing my mind. I'm taking the bus. What do you think? I'm an idiot?"

"Yes!" Again, Gianna and Delanie, twin timing.

"Well, tough."

I sit down to put on my boot. Gianna runs up the stairs crying, and Delanie stomps out the door. Hux follows Delanie, patting me on the back as he passes, "Good Luck, Forrest," he says. "You might want to take a box of chocolates for your bus buddies."

"Get the heck out of here," I scold.

An hour later, Gianna hides at a friend's house for the day, and I stand at the bus stop, thinking maybe the kids are right. Forty-five might be too old for a first bus ride.

Still, after the emergency room debacle, my determination is set. I'm not asking Mark for any more rides. I'm going to be independent.

Even if that means being dependent on the bus company.

Of course, I miss my intended bus and must wait for the next one in the blazing sun. There's no covering over this bus stop because, face it, does anyone in the suburbs ever board a bus?

I have sweated through my new white shirt by now. My pink bra—bad choice—has bled through in spots, but I refuse to succumb and go home.

I count sixteen neighbors riding by. Some wave apprehensively, others have looks of horror on them as if it's Halloween, and they can't quite make out what my costume is—they simply know its frighteningly odd.

I'm only brave enough to stand here because I know Janice Everglade, my soon-to-be best friend, is gone for an extended weekend at the Atlantis Palm, St. Lucia, or, I don't know, some Hilton on a remote island in the West Indies. She doesn't live by me. Her stunning home sits on the edge of Lake Erie, but she frequents our neighborhood because we reside in the same school district. But she's vacationing, so I'm safe.

By the time the bus arrives, I'm drenched in sweat. Imagine my surprise when the doors open, and I stare into the face of a bulldog. He's short, thick, and his face is rowed with wrinkles.

"I've been driving this bus route for twenty years." He pauses. "No one's ever gotten on here."

"Thanks for the history," I say, and we continue staring. He's eyeing me up and down.

"You're sweating," he remarks.

"No kidding."

"It's hot today."

"Who are you, Al Roker?" It slips out of my lips, and I have to stick my boot up to keep him from closing the doors and driving away.

We stare more. He opens the doors again. "Are you getting in, or aren't you?"

This is not a good beginning to my independent bus-ride day, and I wonder if I should retreat, go home, and call Jody. Then I remember she's leaving. I have to learn to live without her.

I peek inside. Several sparsely spaced passengers appear cool and relaxed. I hurry in, select a spot in an empty row only to find the seats are hard and sticky.

When the bus driver takes off, I grab hold of a handrail on the side of my seat, and we bounce all the way into the neighboring city of Erie where the main library is located. I'm sure one pothole dislodges two vertebras in my back, but I say nothing to Al Roker, who speeds along as if he's got somewhere important to be. I don't dare ask where I transfer to the library bus. I gaze up at the schedule and estimate I get off somewhere around Tenth and State Streets. Occasionally, people board and exit until, finally, we turn onto State Street, and I am the only passenger left.

Al pulls up behind a line of buses that are parked on the side of the street. He inches to a halt then announces over the loudspeaker that this is the last stop. Everyone must disembark.

I clomp my way to the front. "Was that necessary?"

"What?" he grunts.

"Making an announcement. I'm your only passenger."

"Protocol," he says, then he jiggles the doors as if he's in a hurry for me to exit when there's no place for him to go. He's parked two inches behind the bus in front of him.

"How do I get to the dock? The library?"

"It's down the hill behind us, about a mile."

I turn palms to the ceiling. "Do you not see I'm wearing a boot?"

"How'd you break your leg?"

"I didn't break my leg."

"Then what's wrong with it?"

"That's a rather personal question."

"Asking what's wrong with your leg?"

"Yeah."

"It's a common courtesy question."

"No, it isn't. It's personal."

"It's just a question, lady. Like how are you today? Are you okay? What happened to your leg? Did you hurt it or were you born with a problem?"

"Really? I'm pretty sure that's personal."

"No, it's not."

"Well, how's this? How tall are you? Are you a midget?"

"Get off my bus."

"This isn't your bus. It's the bus company's."

"Get off."

For a moment, I stand there, wondering what Jody would do. Jody wouldn't be in this predicament. She would have said, "Have a nice day," smiled, and stepped down.

I stomp off the bus and turn. "Where do I catch the library bus?"

"Up the street." He shuts the door.

I look down the hill. The library beckons me from the bayfront, but the distance is too far to walk in my doggone boot, which hugs my leg uncomfortably tight. I turn the other way and trudge up the street, passing seven buses.

Every five minutes, the sign on the top panel of the front of the bus in the number one spot switches, the driver opens the doors, and people board. I wait for the sign to turn to "Blasco Library." At least I am out of the sun, sitting underneath a bus-stop shelter now.

I hold my purse for dear life because what could I do if someone grabbed it? When I was young and working down here, I feared no one. A teenager approached me once, and I yelled, "you better be able to run a long way, kid, if you take my purse. I'm a marathoner." He backed off.

But what could I do now? Take my boot off and beat the purse out of his hands? I couldn't catch him.

So I sit alone. A helpless, feeble woman waiting for her bus. I'm as vulnerable as a ninety-pound octogenarian.

I watch the buses. A fourth bus leaves, a fifth. Al Roker's bus inches forward, getting alarmingly close. Finally, two more buses leave. Al pulls up and sure enough, his sign switches to Blasco Library.

The doors open. People get on. I wait designedly. I want to be last. When the person in front of me turns to take a seat, I'm standing with my arms crossed.

"You couldn't let me wait on the bus," I say. "You had to make me get out and sweat in ninety-degree weather."

"It was my lunchtime."

"I could have sat quietly in the back."

"I doubt that."

"But you should have taken pity on me. I'm practically disabled."

"What happened to your foot?"

It's as if he's never seen me before.

"What did you have for lunch? Prune juice?"

He closes the door and steps on the gas. I have to scramble to a front seat to avert a fall. Five minutes later, he utters secret words as I exit the bus. He slams the door, and I clomp down the street to the library.

I'm hot and sweaty and annoyed by the time I arrive. The cool air of the library relieves me. I sit and enjoy the coolness in a big cushiony chair in the back. My medication still makes me groggy, so I doze in and out and wake with a start when I realize over an hour has passed.

I google the library's card catalog and within a minute my phone dies.

Drat.

I roam around until I locate the library computers that show the available titles, only to find every single novel on my old book club's list is checked out.

A nice lady at the help desk enters me onto three waiting lists. I look around a while; I've always loved the library. There's something mystical about it. So many stories in so many books. I'm tempted to check out a few but decide lugging other books home on a bus might cramp my clomping style. I'm too tired to carry anything.

By now it's five o'clock and I head out. The boot digs into my leg with a vengeance; I'm not usually in it this long. I limp on, arrive at the bus stop at ten minutes after five. The schedule on the pole states the last bus leaves at five-fifteen.

Perfect.

I lean on the bus post, the only passenger waiting. I slip my foot out of the boot and cool my toes on the shady pavement. Minutes pass. The bus approaches, but it's not slowing down.

I squint to read its sign. State Street Transfer. I check the pole schedule. Yes, that's it. I ride the State Street Transfer bus then take the six o'clock Fairview bus.

I put my hand in the air, step into the street, but the bus speeds up. I pick up my boot, whirl it around in the air. The bus races by, and I see Al Roker, waving from behind his steering wheel. I hurl my boot in the air. It smacks the back of the bus, falls, and cracks in half. The bus keeps moving up the hill. I see Al Roker's shadow bending and straightening in laughter as he drives away.

I pull out my phone.

Still dead.

I leave what remains of my boot in the street and begin limping along the path that runs beside the Bayfront Highway. People driving home from work whiz by. I hope and pray I don't know any of them.

About a quarter-mile into the walk, I stop, remove the one shoe I do have, a $125 running sneaker. I chuck it as hard and far as I can into the bay and walk on barefooted. At least my gait is even now, but I don't know what I'm doing or where I'm going. I'm at least ten miles from home.

Should I trudge back to State Street and climb the hill? Or continue along the Bayfront and hope for another bus stop?

My kids were right. I can't even get to the library and home on my own. I picture them in our kitchen, sitting around the dinner table, laughing.

Someone driving by honks and startles me. Someone I know? I see a car turn into a parking lot about a quarter of a mile ahead. It stops, blocking my pathway. Who is it? A thief? Mass murderer?

I don't care. I hobble forward. A man gets out and leans against his car, facing me. His feet are crossed at the ankle and his arms at his chest while he waits.

I near. I recognize his face. That's—

Oh, dear God, it's Blake the Pro.

A little shake of his head back and forth reveals he thinks I'm crazy. When I finally limp up next to him, his smile widens, maddeningly. I don't have a thing to say. I'm out of excuses for the day.

"Where are your shoes?"

"Well, if you must know. One's at home and the other one is at the bottom of the bay."

He blinks a few times. Tries to hide the hilarity he sees in my predicament.

"And you're walking where?"

"Home."

"From here?"

"Yes, because my phone is dead, and I can't call anyone."

"You know they have this thing called a bus."

Thank God I left my boot in the street, or I would have clubbed him to death.

Chapter 9 The pills

"Quit your job, you're a writer," Jeff Zahner
said to CJ when her only sibling was diagnosed with
early-onset dementia.

On the fourth of July, I sit in my back yard and listen to Natasha entertain the entire neighborhood with food, music, alcoholic beverages and, in the evening, a blizzard of fireworks. As if that isn't enough fun for me, the next day, the nursing home calls. My sister had a stroke.

She spends a day in the hospital while doctors argue whether her impairments are the result of her stroke or progressing dementia.

Carol, Laura, Jody, and Val run me back and forth to the nursing home every day for the next week. I'm so exhausted I can barely function. I haven't acclimated to my medication yet; it still wears me down.

Today, I blearily roam the halls of the nursing home, dodging mindless questions from sadly confused residents. "Do you know where my husband is?" "How do I get out of here?" and yes, even, "Is there a bus stop close by?"

That one nearly sends me running.

Barb clings to my arm. She suffered physical setbacks from the stroke, which for her are worse than cognitive impediments. She was once a world-class runner. She twice ran in the women's marathon Olympic trials. To see her so feeble, hurts.

I lead her outside to the Alzheimer unit's garden. We weave slowly around the bright-colored flowers and neatly trimmed trees on an asphalt path with low-to-the-ground lights for evening walks.

This disease has stolen only part of Barb's memory. Our childhood capers remain tucked alive and well in some fertile cranny of her brain. We reminisce about beach times and school days and Mom and Dad because she still recalls those experiences. I treasure these walks and talks in the garden. I know dementia can steal her from me for good any minute.

July drags us along, and I stretch visiting to every other day then every three days because I have children at home and a slew of chores to accomplish before school resumes.

Toward July's end, as if God wasn't already sitting in the clouds tossing spears my way, life spirals further out of control when Mark announces he and his firm's partner are splitting. Mark is about to go it alone. That means longer hours and more trips to Pittsburgh.

The schism had been coming for a while, but Mark had downplayed it. They'd disagreed on a major issue a few months back, but I'd never bothered to ask about it. Honestly, I couldn't pretend to care what happened between Mark and David. I was too caught up in my own—admittedly frivolous—world.

I try to comfort Mark in those first few days he tells me about the split, but he spends less and less time with me and the kids.

I had been seeing a counselor since June, but the man was crazier than I was. He took pictures of my head with some infrared camera and printed out photos that showed psychedelic colors zigzagging across my forehead. The colors represented my inner stress, anger, inhibitions, he said. Each week he snapped a picture and less color showed. He bragged the relaxing techniques he had taught me were working. But I'd never used one, so I politely told him thanks and stopped scheduling appointments.

Then my friend Carolyn suggested I see her counselor, Tracy. I did. It's amazing what a good counselor can do. Tracy helped me realize that I'm not a horrific mother. My kids are simply charting their own courses, not leaving me. I need to plot a new course, too. Learn to love me.

I set up an appointment for Mark to see Tracy. With so much work, he was coming unglued. He became angrier and angrier when he had to drive me places. His business lingered above us in crisis mode. His short fuse shortened, and I avoided his path whenever possible. We were like magnets turned inside out, repelling each other.

Disappointingly, Mark canceled his appointment, blaming his busy schedule. I continued mine.

Tracy's office sits less than a mile from my sister's nursing home, which is wonderful. My stress fracture is healing, so I often walk to see Barb after my counseling session.

At today's visit, I talk excessively about Mark to Tracy, and I continue this conversation at the nursing home. Some days I still bounce problems off my big sister, knowing most of the time she doesn't understand. She walks with a slight curve to her spine and shuffle to her feet now. Her cognizance skips in and out. I'm never able to determine how much she understands or doesn't of our chats.

"Mark is never home, anymore, and I haven't gotten used to this medication. It makes me tired," I admit.

"Sometimes," she replies, "I don't swallow my medication."

I stop walking abruptly. She turns toward me, and the Barb of old surfaces. She sets a hand on my arm. "Don't say anything, Nikki. The medication doesn't help. It makes my headaches worse."

My first inclination is to insist she take her medication, but before I reply, she flashes a familiar look of desperation. "Please?" she begs.

In my head, our childhood resurfaces. Barb is babysitting, and she's broken my mother's prized vase. She glues it back together with superglue, and I say I'm going to tattle. She looks at me with those same desperately sad eyes. "Don't tell, Nikki. Please?"

I hadn't told then, and not telling hadn't changed a single moment of our lives. That vase sat on my mother's shelf fully intact until long after my mother died.

Not telling today is the same. Dementia will take my sister from me whether she swallows those pills or not.

Later, right before Jody comes to pick me up because Mark no-shows and won't answer his phone, my sister admits something else.

"I never liked Mark."

I wasn't sure it was a truth or the illness prompting her to say such a thing.

"You never liked Mark? Why?"

"I never trusted him," she replies. "Dad didn't, either."

"What do you mean? Dad loved Mark."

"Not really. He pretended to because you loved him."

On the way home, I tell Jody and she says, "Nikki, her mind isn't working properly. She didn't even know who I was."

"Of course, she did. She said hello and called you by name."

"No, you said my name, and she repeated it."

Maybe I'm deluding myself into thinking Barb sometimes has good days.

After a quiet drive, Jody turns into my driveway and sighs.

"I hate telling you this, but I wouldn't say anything to anyone else before you. I told Archie not to tell a soul until I talked to you."

"What?" My shoulders sink. I can see the light of the train coming straight at me.

"He got that job in Seattle."

"Oh God, no." I set my head back against the headrest and close my eyes.

"I'm sorry," she says, and when I open my eyes, she's crying.

After a long emotional hug, I leave her and enter my dark, empty house. The rattle on the roof seems louder than ever.

Something has to change in my life. I can't live like this—exhausted, sad, lonely. I remember my sister's words and realize, I can at least fix one problem

I march to the medicine cabinet and remove all of my epilepsy medication. I dump the pills into a plastic bag, crush them with a rolling pin, and empty the bag into the garbage.

I'll take my chances that I don't experience another grand mal seizure without the medication. I won't do anything stupid like smoke dope again.

If I'm not so tired, I can visit my sister more often, have more energy for my kids, be the wife Mark needs me to be during this transition of his business. I can help him. This is why he's been so enamored with John Everglade. He hopes to win his business.

If I learned one important point in recruiting clients during my years working in the business world, it is that contacts matter.

Contacts. Friendship. They're synonymous. My original thoughts had been right all along.

I must refocus and get on Janice Everglade's good side—not only for me but for my marriage.

Chapter 10 The attic

"She's obsessed with this movie to an unhealthy degree," Jessie said to CJ about Layla, who watches Nightmare Before Christmas several times a day.

"You think this guy right here." Evy points. "Is gay?"

It's a Monday swim day. My yard bursts in summer-bloom hues. The pavers of my patio have been weeded, sanded, and sprayed. My energy has tripled since I stopped taking my medication. My friends and I sit on brand-new beige and pink patio furniture that I've purchased. Hux set the old table, chairs, and umbrella out beside the street last night. Someone tossed it in the back of their pickup truck a half-hour later.

Our neighborhood crawls with frugal drive-by trash removers.

None of my friends work this Monday. Everyone arrives early. Now that Jody has revealed she's moving to Seattle, no one wants to miss a swim day—except Reah, of course. She had some family outing. I care but don't fret. I'll see her at our golf league.

"Yes, he's gay," I repeat.

Evy passes me his phone, so I can see Blake the Pro's picture. "You're sure?"

"Where'd you get this?"

"He's a golf pro. Won lots of tournaments. His little tush is all over the internet."

I hand it back. "Think you'd like him? I could fix you up."

"He's not gay, you ninny."

"Let me see that," Ellie says. "I have great gaydar."

"You?" Evy hands her his phone. "Have gaydar?"

"I do." Ellie studies the phone. "He's gay. Look at his tan. Straight guys don't tan."

Evy grabs his phone from Ellie. Jody, Val, and I lean in. "He is tan," Val agrees.

"He's the golf pro at Lake Erie. He's in the sun all day," Evy retorts.

"He's the pro at your golf club?" This surprises me. "Is that a full-time job?"

"Of course it is, darling. He took the job last year. Rumor has it he wanted a small town to stay away from the press."

"He's that good?"

"That good and perfectly straight." Evy stops and shoots upward, stands in his spot. "Leah, sweetheart, let your sister up for a breath of air."

We all glance toward the pool. Leah is holding Penelope's head underwater. Gianna's counting. The other kids stand around watching—except Becca who's not tall enough to stretch her toes to the bottom of the pool. She treads water in her swimmies.

Leah raises her hands, and Penny's head bobs up. She sucks in air and yells, "How long did I hold it?"

"Thank you, Leah." Evy sits down.

Penelope can hold her breath underwater for two full minutes. Unfortunately, Leah thinks she can hold it for three. Evy keeps a careful eye on them. He's a good father. When he and his partner split up there was no question who would raise the kids. Evy has perfect parental peripheral vision.

"I'm telling you he's gay." Ellie continues her studying of Blake the Pro's photo. "I don't know one straight guy that goes to a tanning salon."

"He doesn't get sprayed, that's for sure," Evy asserts. "He's not orange."

Oh, no.

"I tan. I'm not carroty," Ellie retorts.

Evy raises two flat palms, fans them out to flank his mouth, and leans across the table, hollering as if he has a megaphone, "You. Are. Orange. A tangerine Republican overdue to be peeled. If your hair was lighter, people would think you were Donald Trump's sister."

She slams his phone down on the glass table, and I check for cracks. "You're an emaciated, flamboyant charlatan," she says.

"Thank you, darling." Evy raises his coffee cup, his little finger held high.

Ellie sighs.

"Speaking of pompous Republicans," Val quips. "How's your friend recruiting of Janice Everglade going?"

I gulp down coffee and say, "Oh, I forgot to tell you guys my new plan. I go back to school in two weeks. I'm going to volunteer to work at the fall festival. Janice will love that. Every year she begs for help."

What I can't reveal in front of Ellie—because of her secret-spilling skills—is my other plan. I overheard Amy tell Gianna their family goes to dinner every Thursday. This Thursday, they are going to the Sunset Place Restaurant in downtown Erie because John is taking them to a special Erie Philharmonic event for sponsors, and the upscale restaurant sits a block away. Amy didn't want to go. Her mother insisted.

I estimate their reservations must be around six o'clock because the Philharmonic plays at eight, so I'm contemplating doing a little insisting myself. I dream up a

Thursday night dinner for my family, picturing how quaint and preppy we could look, all five of us perched around our seafood at the Sunset Place—except Gianna, of course. I'll camouflage her mustard bread.

I'm confident I can get Mark there. He had to go out of town until Wednesday. Usually, he takes me to dinner a day or two after he returns, snuffing his guilty conscience for leaving me alone.

I simply must find a way to convince Hux and Delanie to agree to go.

That potential dinner reminds me.

"Can someone pick me up from the counselor on Thursday afternoon?" I refuse to ask any of my family members. It may deter them from accepting my family-dinner-night request.

"I can," Jody and Evy say at the same time.

"Why don't I take her. You pick her up," Evy suggests.

"I'll take her home," Val breaks in. "Jody, you have too much to do with the house."

This is embarrassing. I'm like a custody-battle child whom nobody wants. My husband and kids treat me as if I'm a rabid skunk. My friends don't mind carting me around, but I mind. I hate putting people out. Jody is stressed regarding the potential move, Evy teaches summer classes, and Val works hard as a hospice nurse.

"Aren't you on twelve-hour shifts?" I ask Val.

"I am, but I'm off on Thursday. I'd be glad to give you a ride."

When I first met Val, and she explained she worked weekend shifts as a hospice nurse, I was shocked. Val with the staggering sense of humor? Worked with people who were dying? She is hilariously funny, a bit—maybe more than a bit—mischievous. When I considered this amalgamation of character and career, however, I concluded who better to cheer up someone passing from this life to the next?

Val mixes wittiness and compassion perfectly. She was born to do so.

For a moment, I think maybe I'll be all right when Jody leaves. As long as Evy and Val stay close.

"Nikki?" Jody sets her hand on my arm, whispers while the others argue whether Blake the Pro is gay or straight. "Are you taking your medication?"

I snap out of my stare-away.

"I'm fine," I say and ask her about the house. If she's painted the living room.

My stare-aways occur when I try a medication then stop taking it. Temporal lobe epilepsy, or TLE as many refer to it, is the least of the epilepsy curses, usually causing partial seizures that may advance later into full-blown seizures. Until what has come to be known as my marijuana seizure, I never lost consciousness. Not once.

When first diagnosed with this nasty disease, I had been tested because of dizziness. Back during college all-nighters when I stayed up studying for finals, I had a few middle-of-the-night panic attacks. I was tested, but not diagnosed. A few years later, in my twenties, I began running marathons. My blood pressure sometimes dropped so low I became light-headed. I learned when to eat and hydrate, but not before I had an EEG, which showed the TLE.

They took my driver's license away for a day. I signed an affidavit attesting I had never lost consciousness—and I hadn't, never in my life until the marijuana blunder.

My own diagnosis, not the doctor's, is that my epilepsy is nocturnal. I don't worry about having full or partial seizures during the day. As long as I behave myself and refrain from smoking marijuana, I'll be fine.

Jody, of course, is the only person in the entire world who knows this. She worries my self-diagnosis is wrong.

"Another one," she asserts.

I glance at her.

"You just had another one. You're off the medication."

Evy hears her, so later when Val and Ellie leave, he suggests, "Why don't I come and stay tonight since Mark isn't home, and Gianna's spending the night at Amy's."

"No, I'll be fine. You have too much to do."

"Jody and I can both come." Jody has stepped up beside him. They look like two kittens begging to be scratched. "We'll have a movie night. Just the three of us."

The idea tempts me, but inconveniencing Evy and Jody due to a ridiculous fear of sleeping alone in my house encourages my Needy Nikki behavior.

"Absolutely not. Nothing to worry about. Delanie and I have plans. I'm looking forward to it, just the two of us."

I'm lying, but they've lost the battle. They frown and leave at the same time, a united front driving off into the sunset.

Later that night, they keep calling me until I threaten to block them if I get one more call. I promise to text them in the morning, and I settle into my bed, doze and wake until a night jerk, that's what Mark calls my little episodes, startles me into a sitting position.

I check my phone. Neither Hux nor Delanie is coming home. Both sent pleading texts to spend the night at a friend's—a common summer ploy. I don't allow underage drinking. Other mothers do.

I lie back down in bed. This is the first time in my life I've been alone at night. I moved from my parents' house to live with Mark. Before the kids were born, I slept at my parents' when Mark was out of town.

After Delanie came along, Mark installed an alarm system, but I still tilted chairs against doors in case the alarm didn't work, and some stranger decided to break in on the exact night Mark was out of town. When the fearless

Delanie was nine years old and Mark was in Pittsburgh for the evening, she awoke and saw my burglar boobytrap.

"Mom," she said. "Go to bed. No one's going to break in."

Tonight, I refrain from jamming chairs against doors in case someone decides to come home.

I try to sleep again, and I do doze off, but probably because I'm stressed from being alone, I have another frightening night jerk. I scream Mark's name then realize I'm alone in the house.

What if someone does break in?

I can't sleep. Attempting to try will be fruitless. I toss off the covers and get out of bed.

I trudge downstairs to the kitchen and grab a can of diet pop—caffeine-free—and make my way to the family room. I stroll around the circumference of the room, snapping shades shut, then plop into a recliner. I open my soda and grab the remote, but before I turn the television on, I sit and listen to the wind howling, and I hear that sound again—the rattling noise. Where's it coming from? Not the first floor.

I rise, climb back up the stairs, and listen. It's above the second floor, too. It must be in the attic.

I retrieve my cell, turn on its flashlight, yank the cord in the hall ceiling, and the attic steps magically fold down. I creep up the rickety stairs and step into the attic, flashing my light at the ceiling and all around.

I listen. The noise is coming from the roof.

Mark's problem.

Satisfied the trouble is not mine, I turn to leave, but my old hope chest catches my eye. I sit down on the floor beside it and run my fingers over its gritty wood. I open the lid and a world of paintings and pottery pieces stares up at me. Ceramic pencil holders. Santa pictures. Bright-colored turkeys traced from little hands. All the sentimental bits from my children's childhoods.

I miss my kid's younger years. Paint days, beach days, park days. Only Gianna looks forward to swimming days now.

Time sneaks by. Children grow wild and reckless and fast. We barely see them change. One day they're walking, then doing homework, driving, going off to college, making memories of their own.

I pick up three ceramic dishes and run my fingers along the little handprint impressions on each. My kids molded these in preschool. I compare them. Delanie's is near perfect, smooth, no smudges, block-lettered name with a backward L. Hux's is a messy swirl of hand and crevasses, his name etched crookedly across the bottom. Gianna has artistically etched tiny swirls on hers. Each print brags of distinctness.

A sorrow for time passed scrapes my heart.

Maybe this family dinner isn't completely about winning Janice Everglade's friendship. Maybe it's about me, too. Delanie is forever angry with me, Gianna sees me as a servant, and I'm not a person to Hux. I'm just a mom with an extraordinary ability to get under his skin with the simple twist of my lips.

I hope Delanie and Hux will agree to this dinner.

An idea sparks.

I wedge the chest lid open and tap Delanie's number into my cell. It's past midnight. The family rule is they must answer their phone after midnight, or they lose their cell privileges for a week. Delanie answers on the second ring.

"Come home," I tell her. "Your brother is staying out, and you know I've never been alone in a house at night. You have to come home."

"Mom, nothing is going to happen. I am not come home to babysit my mother."

There's not an ounce of inebriation in her, only anger.

"Please?"

"No!"

"All right, don't get mad." I sigh. Try to sound scared, upset, pathetic, which isn't typically hard for me to do. Delanie of all three kids expects wretched dependency of me. "I'll make your brother come home but only on one condition."

"What?" she asks, and I wonder how she can combine four letters and produce such vengeance.

"We have a family dinner Thursday night. You have to come."

"You are such a pain."

"Does that mean yes?"

"Yes."

"Okay, honey, have fun tonight. I love you."

The conversation goes much the same with Hux only less vengeance and a hair of inebriation. I tell him I'll call Delanie if he will agree to the family dinner.

When he agrees, I hang up and sit cross-legged on the floor, happily sifting through the artwork until the light of my phone dies.

I flail one hand around in the dark until my fingers find the light cord. I pull and the attic lights up. I feel a draft and walk to one window. I insisted Mark put screens in when the kids were little. I was afraid they'd suffocate when they hid up here. They used it as a refuge. Now, we open the windows an inch every summer and let a sliver of air in. But tonight, it's cold. I crank one window shut.

I traipse to the other side of the attic and close that one, too. A vacuous surge sweeps from one end of the attic to the other. The dangling overhead light swings, and a loud slamming noise sounds. The stairs.

Oh, no, no, no!

I pray Mark has fixed the ceiling latch. When the stairs spring shut, the latch closes, and the steps lock in place. I've told him countless times someone would eventually be locked up here. I never expected that person would be me.

I run to the collapsed stairs jutting out of the attic floor. I stand on them. Jump up and down. Bang them with an old popcorn popper, but it's no use. They won't release.

I yell and yell, but of course, no one hears me. No one will be home until morning. I'm here for the night.

Delanie is right. I am a born loser.

I succumb to the idea of sleeping in the attic. What choice do I have?

So I sort through a box of old clothes and dress appropriately in Hux's old *Nightmare Before Christmas* pajamas and a white ski cap. It is the first August night in more than forty years that the temperature plummets below sixty degrees.

Of course, the only light bulb burns out before the night ends, and I cry myself to sleep in horrific fear, listening to the whistling wind and the rattling roof.

In the morning, I hear commotion below me. It's Hux. He's home first. I scream and holler and jump up and down until he lowers the staircase and glances up at me in his Jack pajamas.

He yells, "Can you take off your head and recite Shakespeare?"

I'll be the butt of his jokes for the rest of his life.

Chapter 11 The tail

"You holler shit and she comes sliding in," CJ's dad, Pat Filutze, said about her mom, Donna Mae, when Donna embarrassed them.

On Thursday I threaten my family that if one of them breathes a word of my night spent in the attic—even hints of it—I'll leave and never come back.

They celebrate.

So I change my threat to spending every night of the next month watching TV with me. That draws a groan.

I try five dresses on before deciding their tight cut broadcasts my too old and frumpy figure. I slip into a smart blouse, snug-fitting slacks, and loafers and stare at myself in the long mirror. Unfortunately, I've gained a few pounds since my stress-fracture sideline. Most of my wardrobe is form-fitting now. I'm not sure what I'm wearing is she'd-make-a-good-friend worthy, so I google the dress code for the restaurant. Their website says casual chic. I google casual chic and see a picture of Cameron Diaz dressed in a sexy blouse, jeans, and boots.

I change, mirroring Cam's outfit.

The kids are thrilled when I say jeans are fine to wear. I tell them they can pick any dressy shirt they want. They make fine choices. Mark, too. By the time we arrive for our six o'clock reservation, at twenty after six, we look stunning. I thank God they haven't given our table away.

Of course, the Everglades are nowhere to be seen, and my little plan of impressing them with a grand entrance is foiled. After twenty minutes of worrying they won't show, they parade in ostentatiously. The hostess practically carries Janice Everglade to her table, which sits heads above all the others on a front landing next to a beautiful bay window. The platform resembles a stage

That's fine for me. Janice hovers above everyone else, so we make instant eye contact from across the room. I wave slowly. She waves back.

"Mom, what was that?" Gianna asks.

"It's her kiss-ass wave," Delanie grunts. I frown at her then remember Janice is watching. I quickly pat Delanie gently on the back. Sad as it is, I practiced this wave in the mirror.

I can barely contain my pride. For once, my family looks ravishing. Throughout the entire meal, I giggle and brush my hand affectionately against my kids' shoulders even when they're swearing at me. I ignore Delanie when she says, "stop touching me," and pretend to be the perfect mother with my perfect family, laughing elegantly when I think Janice is looking.

Pitiful or not, I'm determined to win her over. Prove our family is deserving of hers. The Everglades hold my ticket back into Reah and Natasha's life. The two idolize Janice.

I rock in my seat daintily and speak sweetly, elevating my voice a touch above the others in the room, hoping Janice can hear me.

"Mom," Gianna says. "Why are you acting so weird?"

"Because the Everglades are here," Delanie grumbles.

"That's not true," I counter. "I'm thrilled we are finally having a lovely family dinner."

"The Everglades are here?" Mark says.

"Lovely?" Delanie huffs. "Really, Mom?"

"Who are the Everglades?" Hux asks a little too loudly.

Mark jumps up, and suddenly my night seems ruined.

"Don't rush over there while they're eating, Mark." I tug at his sleeve.

"It's fine. They're done."

He shuffles off, and I frantically wonder how I'll be able to stop by and say hello to Janice without us seeming overly zealous, stalking, creepy. When Mark returns, I try to coax Gianna into helping me out.

"Gianna," I gush. "Would you like to walk over and say hello to your little friend?"

I don't know why I'm talking like this. It's as if I can't break the I-adore-Janice part I'm playing.

"My little friend?"

"Amy, dear."

My God I'm making myself sick.

"Not really. I waved to her." Gianna keeps eating her bread.

Delanie laughs, and I frown at her. Her perceptiveness can be exhausting. She must feel my desperation, however, because in the middle of dessert, she throws me a life ring.

"Don't you have to go to the bathroom?"

"What? No," I sputter.

She continues shoveling cake into her mouth. "Yes, you do."

I realize then. Yes! The bathroom. It's across the room. Perfect.

I stand, but as I do, a man appears out of nowhere. He's someone Mark knows. I stare over his shoulder while Mark introduces him. I keep watching the Everglades.

The man is an attorney who recently secured a job in Erie. He recognized Mark from a Pittsburgh conference. He and Mark blah blah on as I shift my weight back and forth nervously. If I don't get to the bathroom quick, the Everglades might leave.

"We are moving into that neighborhood," I hear the man, whose name I cannot remember, say. "You live there?"

"Yes, we do," I respond, although I'm not one-hundred percent sure it's my neighborhood he's talking about. I just want to excuse myself.

Just go, Mr. Chatty Attorney Man, will you?

"It would be great if our children could play together. Mine won't know anyone. Where's your youngest girl?"

"Right here." I talk, but I'm not aware of anything I'm saying. "Her name is Gianna."

Oh my God, will he never leave?

My nervousness heightens when the waitress approaches the Everglades.

"No, your younger daughter."

I hold my breath while Mark explains Gianna is our youngest. His partner has a little girl. Everyone gets Mark and David confused. They have for years.

I can't take anymore.

"I'm sorry," I blurt out. "I must excuse myself. It was nice meeting you."

Rudely, I shake his hand and prance away. I scurry toward the restroom without glancing in the direction of the Everglades' table whatsoever. I use the facilities as quickly as possible, wash my hands, splashing water on my hot face, and exit the ladies room, hoping they're still there.

They are. I sigh with relief and stroll casually toward them. For once, I feel like the perfect, quintessential mother instead of a haggard old housewife. I have the right clothes, the right boots, the right kids.

The right friends.

I step gingerly up the stairs to their landing, clutching my purse smartly at my side.

"Hi, Janice, how nice to see you with your family."

"Nice to see you and yours," she responds, but I feel a bit of tension. It's as if I've walked into the middle of a family discussion or argument. They're unusually quiet. Janice, John, the kids, all seemed strained.

"Your older children have grown so much I hardly recognize them," I insist.

Delanie attended school with Janice's oldest daughter, Megan. Simply put, Megan is a bully. Delanie called her Maggots. They hated each other. Maggots, I mean Megan, made fun of the space between Delanie's front teeth until braces correctively forced them together.

"Nice to see you, Megan. How is Boston College?"

"Love it." She answers, smiling, acting a little too happy.

The entire encounter seems tense. Maybe I had done exactly what I accused Mark of doing. Bothered them while they were eating.

"We love having Amy over." I pat Amy's back sweetly. "Hope to see you again soon, honey."

"Yeah." Amy giggles. Does she know I planned this family dinner intentionally? To see them?

"I'm sorry. I'm interrupting your dessert," I apologize.

"No, you're fine," John remarks kindly.

"Well, see you soon, Janice," I say.

Janice nods but doesn't speak.

I turn, a little confused. I step gingerly down the three stairs, so I don't fall flat on my face and embarrass myself. These high-heeled boots are stylish but wobbly. I shouldn't be wearing them because of my stress fracture, so I saunter slowly. Several people smile at me, and for the first time in years, I feel pretty. I see other women in blue jeans and trendy shirts like mine. For once, I fit in.

I strut across the room, swinging my hips a tad more than usual for effect. As I approach my family, I notice Hux has his head resting on top of the table.

My God!

I try to make eye contact, hoping he'll read my mind.

Sit up. Are you kidding? Don't embarrass me in front of the Everglades.

But when his gaze finally meets mine, he snaps his eyes shut and slaps his hand on the table. He's laughing. I glimpse the rest of my family. Mark has his head down. Delanie is covering her face. I think Gianna is crying.

"What is with you people?" I say when I reach them.

"TP," Hux blurts out.

"TP? What the heck does that mean?"

"Toilet paper," Mark whispers.

Oh, no.

Hux slaps his hand on the table again. He's howling, crying. People are beginning to look.

I glance toward my boots, but there's nothing there. I raise a palm upward and annoyedly pantomime, "What?"

Hux pounds a fist on the table again and again. He's dying laughing.

"On the back of your pants," Delanie groans, disgustedly.

I turn around and eight or nine crumply squares are flailing behind me, caught by a draft from the front door. The top square is lodged in the top of my jeans, perfectly centered. I have a long, TP tail.

I swing one hand around and rip it off. Roll the toilet paper around my fingers. I cringe, and my face reveals to the entire room what I'm thinking.

Oh my God, it's damp.

My eyes meet Janice's. She's laughing as hard as Hux.

Chapter 12 The school

"If you find yourself in need of friends, cast a wider net," Heather said to encourage women to tap into multigenerational friends.

"Hux said never in his wildest dreams did he think I could top the Jack in the attic caper, but that I did. He's calling me TPN."

"TPN?" Evy asks.

"Toilet-papered Nikki."

"Perfect, darling. Has a ring to it."

It's Monday at the pool again, and I might as well tell my friends about the family-dinner night because Janice Everglade has blabbed it all over Fairview. She couldn't have notified more people if she purchased a megaphone and drove two miles an hour shouting TP Nikki out her car window.

"And the place was packed?" This question sounds heartlessly too happy crossing Ellie's lips.

"Packed. People were crowded into the entranceway, and I paraded right up onto the front landing, so everyone could see. You know me. I'm all-inclusive."

Val snorts. "How embarrassed was Marky?"

"Terribly."

"What did he say?"

"He said, 'someone hollers shit and you come sliding in'." I give my best Mark imitation.

They roar so loud the kids in the pool stop to see what's going on then swim away disappointedly when they see nothing but a circle of old people laughing.

"Clearly, this Janice Everglade friendship isn't working out for you, girlfriend," Evy remarks. "That's better, too. You can't be friends with me and her both. You know that, don't you?"

"Why do you keep saying that?"

"Because she hates me. Loathes me passionately."

"She does," Val affirms.

"You say that as if you're proud, Evy."

"I am. Very."

"What did you do?"

"Embarrassed her in front of her own."

"How?"

"Words. Sticks-and-stones words."

None of us can pry what happened out of Evy. If Val knows, she's not saying. We've been asking what Evy did for two years—ever since Janice took up arms about the LGBT spring parade. We're sure she's trying to get back at him, but he won't say why.

"Have you learned yet that you don't need her?" Evy scolds.

"You're right. I don't need her. But I need Reah and Natasha back in my life so, consequently, I must impress Janice. Last year my Christmas was so boring the kids hightailed off to friends' houses."

"You can come to mine," Evy offers.

"Thanks, I love you, Evy, but you know Delanie and Hux won't want to spend Christmas with the little ones."

"He could let them drink," Val suggests.

"No, thanks."

We never see Mark's sisters anymore. They fly back and forth between Texas and Florida, pretty much ignoring Mark. And of course, I have no one. No family left at all.

I think about this coming Christmas. It will be dull and boring like last year. Reah used to spend Christmas Day at our house. Natasha would stop by, too.

"Mark and the kids say I make Christmas boring. No matter what I try, they get angry with me. I'm like a bullied grade-school kid in my own home. Mark says I get treated that way because I act like a pathetic grade-schooler."

Even though I joke about the kids and Mark, that they think I'm a bore hurts me.

"Why is everything my fault?" I blurt out.

"Nothing is your fault," Jody consoles. "Your Catholic guilt makes you feel that way."

"Please tell Mark that, will you? If I do something wrong, it's my fault, and if he does something wrong, it's my fault. He's got the kids convinced their faults and shortcomings are caused by some deep-rooted evil in their mother."

"It's always the mother's fault," Val chimes in. "Bruce says I'm the reason our kids are bad."

"That's not helping," Evy says. "You were a complete delinquent as a child."

"So was he," she yells. "He was arrested six times. Spent a week in jail once."

"How many times were you arrested?" I dare to ask.

She counts on her fingers. "Four times. But I never spent a single night in jail."

"That's because Daddy got you out." Evy, again.

"You male chauvinist. Daddy, hell." She stands and points her finger at him. "I'll have you know my mother rescued me every time. Why do you assume my father defended me? Hands down, a mother always protects her child."

"She does," Ellie agrees. "It's always we mothers who run to our kids' defense."

"Then what do they do?" I fume. "Say, isn't it nice daddy got the Jeep he always wanted. Let him go for his weekend with the guys, Mom. He deserves it. Poor Dad, he worked all day."

"Mine do the same thing."

"That's why we need more friends," I insist, convinced once again that friendship is the answer to all my problems.

"So what's the plan?" Evy combines exasperation and curiosity into the tone of his voice. "You'll be back to school in two weeks. You won't have as much time to draw up a new blueprint."

I sit mulling over this. But, wait—Evy is brilliant. Yes! I'll be back in school. Working for Mrs. Higgins, who loves me. Whom Janice loves.

"Multigenerational friends," I announce, enthusiastically. "I'll invest in multigenerational friends."

Mrs. Higgins is approaching seventy.

"Um, no offense but the last time you made nice-nice with the older generation you took a line drive to the temple," Jody reminds me.

"True, but all friendships have their ups and downs."

"Yes, they do." Evy looks flatly at me.

"Wait, are you talking about Mrs. Higgins?" Ellie perks up because she's still in the book club, and she knows Janice Everglade would polish Mrs. Higgins' shoes with an eyelash brush if she could. Megan Everglade is majoring in elementary education. She'll need a job in two years, and jobs are scarce in Fairview.

"You got it," I say.

"That just might do it," she nods, pensively.

The gate to the backyard springs open, thumps against the house, and slams shut. Hux runs to the pool and splashes the girls in their faces. They splash back and scream, all of them in love with Gianna's big brother. When he's finished, he runs, sopping wet, toward me. He retrieves a damp sheet of paper from his pocket.

"Mom, look what came."

The University of Virginia Admission Department sprawls across the subject line.

Oh, no. Virginia is so much farther than Slippery Rock.

"I got in," he shouts. "They admitted some of us from the waitlist. I'm in!"

I choke back all the things I don't want to say to him, and I jump up like everyone else. Hug him. He's so excited he shocks me with a bear hug. He won't let go. I think he is going to cry. I think I'll cry, but then Evy pats him on the back. Hux releases me, kisses my cheek, and everyone else has a turn at hugging him. Evy, Jody, Val, and Ellie congratulate him while I try to come to terms with the fact that my son probably won't be coming home every few weeks. That he might never be home again other than for a few short summers.

"Congratulations, honey. I'm happy for you."

"I'm going to call Dad. See if I can get through." He bounces into the house, and when the door slams behind him, I collapse into my chair and cry.

Evy slides his chair close to mine, puts his arm around my shoulders, and I set my head on his chest, sobbing.

I glance across the table and see Jody.

I'm losing everyone I love.

Chapter 13 The ride

"No matter where you go or who you meet in life, remember, no one loves you like your mother," CJ Zahner says over and over to Jessie, Zak, and Jilly.

By the time I pack Hux up and we head to Virginia, my attitude has changed. Twice in the last week, he was inebriated when kids dropped him off at home.

He's only eighteen! How did this happen? My God, what was I thinking? Smoking marijuana? Such bad mothering.

One of those nights when Mark worked late, and the girls and I fell asleep in the family room in front of the television, I heard a thumping at the front door. The bumping and banging continued until I was fully awake. I grabbed a bat and tiptoed toward the door, careful to stay out of sight of the side windows.

A figure hovered in the shadows. I flicked on the light, and a peal of deep, muffled laughter sounded from my front porch. I peeked outside. One of Hux's friend's cars sat idling in the street, exhaust puffing out its tailpipe.

I stepped toward the window. Hux was leaning on the door. I wrenched it open, and he fell onto the tile foyer, cracking his head open. Blood gushed from him. He felt nothing.

"Hello, Mommy dearest." He smiled from the floor.

Naturally, I couldn't take him for stitches in such an intoxicated state. He'll wear a memory of that night forevermore on the edge of his hairline. A gash about an inch long. It took me two days to get his blood out of the foyer's grout.

"Sorry about the last few weeks, Momma," he says when we are three hours away from the hotel. He's slept until then. I faked running out of ibuprofen to ensure he felt the pain of his sins.

Mark couldn't come, of course. Delanie drove us. I expected a hard-core attitude when I revealed she'd have to drive, but the strangest thing happened.

She smiled and said okay.

So the four of us journey together toward Virginia. Hux curls up next to one side of the backseat, drooling and snoring. Gianna crowds the other side, reading and shoving her brother once in a while when his snores annoy her.

Delanie is at the wheel, and I read next to her, feeling as if I'm the worst mother in the world. If it hadn't been for the marijuana, Delanie would be at home enjoying her last few summer-break days with high-school friends instead of driving her brother to Virginia.

We stop for dinner at a road-side diner, and surprisingly, the food is tasty and the conversation, excellent.

Seems I'm not the only family member feeling sentimental over Hux's leaving. All three kids reminisce pranks and shenanigans, most of which I've never heard before. Yes, I'm still the butt of their jokes, but not in a bad way this time.

I'm sorry Mark misses this. Halfway through dinner, I realize our three kids genuinely care for each other. I've been so busy feeling bad because I annoy them that I've missed something more important. I've taught them to love each other.

Relationships are unique. They range from firm to fragile. What I witness among my kids is a strong, unfaltering connection. The hard-to-sever kind. They'll miss the comfort of each other, of our family, during the school year.

I bit my lip and, for some reason, hope nothing changes us.

Two hours later, we spend time in a hotel pool before heading to bed.

I sit with my feet in the water and watch them. Hux tosses Gianna into the deep end. Delanie pulls her back and twirls her around in the shallow end. For a moment in time, they aren't twenty, eighteen, and twelve. They're ten, eight, and two, and we've just installed the pool. They plunge from the deck into the water. Hux and Delanie dodge pink swans and black sharks as they carefully drag Gianna around the pool. Noodles fly left and right. A floating basketball net bounces in the waves.

By the time we jump in bed for the night, I'm not mad any longer about the underage drinking. I sit in a chair and watch them sleep. I don't know how many more times I'll have them all to myself.

They were nice to me tonight. Kind. Loving. Even Delanie.

Tears well in my eyes. I snap a tissue from a box and cry silently. I love these kids more than life itself. I don't know how to let go. Allow them to live their lives without me.

Hux lifts his head off his pillow. Snot and tears mix unbecomingly on my face as I try to muffle my sniffing. I turn away, so he can't see me. I hear Delanie.

"Yep. She's crying."

"Ah, Mom, don't cry," Hux says. "Want me to make you feel better?"

Then he lets out a thunderous fart. Gianna gags, and Delanie runs to the bathroom shouting.

Just like that, my tears stop.

We laugh off and on throughout the night. People in the room next to us bang on the wall. Hux bangs back. We get a chastising call from the front office. The laughter goes on and on like a faucet that won't shut off. We're tired in the morning, but we rise, eat breakfast, and take Hux to his dorm.

Delanie and Gianna kiss him good-bye while older students grab his bags and haul them off toward his dorm.

He doesn't want me to come inside, the brat.

I step up to him. Try to hold back the tears. "Okay, don't drink too much. Be nice to the girls. Go to class."

He flashes that dynamic Hux smile that has gotten him out of so many jams in his youth. "I love you, Momma."

"And don't run naked in the courtyard."

His eyes widen.

"Yeah," I brag. "I did my homework on this school."

He laughs. His mien changes. For once, my overactive, never-stop child looks—what is that? Still and loving? This registers hard. He loves me.

"Remember." I can't keep the tears from falling, but I don't care. I love these three kids so much I hurt. They are the best of me. What little that is, they've grabbed and run with. "Nobody loves you like your mother."

He hugs me, whispers, "I know that, Mom. I love you."

Then just like that, he's gone.

I have a nice ride home with my girls. Delanie leaves two days later, and I can barely keep from crying. We've had our old car fixed—the one Hux ran into a stop sign—and we let her take it to Slippery Rock.

"Call me when you get there," I say the morning she leaves. She's standing in shorts and a t-shirt, the car stuffed to its ceiling. "I hate it that I can't drive you. We had such fun taking Hux. I wanted the same for you."

"Oh my God, don't cry again, Mom."

Crying won't go over as well with Delanie. I wipe my face and say, "Okay, okay, don't get mad. Call me when you get there. And no texting while you're driving."

She sighs. I hug her. Then I repeat my mantra, the same words I uttered to Hux before he turned and left me. This is my staunch reminder that I bombard my kids with over and over and over. I'm like a bad movie they can't turn off.

"Remember, no one loves you like your mother." I swear they'll write that on my tombstone.

"I know, Mom." She hugs and kisses me. Then she picks up her sister and swings her around, drops her on the grass, and shouts, "You're gonna miss me, peanut."

Right before she drives away, she blows me a kiss. Like. She. Used. To. do. When she was little. When I was still her best friend, her idol, her world.

I can't stand it. I linger in the driveway waving dramatically until she turns the corner and disappears from my view. Then I break down into my ugly cry.

"O. M. G.," Gianna barks. "You are such a sap."

Just like that the cycle continues. Gianna slams the front door, and three hours later, I cry at the counselor's office as if there is nothing left in life for me.

Gianna's right. I'm such a sap.

Chapter 14 The scramble

*"No, I don't want a golf lesson. I can throw my
golf club farther than I can hit the ball," CJ told her
friend, PGA & LPGA Golf Pro Karen Bukowski.*

On the first day back to work, I triumph, majorly. I meet
with Mrs. Higgins, the assistant superintendent, and admit I
suffered a seizure.

"Oh, my sweet little, Nikki, do they know what caused
it?" she asks.

"Stress and insomnia," I answer, all remorseful and
dejected. I'd practiced the reply. I'm fairly certain she won't
believe the rumors that I smoked dope. Mrs. Higgins tends
to see only the good in people she loves.

"So that's why you're here early this morning?"

"Yes," I reply, sadly. "Mark dropped me off before he
drove to the office."

Coworkers who once scoffed behind my back about my
tardy reputation won't comment to Mrs. H. about it now. As
much as I hate everyone knowing my business, their
attitudes change from "She's always late" to "Poor Nikki
Grey, I wonder if that's why she's been late all these years—
epilepsy."

People drop by my little cubicle and say hello. Ask how
my summer was. Everyone smiles and waves to me in the
halls and during lunch. Even the short, nasty woman in the
computer department, who usually frowns when I ask for
favors, remarks, "Nice to have you back."

I'm not proud of wallowing in the pity for my disease. I'd rather drag my knees across nails than worry about epilepsy, but you know the saying about lemons.

Stick the lemon in the bottle and drink the beer.

Evy says lemon juice counteracts the alcohol on your liver. Likewise, my diagnosis offsets the book club ostracism. I'm getting closer and closer to being invited back.

"I'm going to pick you up in the morning." Mrs. H. nods her head and rubs my arm. "No debate. Until you get your driver's license back—and you will—I'm picking you up every Tuesday and Thursday."

With this, Mrs. Higgins raises me up and catapults my reputation into near sainthood. Every day when she picks me up, I wave from the passenger window to Reah and Natasha and anyone else who might tell Janice Everglade I'm riding with Mrs. H.

On one of those wondrous mornings, I slip the topic of the fall fest into our conversation, and I don't have to ask Mrs. H. if Janice Everglade needs help; she implores me to volunteer. She and Janice are co-chairing this year's fest.

"Could you possibly help us with addressing the invitations and ordering the decorations, too?"

"I'd love to," I beam.

Later, I hurry home and text Jody, Val, and Evy—not Ellie, she'd tell Reah for sure—that my plan is a success. I send a picture of the fall fest invitation and a thumbs up.

"You're working it?" Evy calls first.

"Yes!"

"Does Janice Everglade know that we're friends?"

"I have no idea." This is the first I feel a bit guilty. She does give the LGBT community trouble every year at their spring parade.

"Well, don't tell her, darling, or you'll be out before you're in."

I smile. Everyone should have a friend like Evy. He hasn't a worry for himself. Just me. He hates that I love Reah and Natasha, but he supports me in my quest to win them back.

"I love you, Evy."

"Well, you won't if Janice finds out you do."

"Maybe if Janice and I become friends, I can get her to lay off about next year's parade."

"Oh, darling, don't go there. We plan on parking our homemade floats in front of her house next year."

I laugh hysterically. That's too far away for me to care.

We close the pool up on the weekend after Labor Day, and Mark and I hit whiffle balls around the back yard every night, practicing for some golf scramble. Evidently, last September, Blake the Pro rounded up his golf-lesson fans and conducted this you-hit-then-I'll-hit scramble that went over like hotcakes and chicken. Mark is giddy waiting for the event.

Despite the TPN dinner, Mark successfully landed John Everglade's account. I guess sucking up all summer long worked well for him. The lessons from Blake the Pro helped him lower his handicap and impress John.

I continued to hate my lessons, but that worked out, as well. I still stunk. And that was okay because, at the end of each week, our scores were posted online, and I never wanted to beat Janice Everglade's score—not that I could. Janice seemed to take a personal affront to any woman beating her.

I was finding out Maggots, I mean Megan, had learned to bully from the best. And even though I was fine having the highest score in the league week after week, Blake the Pro didn't like that. I doubt he told anyone I took lessons from him.

"You could hit the ball much farther if you used a wood when you're far from the hole instead of an iron," he said during one lesson.

"Really? Off the grass?"

"Yes."

"I can't use a wood unless I hit off a tee. I dig up too much earth. Mark says I bend my clubs."

He laughed a bit. "You're taking your eye off the ball. You need to watch the club strike it. If you do, you'll hit smoother and farther."

"I'd be happy if I could keep my ball on the fairway."

I tend to knock my balls far into the woods. Fellow golfers grow impatient waiting for me to rustle through the plants and trees searching for it. Earlier this summer, I began stuffing extra balls in my pocket. If I couldn't see my ball from the edge of the woods, I'd drop another just inside the trees by the fairway, kick it to a spot where I had a straight shot toward the hole, and lob it out without taking an extra stroke.

And while throughout most of my life guilt has been the bile of my existence, this I did not remotely feel guilty about.

"You do hit deep into the woods," he said on the last official night of our league.

"Are you trying to make me hit farther into the woods, so I never come back?"

"No, I'm trying to make you honest," he had said with a smirk.

I stared at him, daring him to say it. That I'm a cheater. Wordlessly, he returned my stare, eyes twinkling.

A few minutes later when everyone was warming up, he walked around giving tips, and I couldn't help myself. When he stepped close to me, I pretended not to see him. I swung as hard and quickly as I could, nearly hitting him with my club. He dove out of the way onto the ground.

"Nikki!" Unfortunately, Janice saw this. "You almost hit Blake."

Mark and John Everglade ran to help him, and I faked remorse. Blake stood up smiling.

"Oh, I'm sorry." I put one hand on the side of my face and one hand on Blake the Pro's arm. "Please accept my humble apology. I didn't see you there—honestly."

That was the last I saw of him until today's scramble, which I'm not swimming in excitement about. But as in much of life, good trumps bad. During that last league game, Janice had brought up the book club. Then someone rudely interrupted, and I couldn't catch her attention again.

This scramble is my last shot.

Mark had called an hour beforehand and asked if I could catch a ride with Janice Everglade. He'd mentioned I might need a ride to John earlier in the week.

My God. All my dreams come true!

"Sure, honey. I'll call them right now."

"And oh, God, Nikki, please keep your mouth shut. Try not to embarrass me. Don't bring up the book club again."

"I won't. I won't," I say apologetically, but right off the bat, I can't help myself. Practically before I shut the car door I ask, "Have you read *Crawdads* yet?"

Right away I hate myself. It's like when Mark told me not to mention Mary Yeager in front of Ken Morris's wife at the office party. Ken, a paralegal, was having an affair with the office clerk, Mary, of the law firm next door. Throughout the evening, I chanted, "Don't mention Mary Yeager. Don't mention Mary Yeager," in my head. Then Ken's wife introduces me to someone I don't know. She says, "Do you know Mary?" I blurt out, "Mary Yeager?" She says, "No, this is Mary Allen," and everyone glares at me. Mark never invited me to another office party.

That was the longest ride home of my life.

So I hope he never finds out I ask Janice about *Crawdads* right away.

Janice doesn't seem bothered. "I just started it. That's the book we're reading for book club."

"Is it?" My nonchalance has been perfected.

"Yes." Janice shoots me a pensive look.

She's aware Mrs. Higgins loves me. I hold my breath, hoping she wants to befriend me as much as I want to befriend her. "I have to ask, Nikki. Why did you get kicked out of the book club?"

That's not the question I expected. I concentrate on not changing my face and revealing my disappointment.

Janice was not in attendance for the infamous night. She was off in Punta Cana, Greece, Paris? Who knows where? Natasha had been posting pictures all over Facebook the prior month, flaunting it in my face that she and Reah no longer wanted me in their lives. They and their husbands, the six of us, used to visit the annual wine festival, take a spring ride on a Lake Erie dinner boat, and spend a weekend at Niagara Falls together. So Natasha's posting pictures of those occasions with the four of them and not us devastated me.

I cried for days.

Unfortunately, I sometimes camouflage my hurt with anger. This is a major glitch in my DNA.

On that night, a warm eighty-six-degree summer breeze swept across Fairview, and the neighbor four doors down was hosting. We'd all had a bit too much to drink. It was a Friday night. No one had to work the next day, and none of us had to drive home.

Natasha stood beside the pool, drink in hand, delivering an exasperating account of how she and her husband were planning a cruise with Reah and her husband. Like Janice, Reah wasn't there that night, either. Natasha yakked on and on, glancing at me occasionally, snickering and sipping her wine.

In my defense, she asked for it.

After about twenty minutes of her blabbing on, I walked toward her. Whoever she was talking to, I can't remember the woman, remarked, "How exciting," and Natasha said, "Yes, a Caribbean cruise with my best friend. I can't wait."

Your best friend? She was my best friend, and you stole her.

Natasha emphasized "best" as she glowered at me.

That was a slash to the jugular. I had introduced Natasha to Reah. She hadn't a clue who Reah was until the six of us began hanging out together. Natasha had deceitfully lured her away. She'd done this before with other neighbor friends, but this time she'd crossed the friendship etiquette line. Reah had been a body friend.

So I said, "You're going on a cruise?"

She nodded, smiling wickedly.

"With Reah?"

"Yes." She folds a little laugh into the attitude she's been cooking up all night.

"Then how about a swim lesson?" I shoved her, sequined outfit, designer shoes, and all, into the pool.

That was two years ago. I haven't been invited back since.

The dynamics of the club have changed since then, so my hope of being asked back glimmers. Several women left Fairview. Others moved in and became members. Only three or four of the club's original women witnessed the fatal push—my fatality, not Natasha's.

Had Janice heard the story? Was she baiting me? Regardless, I wasn't about to mention the shove.

"Natasha said something terrible on Facebook about me," I fabricated.

It wasn't as if Natasha hadn't bad-mouthed me hundreds of times on Facebook, anyway. She had a habit of downing a few glasses of wine, staring out her back window, opening her computer, and letting me know exactly how she felt about me without mentioning my name. "I'm afraid I let my hurt turn to anger. I said worse things back. I've regretted it for years. It was horrible of me."

"Well, I think it's about time to bury the hatchet," she said, eyebrows raised. "Don't you?"

I nearly flung myself forward and kissed her. "I'd like that," I replied calmly.

I wanted to call Evy and Jody and Val and let them know I was on the verge of reentry, but I refrained. I was still wallowing in my success when the scramble started. I didn't even realize Mark wasn't there. Blake the Pro reassigned the tee times and scheduled Mark and me last.

By the time the second-to-last golfers teed off, I started to worry. I'd called him twice by then.

I texted. No answer.

"I'll golf with you until he gets here," Blake the Pro said.

I glanced around. Everyone was on the green.

"I guess that's okay."

"Sure, it is. I'd enjoy playing a few holes with you." Sympathetically, he set the palm of his hand on my back. "Mark will be along soon."

Oddly, a warm rush swept through me, and I spent the entire first hole flustered. I swung mindlessly. Missed the ball entirely four times. I couldn't figure out whether I was struck by Mark's inconsiderateness or smitten with Blake's sweetness.

Three holes later, I get a text. "I'm sorry, Nikki. I'm tied up at work. Please give Blake and John my apologies. I'll try to make it for the dinner afterward."

I was furious. The text arrived right as Blake the Pro encouraged me to swing a three wood at a ball on the fairway. He said I didn't need to tee it up. I dug a hole deep enough for the ground keeper to plant an evergreen in.

"And that's why I never swing a wood unless I'm standing in front of a tee," I yelled at Blake.

Unlike Mark, who would have lectured on disgustedly, Blake the Pro simply muffled a chuckle and attempted to fix the trench I'd carved in the earth.

Mark did eventually make it but not for the scramble. He swooped in halfway through dinner. Despite being angry enough to order a whiskey on the rocks, something I never do, once he sat down beside me, my anger lightened. I was happy the chair beside me wasn't broadcasting "Nikki Grey golfed alone" across the room any longer.

Even Janice Everglade had felt sorry for me. She kept rubbing my shoulder and shaking her head in the clubhouse before dinner.

Blake felt sorry for me, too. He had been kind during the scramble. He never once laughed when I knocked my ball into the woods. There was also a terrible calamity when I mistook one of his clubs for mine. And I hit three balls into one pond. He let me hit from the other side of the pond on the ninth hole instead of teeing up in front of it because we had fallen so far behind the group. I think he was nervous we'd miss dinner.

The entire game proved disastrous. I couldn't concentrate. But Blake kindly kept his composure.

Golfing with him might not have been bad, but being stood up by my husband at the much-talked-about scramble shamed me.

Still, I didn't have to put up with Mark's constant badgering: "For the love of God, you're not playing lacrosse, you're putting." "You've replaced so much turf they're going charge us a landscaping fee." "Does your ball need to be washed again?" (I love pumping those little ball washers.) "How can you hit the same tree three times in a row?" "I'm not giving you any more balls; fish one out of the pond." "Don't talk when someone's swinging."

I also had the bad habit of knocking the ball off my tee when I lined my club up with it at the beginning of each hole. Mark compared this to running fingernails down a chalkboard. After a while, I did it on purpose to irritate him.

So even though I was relieved when he showed, I barely talked to him and hardly said goodbye to anyone—other than Janice and John. The night was nearly over, and Mark had rained nails on my back-to-book-club chances.

Then out of nowhere, the oddest thing happened. Mark and I had arrived at our car to leave when I heard, "Nikki."

Janice wiggled down the sidewalk toward me.

"Book Club is at my house next month," she said. "How would you like to come? We're reading *Crawdads*."

"I'll check my schedule but if I'm free, I'd love to."

Chapter 15 The club

"Remaining calm is a big part of golf," Pro golfer Karen Bukowski said to CJ when she attempted to give her a golf lesson.

"I'm glad you're back in the book club." Ellie slaps another invitation onto the pile in the middle of my kitchen table.

"Me, too." Reah has graced us with her presence. Now that Janice invited me back, Reah's less stressed about admitting she's my friend. "Janice is not as bad as everyone thinks."

Evy turns his nose up. He doesn't trust Reah. They share a mutual exasperation for each other.

My invitation to rejoin the neighborhood reading clique has caused tension with Evy. Right now, you couldn't tender the room with a mallet.

"Your taste has always been questionable." Evy's like a chef stirring a stew, trying to bring it to a boil without overflowing it.

Reah turns up the heat. "She's Fairview's greatest philanthropist."

Evy continues stirring. "She waves her money over every nonprofit's head as if one wrong move, and they're out."

We all hold our breath, hoping the broth doesn't boil over the sides and flood our little get-together. Reah, smartly, adds no spice. She remains silent.

I keep still. It's as if I'm awaiting a turn at a chess game. I don't cheer for either player because I'm not sure whom I'd rather play against.

"Regardless, it's good Nikki is back in the book club." Jody turns the attention away from Reah. "She was stressing too much about it."

"While you're doing your happy dance over Naggy's reemergence to novel land," Evy tells her, "let me remind you, Janice is circulating a petition to stop our spring parade."

Oh, yes, and then there's that.

"Did you do that intentionally?" Val asks. "Schedule the parade on the same day of the Everglades' spring garden party?"

"Do you really believe I would be so vicious?"

"Yes!" We all say it at the same time, even Jody.

He stacks his invitations into a perfect pile. "Well, thank you for the unified vote of confidence. As if the entire gay community is willing to fan my fever. The parade always takes place on the second weekend in May. It has for five years."

This reminds me.

"Oh! By the way, Evy. Blake the Pro?"

"Yes?"

"Gay," I announce. "He was at last year's parade. He has one of those little rainbow thing-a-ma-jigs with people holding hands."

"Dog tags?" Evy asks.

"Yeah, the rainbow-people dog tags. It was hanging off his golf bag." I pick up the stack of invitations I've addressed and place them in the middle. Then I grasp the sides of the big box, stand, and slide a bunch of invitations off the table into the box. "I told you."

"See." Ellie nudges Evy with a shoulder. "You get all the good ones."

Evy pulls out his cell and presents a picture of Blake the Pro. He eyes him up and down. "I'd set my feet on the coffee table beside him any day. But he's not part of the family."

"He is," I insist. "Someone asked if the dog tags were from last year's parade, and he said yes."

"Girlfriend, you are teasing me." Evy gives one of his little head shakes. "But mm, mm, mm, he is fine."

"Janice loves Blake the Pro," Reah announces. "Maybe she'll forget the petition."

"You should ask him out," I encourage Evy. "He's a nice guy. Didn't get mad at me in the slightest when I threw his golf club in the pond."

The room goes silent.

"Excuse me?" Evy's intrigued. He golfs a little himself. "You did what?"

"I threw his three wood into the pond. I thought it was mine."

Instantly Val screeches, "Don't you hate when that happens? When you mix your discount clubs up with a pro's?"

"It's not that funny," I reprimand because Val's laughing hysterically. "It was a mistake. Haven't you ever made a mistake before?"

"Girl, do you know he's a professional?" Evy, again. "I hope you wiggled your little fins and went for a swim, fished it out."

"No. I wasn't getting my eighty-dollar golf skirt wet."

"So you have to buy him a new one?"

"No, I offered him mine."

"You offered to replace his three wood with yours?"

"Right."

"A professional golfer?"

"Who cares? It's not like he lost a leg or anything."

Evy sets his pen down, places elbows on the table, and tucks his chin on top of his fingers. "Every time I think you can't surprise me more, you do. What did he say?"

"He said it was fine." I give the table a once-around glance. Everyone has stopped working. "What's the big deal? He needed a new one. He'd had that one over two years."

"He wasn't mad?" Evy raises his eyebrows.

"Not a bit."

"Tell me more."

"Well." I had to think. "I said I'd had my three wood longer than that, so it could keep his company. Then I threw mine in."

Val, Ellie, Reah, and Jody burst into a unified laugh.

Evy says, "Girl, if I wasn't familiar with your utter carelessness with the American dollar, I'd think you were kidding. Go on. What did he say?"

"He smirked and said I'd just thrown my four-hundred-dollar club in the pond'."

Again, heartfelt laughter.

Evy waves his hand, beckoning. "More."

That this has them crying in amusement baffles me. "Um." I stare at the ceiling, trying to remember. "I said, 'Are you kidding me? Why would Mark spend that much money on a club for me?'"

Everyone waits, eyes wide.

"Then he said Mark must think I'm worth it." I resume writing. "I'm not sure why he said that."

"What did you say?"

"I asked him how much his club was, and he said a tad more than mine."

"Girlfriend, you tossed a thousand-dollar club in the pond." Evy picks up his pen and finishes addressing his last invitation. "I'm going over there later and fish it out."

"Everyone done?" I change the subject. Golf is such a bore. "Mrs. Higgins wants these in the mail today. I'm not screwing this up."

My remark unifies the room. They gaze at each other as if me not screwing something up is a joke. Reah assures them I won't. She's going to drive me directly to the post office then take me shopping for a dress.

Everyone calms down, finishes up, and we stack the rest of the invites in the box.

"Did Mrs. Higgins say more about the layoffs?" Jody asks when she's heading out the door.

Ugh, another spear tossed at my world.

"No, only that they are looking at part-timers."

Our school district is in crisis. I may lose my job. Mrs. Higgins is fighting to keep me, but it's not looking good. I'm contemplating updating my resume and considering full-time openings. Jody thinks I'm too stressed right now to work five days a week. But I'm running again, and I'll have my license back in under three months. Delanie and Hux are gone. Gianna's at that recalcitrant age where she'd rather do anything other than spend time with her mother.

"Something part-time will open up," positive Jody says. "Maybe after the first of the year, when you can drive again."

"And you're gone?" I glower.

She shoots me a sad and gloomy frown then lingers in the front foyer attempting to convince me her move won't be bad. Gianna and I can visit Seattle for a long weekend when Mark is working. She knows about him buying his partner out. I haven't told the others.

The conversation turns back to the fall festival when Ellie, Val, and Evy join us to say their goodbyes. Stiffly, Evy leans toward my ear.

"Happy dress shopping." He points toward Reah and whispers, "Pick her something green and vile."

No one hears but me. The others go out after him.

Reah and I drop the invitations in the mail and head for the mall. We giggle from dressing room to dressing room like two girls trying on dresses for their first dance. Reah buys a chestnut-brown dress that highlights her auburn hair, and I select black because I'm down to my post-stress fracture weight, and I want everyone to know it.

My stomach flutters with excitement after we purchase our dresses. We're meeting Natasha for lunch. This is sad of me to delight in reconnecting with someone who wished me dead on Facebook, rallied the entire neighborhood against me, and coaxed my childhood friend away from me, but I can't help myself. I lust for friendship.

Neither she nor Reah apologizes for ejecting me from their lives last year, so I don't say I'm sorry for my infamous push into the pool, but somehow, we become comfortable in each other's presence.

A few times while sitting in the restaurant, leaning toward each other, elbows on the table, sharing stories about other book-club members, my world feels somehow back in order.

Sad, I know. My running friends spent miles instilling positivity in me and rebuilding my ego after Reah's and Natasha's boot. They worry I'm jumping back into the flames, but I can't help myself. The risk is worth it. Next to losing my parents, losing Reah and Natasha was the worst crisis in my life.

Mark's not thrilled about replanting friendship seeds with them and their husbands, but snaking my roots into Reah's and Natasha's soil is a start. I'll work on him over the holidays.

When Reah drops me off at home, I am happier than I've been in a year. My mother used to insist God didn't give you more than you could handle.

"Pray for strength," she'd taught.

I'd pray for what I wanted instead.

But maybe God realized without Jody, I needed Reah and Natasha in my life.

I call Ellie and tell her how the day progressed because she's spent time with her mother and sisters today. She's happy. This has been tough for her. Perched solidly in the center, trying to balance two teeter-tottering friends forced her to make choices she didn't want to make. At times, she went out with them, hoping I didn't hear, and occasionally, she spent time with me and prayed they didn't find out. Straddling that middle weakened her friendship with Reah.

Ellie is simply hanging on like me. This reconciliation is good for everyone.

I make Mark take Gianna and me to church the next two Sundays. Both of them whine and complain. But now that God has miraculously answered my prayers, I owe Him attention, too.

On the Sunday before the big fall festival, I pray that I become a better mom to my kids, wife to Mark, supporter of my friends, and child of God. Then I pray no one else has purchased the same black dress as me and if someone has, I pray I'm thinner than them.

Chapter 16 The festival

"Lord, if I can't be thin, please let my friends be fatter than me," said the little picture Patty gave CJ.

"Wow," Mark compliments. "You look delicious."

It's two months from my no-driving prison jailbreak. I'm back pounding the pavement with my running friends. My bathroom scale tips one pound less than my pre-stress-fracture weight. Reah and Natasha are back in my life. Jody hasn't sold her house. My stare-aways have ceased to exist. And Mark and I are getting along spectacularly, better than in years.

Now if I could only get my kids to like me, my life would be complete.

"You're never satisfied." Mark grins when I tell him this. "Your kids love you. They're just showing their independence."

He sets a hand on my hip while I knot his tie perfectly. "I know. Sorry. Done with negativity. I'm positive-me, now."

I pat down his tie; he pulls me close and kisses the tip of my nose. "I like positive me."

"Gross, really gross, Dad." Gianna has come into our bedroom. We're dropping her off to spend the night at Amy Everglade's. It's the first she's been there in a while, but Amy invited Kate, Natasha's daughter, and Olivia, Ellie's daughter. The four of them are having a sleepover.

"Doesn't your mother look good?" Mark steps aside, and Gianna eyes me up and down.

"Why do you always wear black?"

"Because it's formal, elegant." I'm annoyed that she's noticed. I wear black because it's slenderizing.

"You're not wearing those shoes, are you?"

I gaze at my feet. "Why? What's wrong with them?"

"Mom, they're ten years old."

"They're still in style."

Immediately, she heads to my closet, drops to her knees, inspects my shoe shelves, and removes a pair of high heels Mark bought me two years ago, but I never dared to wear.

"Try these," she suggests.

"I'll kill myself. I just started running. I don't want to be out of commission again."

"Then find another pair, but you can't wear those. They're creepy crone shoes. That's what we call Mrs. Higgins' shoes when she visits our school. You've been hanging around her too much. She's wearing off on you."

She hands me the shoes and hurries away, hollering over her shoulder, "When are we leaving? You were supposed to drop me off fifteen minutes ago."

I glance at the clock. Late, again. I kick off the crone shoes and hop into the high heels. Practice walking around the room, thinking this could go badly.

But once I arrive, Reah hustles toward me. She gazes enviously at my shoes. "You look gorgeous."

"Thanks, so do you," I say, and a delightful evening begins.

We dance and laugh; Mark toasts John, who has sent much business his way. They bore Janice and me for a few minutes with business, then Mark says, "If you don't mind, John, I'm going to ask this lovely lady to dance."

I glance around, wondering who he's talking to, then realize he's holding his hand out to me. I flush all over, and we head out to the dance floor. The lights dim, and Fairview's favorite band plays soft, classy music.

After dinner, the band's tempo speeds up. Mark and I were once great dancers, so we hurry to the floor, and more than our minds remember. Our bodies flow back and forth in harmony, twisting smoothly across the floor.

Twice I nearly stumble in my heels. Mark catches me.

"Take them off," he urges, and I glance around, searching for Natasha and Janice. I spot Natasha's feet first, fully shoed. Then Janice's, bare as a newborn baby. I kick mine off, and my worries of tumbling to the ground disappear.

There's a Chinese auction to raise money for the veterans' home, and Mark bids on several pieces. While we await the big reveal of the auction, I see Janice Everglade approaching with her clipboard.

Oh, no, the petition.

Janice meanders around the room, and even though I'm indebted to her for inviting me back into the book club, it's hard to ignore her true colors with that clipboard in her hand. She's a predator in a grey dress.

A wolf among coyotes.

She steps toward a man and, I don't know how I didn't see him earlier, but it's Blake the Pro. He shakes his head, and a discussion ensues between them. Their discourse seems cordial, but I notice he frowns when Janice proceeds to the next person. Of course, he hasn't signed it. I watch him stroll to the bar, order what looks to be a martini? Appletini?

Janice continues to swoop her way through the crowd. When she reaches Natasha, I see Natasha sign, pass the petition to her husband, and wave Reah in for the kill. Reah glances my way. I pretend not to watch. She signs quickly and passes it on.

"Listen." I practically jump out of my skin when Mark whispers in my ear.

I put a hand on my heart. "You scared me."

He picks up a strand of my hair and rubs the end of it against my neck. Kisses me softly, his lips half grazing my cheek, half nibbling my earlobe. A chill rushes through me.

"I know you are watching Janice." He hesitates for a moment. I try to concentrate. He releases the strand. "You're going to have to sign it, Nikki."

Quickly, my mind shifts out of reverse. I love Mark but backstabbing Evy isn't an option.

"I can't, Mark."

His flirtatious mien melts. "I understand your allegiance to Evy but signing to stop the gay parade from ruining the Everglades' garden party doesn't mean you suddenly condemn the LGBT community. It simply means you want them to shift their venue."

"Mark." I don't want to start an argument, but signing that petition surely means the end of my friendship with Evy. "I'm not signing."

Mark's phone rings right as Janice makes her way to us and begins her spiel. He hands me his phone, nodding at her and John as if he totally supports the petition. I answer the phone.

"May I speak to Attorney Grey?"

"He's busy. Can he call you back?"

"This is an emergency."

"An emergency?" I look at the area code. It's a Pittsburgh number, so I don't worry. "He can't come to the phone right now."

Mark shoves the petition toward me and says, "Sign it."

I tuck the phone under my chin. "No, I'm not signing."

Mark glances over his shoulder then writes on the line below his signature. He's signing another name—forging mine?

I slip my fingers around his wrist at the same time the woman on the phone says, "This is a family emergency. I'm calling from UPMC hospital in Pittsburgh."

Everything from here on out happens quickly. Instantly, I shudder as if a bolt of lightning has hit the ground, and I'm standing in a nearby puddle.

"Oh my God, this is his wife. Has something happened to our daughter?"

It strikes me that Delanie drives to Pittsburgh to visit friends, watch football games, shop. Did she not tell me she was going? "Has our daughter been hurt?"

Mark hands the clipboard to the man standing next to him and grabs the phone. "This is Mark Grey."

I listen, hear the woman say, "Your daughter is in intensive care."

But I'm already punching Delanie's number into my phone. I glimpse the time. It's after midnight. Delanie picks up on the first ring. "Mom, what do you want?"

I glimpse at Mark. His hand grips his forehead. "How bad is she?" he asks.

"Where are you?" I holler into the phone. "In Pittsburgh?"

"No, I'm in Slippery Rock."

"Are you okay?"

"I'm fine."

"Did you lend someone your license?"

"No. What's wrong?"

I hang up. Mark is hurrying toward the door. I catch up. Grab his arm.

"Is it Gianna?"

He shakes his head, no.

Our franticness attracts attention. People begin noticing our distress. Am I speaking too loudly? Screaming? I hear Hux's voice even before I realize I've called him. Just to make sure they didn't mean our son.

"Hello, Momma," he chirps.

"Are you okay?'

"I'm great, how—" I hang up before he says more. Delanie is calling me back, but I'm clutching at Mark's arm.

"Is it Gianna?" I yell. "Has something happened to Gianna?"

"No," Mark quavers. "It's—'"

Janice steps up. She has the phone to her ear. "The girls are fine. Gianna is fine."

I turn toward Mark.

"It's not Gianna." Mark has hung up the phone. His face is white. Is he going to pass out?

"Who is it? Who?" I'm frantic now. Is it one of his sister's kids?

"It's—it's my daughter," he trembles. "I'm sorry. I have to go to Pittsburgh."

Then he hurries toward the door, leaving me standing, my mouth agape with confusion.

Janice holds her phone to my ear. "Mom, what's going on?" Gianna asks.

Her words echo in my head.

What's going on? What's going on?

Ellie comes tearing across the room. I glance at her, then back at Mark as he slips out the front door. My eyes search the room. Everyone is looking at me. The music has stopped. I stare at the eyes and the faces and the horrific expressions. Then I see him. The attorney from the restaurant. The one who asked Mark about his younger child when Gianna was sitting right there. The man's expression tells me exactly what's going on.

Mark has another daughter.

Chapter 17 The lie

*"Don't believe anything you hear and only half
of what you see," CJ's grandmother used to say.*

I don't know how I end up in Blake's car, but he drives
me home while Ellie drops her husband off and picks up
Jody. They'll be at my house any minute.

My hands shake when I try to turn off our home alarm
system. I can't get my fingers to work.

"What's the code?" Blake gently nudges me aside when
the beeping begins. I fire off one number then correct
myself. Call out another. He punches keys on the pad and
disables the alarm. The beeping stops.

He flits around the house, switching on lights, and I
stand in the hall of my own home. Everything looks
different. Is this my house? Mark's? Who is Mark?

I punch his number into my cell, call him for the thirty-
something time, but now the call doesn't go directly to
voicemail. He picks up.

"Nikki," he says. "You have to stop calling me. I'll
explain. I'm sorry. I love you, but right now I have to get to
the hospital."

"Are you serious? You have a child? With someone
else?"

Blake appears out of nowhere, helps me sit down on the
big white couch in my living room. Wait. My couch?
Mark's? The confusion begins again. I've been cast in some
foreign and unfathomable reality-TV calamity.

This must be a bad dream. I'll wake up.

But then Mark mumbles, "This is a terrible way for you to find out. I should have told you. I wanted to tell you, but I can't talk now. She's in intensive care. There's been a car accident."

"My God, how could you keep this from me?"

"Nikki, I can't do this, not now."

A million scenarios run through my head. Is she little? That attorney asked about a younger child. Was he mistaken? My mind toys with me. Was Mark's child born long ago, and could this little girl he saw be Mark's granddaughter?

Mark is old enough to have a grandchild. If he slept with someone before me. If he cheated on me when we were young.

How can this be something I'm hoping for?

Memories flash in my head like warning lights I ignored. Words, phrases, the Pittsburgh conferences, weekends out of town. How many years have we been together? I never once questioned his fidelity. Or have I?

Have you, Nikki? Have you known all along?

It doesn't matter. Nothing matters. No scenario is survivable.

How stupid of me.

Dumb, dumb, dumb.

When did we last make love? A week ago? A month? Everything's a blur.

"You have a daughter? With someone else? Not with me?"

I'm no longer in control of myself. I'm standing outside my body, watching a horrible episode in Nikki Grey's life. My heart speeds up. My head spins.

I shouldn't have stopped my medication.

Blake drags a chair over and sits close as if he's afraid I might collapse. My hands are cold and clammy, my face warm. Blood rushes through my veins like a hydrant unhinged.

"It was a terrible accident. Several people are hurt." Mark's voice is cracking. He's crying, and I wonder who else he's rushing to see.

Was this woman with whom my husband has had another life—a child with—in the accident, too? Is he rushing to see a lover? Or some shadow of the past?

Again, profound hope surfaces. "How old is she, Mark?"

The doorbell rings. Blake springs to open it. Jody and Ellie step in. I look straight into Jody's eyes, but I don't see her.

"Three," Mark answers.

"Your daughter has a three-year-old?"

Then he says something to me that I absolutely can't register.

"No. My daughter is three years old."

Younger than Gianna.

I repeat what he says to Jody and Ellie and Blake. "Your daughter is three-years-old."

"I'm sorry, Nikki."

"Mark, she can't be three. Gianna's twelve—"

"I'm sorry. I'll be home as soon as I can. Please tell the kids I love them. I will call. I will come home."

With that, the call clicks off.

Jody stares in disbelief. "He has a daughter? A three-year-old?"

Ellie covers her face and begins crying.

"I don't know," I stammer. "I just…I'm not feeling well. I can't…I—"

"Can you get her some water?" Jody asks Blake.

Then Ellie and Jody sit on opposite sides of me, inch close, and hug my shoulders. I sink deep into the cushion, hoping to be swallowed up, lost, hidden, safe from this new world I know nothing about.

The darkness behind me seeps through my window, falls on my shoulders, and closes around me like a cloak and veil. The dark. The cold. The secrets. The strange unfamiliarity of Mark's world is out there in the blackness, hiding. Yet it bleeds through the glass and chokes me.

I grasp for Ellie's hand and rest my head on Jody's shoulder. We don't talk. Tonight, there is nothing to say.

Chapter 18 The morning

"I'm too lonely for this. This isn't the life I planned," CJ told Jeff after their third child, Jilly, moved out of town.

I wake when Furgy barks. I've fallen asleep in my plush front room. My sticky, tangled dress tugs here and there at my skin. Confusedly, I push up onto the palms of my hands. Who's beside me?

Jody.

Two water glasses have stained my custom-made coffee table. My temples throb agonizingly. A rawness, as if I've swallowed witch hazel, burns my stomach. Every muscle and tendon screams with pain.

Have I run a marathon without training? Had another seizure? Where's Mark?

The morning's soft light filters through the window and touches my face. The room around me clears. Confusion fades.

I remember.

"You're awake," Jody sits up. Furgy has woken her, too. "How are you?"

How am I? I do a quick assessment of myself. I have epilepsy. I've stopped the pills. But I am alive.

"Did I have a seizure?"

"No. You cried yourself to sleep."

"Thank God." My forehead drops into the palm of my hand.

I can't have a seizure, not now.

Now that my life—Mark's life—has turned me inside out, spun me around, and dropped me into a world where love and money and friends and book clubs and nothing matters.

Words of my doctor, Mark's friend, invade my brain. Slap me. "With epilepsy, it's essential to get lots of sleep. Try not to stress."

I want to laugh but not an ounce of energy can muscle a chuckle.

"What time is it?"

Before Jody can answer, I hear a tapping sound. Someone's entering our security code. Furgy stands wagging her tail at the front door when Gianna spills into the foyer. She slams the door. I gaze out the front window. Janice Everglade is waltzing up the cobblestone path that winds through my front yard.

"Dad ruined my life." Gianna's shrill scream echoes through the house as she climbs the stairs two and three at a time.

I jump up.

"Go," Jody commands. "I'll take care of Janice."

I follow Gianna upstairs, but she's locked her bedroom door.

"Gianna let me in."

"No, you ruined my life."

"Me?" It's reactive. Instinctive.

"Dad, okay? Dad." She swings open the door. "How could you let this happen? You're mean to him. This is your fault. He hates you. Now he's ruined my life."

She slams the door so hard that a picture in the hall, a family photo, drops to the floor. Its glass shatters.

Like our world.

This can't be happening, I think. How does she know? Janice? Amy? I should have been the person to tell my daughter. Hard to believe twenty-four hours ago we were a normal Fairview family, and now our lives lie shattered on the hallway floor.

"Gianna, open the door."

"No. Go away. I hate you!"

Yesterday, happiness danced around us. We were jubilant. We'd been invited into the inner sanctuary of the Everglades' infamous world.

"I'm sorry." I try to hold in my tears but, as usual, my untimely, emotionally debilitating weakness cripples me. I sob. "I don't know what to say."

"You never know what to say. Go away. Stay out of my life!"

She's hurled something at the door. I feel the vibration because my palms are pressed flat against it. Gianna sobs inside her room. I fall against her door.

"Please, Gianna, let me in." I sound like a child, not a mother.

"Go," she screams and through my sobs, I hear her. She's got Delanie on the phone.

It's horrid to be so selfish, but my first thought is that they'll both hate me now. My greatest fear rises like a blistering sun. The inevitable, embossed by light. My daughters, my husband, my friends will abandon me. I don't deserve them. How could I allow this to happen? Instinctively, the urge to run and hide tempts me.

You're the mother, Nikki; stay strong for Gianna.

I don't listen to the voice inside me. I slide down her door whispering, "I cannot lose my girls."

Jody appears to help me to my feet and convince me to allow Delanie to talk to Gianna. She leads me to my room. I slip out of my fancy dress and pick up the shorts and t-shirt I had on last night, before the party, before the end of my world.

I try once again to coax Gianna to open her door but retreat to the kitchen when she screams for me to leave.

I sit for a long time, not speaking.

Jody urges, "You've got to start your medication."

I close my eyes.

Not now, Jody, please.

The doorbell rings and, in seconds, three of my best running buddies are standing in the foyer, pelting questions at Jody, their voices strained. Did something happen? Another seizure? Why didn't Nikki show up to run?

Oh my God, I was supposed to run with them this morning.

"It's not the epilepsy," Jody apprises.

When I shuffle into their view, I see Carol, Laura, and Jan. Carol gasps. I glance at the little mirror in the hallway and don't recognize myself. I'm pale, old. Grey half-moons sit beneath my eyes. Puffy cheeks distort my face. My lips are colorless.

That's not Nikki. Nikki has died.

Apprehensively, Jody gazes at me. I nod. I trust these three women. They spent miles counseling me through every bend of the road: my children growing too fast, my sister's dementia, my health, the loss of Reah's and Natasha's friendship, but I can't bear to tell them this—this what? Tragedy? Catastrophe? Utter betrayal?

I meander toward them and do what I always do when problems overwhelm me. I hide within my girlfriends' warm support. They surround me, my team.

My friends who move bodies.

These girls love me unconditionally. They extend their sturdy arms down into my dark tunnel and wrench me out into the light. With them at my side, I muster the courage to explain what I don't understand myself.

This has been my life since I was little. Loneliness has been my evil companion since age nine. My father worked three jobs, and my mother worked full-time along with tending the house and caring for her parents. I had no cousins, aunts, or uncles. I spent days alone. Evenings. Weekends. My much-older sister moved out of our house, and now? Now I have no sister at all.

But you do, Nikki. Your friends are your sisters.

The doorbell rings; Val arrives. Mary and Carolyn after her.

For minutes they coddle me. We amble to the kitchen where they plan how to get me through this. I sit listening, wounded and helpless, enslaved in a mindless, treacherous tailspin of confusion.

Wasn't I one of them yesterday?

"I'll come tomorrow," Carol mutters. "I'm not working."

"I've got Monday," Val adds.

"Tuesday." Laura.

"Wednesday." Carolyn.

Jody draws a schedule on a paper. She whispers. The soft undertone of the word medication frightens me. I cry because I can't deal with my epilepsy now. I must concentrate on Mark, our lives, my children.

His child.

When I lose myself in sobs, my friends swarm around me, and I wonder if this is what a nervous breakdown feels like.

"Be strong for your kids, Nikki," someone says.

For minutes, I wallow in the warm embrace of friendship, but then the cold hard facts break through again, and I stagger.

The doorbell rings, and Ellie is suddenly in the room.

Another friend to help me. A true friend.

I hear Evy's voice in my head—*friends who move bodies, not couches.*

"Where's Evy?"

"He's not coming." Val can't look me in the eye.

"Why not?"

Her eyes seek out Jody because that's what we do when we need strength. We run to Jody.

"We'll straighten it out." Jody sets a hand on my shoulder.

"What?"

Jody hesitates. "The petition."

The petition? From last night? I'd forgotten.

"Did I sign it?"

I thought I'd refused, but the night had spiraled quickly out of control. Had I signed it in the confusion? Could I have? I can't think long about this because I hear a familiar voice yelling from the front door.

"Mom! Mom!" Delanie barrels into the kitchen. She makes a beeline straight toward me. Her face is streaked and weary. She throws her arms around me. She's weeping. Her hands grip my back. Her chin nuzzles into my neck.

"Mom," she whispers over and over.

After minutes of sharing raw anguish, I muster the courage to say, "I love you, Delanie."

"I love you, Mom."

There's nothing more to say.

Chapter 19 The homecoming

"I really like Tracy. I want her as a friend, not a counselor," CJ told Carolyn about the counselor who DID NOT photograph her forehead.

"Why do you believe you failed them?" Tracy the counselor asks.

She's fabulous, but I hate it when she presses me about my opinion of myself.

I'm perched inside her cozy, dim office, my hands tucked nervously beneath my legs in a chair that is more comfortable than I deserve. I tense my shoulders and bite my lip like a child in a principal's office—a nice principal.

Nearly a week has passed since my grievous ordeal, and I've ridden the roller coaster of shame and anxiety up and down, in and out, around into a tailspin and through tunnels so low in the ground I've discovered hidden secrets of the inner core. If I had frequent flyer miles for my emotional journey, I'd have earned a companion pass and first-class rights for life.

A companion pass. Hilarious.

"Obviously, I wasn't good enough for Mark if he found refuge in some other woman."

"You can't blame yourself for Mark's actions."

"No, but that doesn't mean I haven't failed my kids—especially my girls. I've been emotionally crippled all my life. I can't face losing anyone. Not even Mark. He called me on Monday, and I broke down and cried pathetically, apologizing. Do you believe that? I apologized to him. Begged him to come home."

I cover my face, ashamed. "What's wrong with me?"

Tracy has been kind and supportive, but I see the sorrow in her eyes and, where normally I'm appreciative, now pity pierces me. There is I-feel-sorry-for-you pity and then there's how-will-you-survive pity.

By Wednesday afternoon, I had learned the whole truth. *The whole truth and nothing but the truth, so help me God. Haha. I'm losing it. Deranged.*

The automobile accident on I-279 that began this curse of an event involved a five-car collision. The second car, submerged in a tangle of metal, tire, and smoke, held two passengers. A mother and a three-year-old child. A girl.

Melissa Briggs and her daughter, Rosalee—*Rosalee! He named her Rosalee, which we considered for Gianna—* were flown to UPMC hospital, but Rosalee was transported to Children's Hospital on Tuesday after she stabilized. She isn't out of the woods, but Mark said there's hope she'll live.

The future for the mother is not as optimistic.

The mother. The mistress. What shall I call her?

Mark is sleeping at some Ronald McDonald, Peppa Pig, or Betty Brothel house. I don't know where he's sleeping.

Does it matter where your husband sleeps after the fact?

Maybe he's staying at her apartment. I don't care. His sleeping arrangements are the least of my worries. I'm embattled in a war on the home front, extinguishing fires he's left behind.

Over the phone, he enlightens me that he spends all day working beside the three-year-old while the child's maternal grandparents bounce back and forth between hospitals.

They are heartbroken.

I don't care how your mistress's parents feel, Mark. I'm not that big of a person.

"I don't want them to die," I tell Tracy, wondering if that is the truth.

I think about this. I've said prayers for the little girl who through no fault of her own has catapulted my life and the life of her half-siblings into chaos. But the mother? I block her from my mind.

Guilt climbs my neck and strangles me the moment my foot hits the inside of a church, which is often now as I'm attending daily mass. Defiantly, I say one prayer for the child's mother, but it's selfishly recited. I don't want to go to hell for inhumanness if this woman dies. She's already turned my life into hell on earth.

"What are your plans?" Tracy asks.

"I don't know. I'm losing my mind."

I stifle a laugh. I'm one-hundred-percent sure my current thought proves my insanity.

I'll invest in a larger kitchen knife—like Lorena Bobbitt.

"When will you see him?" Tracy lures me back from my fantasy.

"He's coming home tonight because the girl's sister is flying in and will sit with the child until Sunday night. She's stabilized."

"Have you started back on your medication?"

"I have," I lie.

Does honesty matter anymore?

She sends me home with her cell phone number, an anti-anxiety prescription that interacts well with the epilepsy medication that I'm not taking, and a list of instructions, calming techniques, pamphlets about self-esteem, self-worth, and a short novel titled *The Workings of the Higher Self.*

She hugs me warmly when I leave, and I think I've won another comrade. Tracy is sincere, supportive, and helpful. I don't want her as my counselor anymore. I want her as my friend.

You never change, Nikki.

Instead of filling the prescription and reading the brochures, I go home and self-medicate.

I open a bottle of wine.

Val has dropped me at my door and headed to her 3 p.m. to 3 a.m. shift. Ellie has Gianna for the night, and I'm alone with my thoughts waiting for Mark, deciding what words to use.

I sit quietly, sipping my wine and listening to that damn rattling noise on the roof, which has astoundingly become the bane of my existence.

What is up there?

I traipse outside and look upward, inspecting the roof. I see something on the corner of our chimney top. A five- or six-inch space separates the top brick of the chimney with the metal platform above it where the smoke filters out. I see something in one corner. A mesh bag flapping in the wind. What's inside it? Golf balls?

Hux!

He'll be home for Thanksgiving in two weeks. He can climb up there then and relieve me of this bother. I have lived in this house with my husband's ghosts following me around for a week, I can live with the sound of rustling golf balls for two.

I trudge back inside.

Even though I haven't run a step in a week, I've lost weight. Despite the stress and insomnia, I haven't seized, but I do continue to jerk awake at night. I pray the epilepsy doesn't worsen.

At least one friend arrives every day to either drive me to mass or check on Gianna and me. They spend time chatting with and encouraging us. Sometimes they fry hamburgers on the stove or toss vegetables in the steamer. The bulk of what we eat, however, is carried across our threshold, steaming hot, by Mary and Carolyn.

I'm blessed to have friends.

Yet.

Am I relying on them too much? Transferring my dependency on Mark to my friends? Eventually, I'm going to have to stand on my own.

His Jeep rolls into the driveway at about 7 p.m. I'm a little drunk, which might help. I'm not as needy when I'm drinking.

Don't let him convince you to take him back.

He walks through the front door and—

O. M. G.

He carries flowers in with him. Two dozen roses.

"Are you kidding me?" I fume.

He's never looked this bad in his life. He appears to have spent the entire week in the same clothes. His suit from the festival reeks of filth. His face is haggard, gaunt. He slumps, packing all six feet of him into less space. He's shrunk into himself.

He holds out his hand. I whisk the flowers from him, stomp to the kitchen, and cram them into the garbage can. Then I pour myself another glass of wine and slam the bottle on the counter. "Help yourself. I trust you won't be driving for the evening."

I take my wine and my pride, and I walk to the family room, which sits off the kitchen toward the back yard. I choose this room for our little chat because in between the glistening long windows, the soft white walls sport picture after picture of our once happy family. Little decorative signs, in case the photos aren't enough, display pleasant little sayings like "Live, Laugh, Love," "There's No Place Like Home," and my favorite, "The World's Greatest Dad Lives Here."

I take a seat in the leather recliner closest to that sign, so he has to stare at it all evening.

He pours himself a glass of wine and trudges in. He sits down on the couch, removes his jacket, and I wonder how I've come to feel awkward in a room with a man whom I've slept with hundreds of times. He raises the glass to his lips, then stops mid-air—I think he sees the dad sign—before downing the contents of his glass.

"I've been thinking." I pounce quickly, a spider to a trapped fly. "Four years ago. Hmm. Wait. When exactly did you impregnate her? This woman? Oops. I mean girl because she's young, right? Twenty-seven now? That made her about twenty-three? And you? Forty-two? Delanie, fifteen. Hux, thirteen. Gianna, eight. Was she your backup when I couldn't get pregnant again?"

Mark wanted two children when we married. He made that clear.

"Two kids are company. With three there's always an odd man out."

We carted our baby paraphernalia to a local second-hand shop after Hux's second birthday. Mark argued our two healthy children, boy and girl, were enough. God had blessed us with the perfect family.

Four years later, I secretly celebrated my surprise pregnancy with Gianna. The doctor had told us I was experiencing early-onset menopause.

Apparently, not.

After Gianna was born, I used Mark's own words to coax him into trying for a fourth. I debated, cajoled, flirted, and wheedled. God wanted another Delanie and Hux for us all over again, I argued. Our fourth would be a babbling boy as favored in temperament as his brother, I promised.

"Life is cyclical," I contended. "Four children would be better than having that odd man out."

Convinced, Mark and I set out on a fourth-child adventure. When I didn't become pregnant the first, second, and twelfth month, I purchased charts and studied infertility.

I bought an expensive thermometer and recorded my ovulating course. Mark and I made love religiously, repeatedly, rapturously whenever my temperature rose a degree in the middle of the month or at any other time, regardless of whether it might be unexpected ovulation or a sinus infection.

Still, no baby bump. There was never going to be another pickle in the jar. My glass vessel was sealed.

But Mark's wasn't.

"I guess this is my fault." I drink deeply and flat-hand my chest above my heart when I begin my speech. "I couldn't get pregnant and you, being the wonderful dad you are, sacrificed and had that fourth child with another woman—oops, girl."

"Nikki, please. Don't you think I feel bad enough?"

I stand.

"Shut up," I say, but I'm not yelling. The counselor explained he wouldn't listen if I yelled, so I keep my voice low. "You don't get to talk. What you've done is uprooted the lives of your other three children. Ripped the floor out from under them. Do you realize I had to call a counselor to our house to get Gianna to go back to school? It took three days and Delanie missing two days' worth of classes to get Gianna back to school. And Hux? Our sweet, happy-go-lucky, Hux? He's called home sixty-seven times—"

I pick up my phone, punch buttons until the recent phone calls appear, and face the screen at him.

"Sixty-seven calls in a week. He wants to come home. You've ruined his dreams of Virginia. Political Science. Law school. You've reduced our big, hearty son to a crying schoolboy. He wants to quit."

Hux never cries. Mark and I have talked about his lack of tears for years, so this hits Mark hard.

He sets his wine down and drops his head into his hands. He begins crying. He sobs and whimpers like the worthless being he's been reduced to, and the match between us goes on for a long time—me swinging, him ducking—until my stamina withers, and I must sit down and lean back in my chair, exhausted. Not an ounce of regret for a single swing softens me. In the twenty-seven years we've been together, this is the first time Mark has shed a tear of regret or showed a morsel of emotional pain.

"How does it feel, Mark? To be the bad guy in the marriage? All these years, you've blamed me for everything. Our financial problems, our parenting problems, our friend problems, family problems, not to mention the arguments we've had over your work hours. How much were you actually working? Was it all a lie to allow you to spread your seed up and down I-79 on your trips to Pittsburgh? How many others are there?"

I get a second wind and go on again long into the night until my throat is parched and sore.

Mark cries and begs me not to leave.

"Leave?" I laugh. "I'm not leaving. You're leaving. You left a long time ago."

At one point he gets on the floor in front of me and pleads for me to take him back. This is the first time in my life I've had the upper hand with him, and I wave it wildly in the air above him.

We drink ourselves to sleep that Friday night. In the morning, Jody stops to check on me. Mark says hello from the family room when she steps into the kitchen. Loyal Jody ignores him. She turns her gaze to me, her eyelids fluttering with disgust. She asks what I need at the grocery store.

"I'm going to ride along with you if you don't mind."

"Great." Her expression softens. Her head bobs with a little yeah-get-away-from-him gesture.

"I can count on you to be here when Gianna gets home, correct?" I say to Mark. "Ellie is dropping her off by noon.

Hopefully, I'll be home by then. If not? You can face her on your own."

He nods, and Jody and I go out the door.

"How bad was it?" she asks, once we are safely inside her car.

"I was an absolute horrible bitch."

"Good. You're learning."

We hurry through shopping because, despite wishing Mark has to face Gianna alone, I can't bear to do that to Gianna.

When we pull into the driveway, I open my door to get out, but Jody sets a hand on my arm.

"Close the door," she says, and I think she is going to lecture me about the epilepsy medication again.

"I can't do it," I respond before she has a chance. "I can't take the pills right now."

"It's not that."

When I gaze back at Jody, she's crying.

Oh God, no.

"We sold the house," she bawls.

There's nothing worse than a friendship divided. Getting through life with someone you love and trust beside you is so much easier than traipsing alone with no hand to help you up.

Maybe because of my loss of Reah's friendship, and maybe because of my small family, I value the friendships I do have more than others. I don't think all women love as I do.

Everyone needs a Jody in their life. Someone strong enough to help them rise from the ashes. But they need a Nikki, too. A person who loves them more than they love themselves. A friend who offers absolute, unconditional love.

Because of Jody's strength and my tenacious devotion to friendship, the bond between Jody and I will never sever. We'll love each other from a distance.

But she won't be beside me. I must learn to stand on my own.

I go into the house with an emptiness festering deep inside me. Funny how words affect physicality. I'm like a negative number. My emotions have zeroed out. I'm so low that I'm getting farther and farther away from rock bottom. My emotions are ceasing to exist. So for once, I'm quieter than usual. I allow Mark and Gianna to do the talking.

Somehow, the three of us survive several hours of tears and yelling and disbelief. When Mark and Gianna finally quiet, the front door opens. Delanie steps in. Gianna runs to her, and we begin all over again.

I sit, feeling nothing, as I watch the love of two daughters for their father liquify before my eyes.

I don't self-medicate Sunday night when he leaves. Val takes me to the drug store, and I refill my epilepsy prescription before Delanie goes back to Slippery Rock. I'm not totally convinced I should take pills again, but the last thing in the world I need now is to have a seizure.

Mark returns for a day later in the week. The highway has become his seesaw. He's balancing Pittsburgh and Fairview.

Two families.

He's assumed a weak and timorous manner, now. He marches to Gianna's bedroom door several times but doesn't knock.

"And that's karma," I murmur when I pass him once in the hall. So many times, he accused me of being afraid of my kids.

Finally, before he leaves, he musters the courage to rap on her door.

"I'm leaving, Gianna." He stands in the hall, his face twisted with hurt. She doesn't respond. He turns the knob, but the door remains locked. "I love you. I'm sorry. I'll be home in a few days."

She says nothing. He steps closer, turns sideways to listen with one ear. He no longer looks like himself.

"Okay, well, bye." He glances up, realizing I'm watching.

Reactively, I fold my arms. He hangs his head, and as he passes me, I pounce. "You can hurt me all you want, but that's my daughter in there you've devastated. I hate you for that."

I walk away.

A few minutes later, Mark sits down beside me in the kitchen, tries to hold my hand.

"I love you, Nikki. I always have. I haven't been the best husband."

"You can say that again."

"I'll make this up to you and the kids."

I look abhorrently at him but say nothing.

"I never meant to hurt any of you. This was a mistake. A horrid, stupid mistake, and we are going to get through this. I am going to spend the rest of my life making this up to you."

A light bulb goes off inside my head, and I realize something that makes me angrier than his cheating, than his creating a life with some other woman.

There is not a speck of belief in him that I would ever leave.

He stands up, gently places a hand on my shoulder and kisses the top of my head. "You'll see."

He's completely sure that even though he's done this horrible thing to me, I'm not strong enough to leave him. I've never been strong enough to leave him.

He goes out the door, gets in his fancy Jeep, and heads south toward his other family.

I sit thinking, not about him but me.

Am I strong enough?

Chapter 20 The war

"Don't you ever mention my mother's name ever
again," Jessie posted on Facebook when someone
criticized CJ by name.

The Sunday after Thanksgiving, I wake to a phone call around 6:45 a.m. All three kids are at home sleeping in their rooms, so I'm not as frantic as I would be if Delanie and Hux were at school.

Mark has been coming home for long weekends, sleeping in Hux's room if Hux is at school and in the basement if he's home. The child's mother, his mistress, ex-girlfriend, girlfriend—whoever—is not doing well, so he isn't home this weekend. He's in Pittsburgh with Rosalee because Rosalee's grandparents won't leave their daughter's bedside.

So when the phone rings, I think it's him calling. I glance at the name on the screen, however, and see my friend's name.

"Mary?"

"Hi," she murmurs. "How are you?"

"Okay. Is everything all right with you?"

"I'm fine."

"What's up? I know you're not calling this early for no reason."

My high school friends and I text each other several times a week, but we rarely call each other.

"I can tell you haven't seen Facebook," she responds.

"No, what's going on?"

"Janice and Natasha are at it again. They made some nasty comments."

I called Janice last week and told her to take my name off her petition. I informed her Mark had forged my signature. Evy has been out of town for his college for a few weeks, but I still haven't heard from him. Once again, I'm trying to right another blunder of Mark's. Running around with a rug, putting out Mark's fires, is wearing me down. At least Gianna is talking to me. Delanie convinced her that Mark's choices are not my fault. I'm hoping Evy will speak to me once he's back in town.

"What did they say?" Despite the fact my life is caught in a whirlpool of deceit, a slight hope springs that she has juicy gossip about someone else to save me from the limelight. I can't shake my resilient suburban-wife pettiness. "Something about me?"

"Yes."

My flicker of hope disappears. I wish this neighborhood would get out of my yard and into someone else's.

"They're mad because I won't return their calls." I swing my feet over the side of my bed. I won't look online. I refuse to sift through Janice or Natasha's Facebook posts. I didn't attend Janice's November book club party, and she had the nerve to call and ask why. She said I'd forced her to rearrange her place seating at the last minute.

Give me a break.

She had probably sat me at the head of the table with a single fork—to stab the tomatoes they tossed.

"You don't understand why I didn't show?" I couldn't hide my anger when she called.

"No, it was rude."

"Rude?"

"Yes, rude, Nikki. We're all concerned over... well, Mark. We are also aware you may lose your job with the budget cuts. We're your friends. Natasha and I want to be there for you. You should have come."

"Janice," I said. I was having a bad day. A news clip kibitzed in the background. Something about North Korea. "You'd give Kim Jong-un a run for his money in the friend department, and Natasha? She's backstabbed me so much in the past month, I feel like Julius Caesar."

Natasha told the entire school district Mark had a three-year-old daughter. Women kept stopping me in the halls at the administration building, whispering, "I'm sorry. How are you doing?" from behind wrinkled little thank-god-it's-not-me faces.

Mrs. Higgins chastised Natasha for her gossiping. Told her to keep her opinions outside school district property. But it was too late. The scolding was like tossing a shot glass of water on a wildfire.

"Since you haven't seen it, stay off Facebook," Mary advises. "Let your friends take care of this."

"What started everything?"

"A post by Janice."

"Of course. Did she mention my name?"

"No, she's not ballsy enough to do that. She wants that job for her daughter in the district."

"Right."

"What infuriated me about her post is several people liked it." Mary, who doesn't have a molecule of meanness in her, is appalled. "All from your old book club."

I don't ask for the names. I'm afraid Reah's name is one of them, and I can't take one more feather on my back. I'll fall flat on my face.

"So Carolyn posted true friendship posts. Roselle, Nancy, and I kept liking them. I'm sorry. It got out of hand."

These are my high school friends. They will defend me until my dying day, and I, them.

"I love you guys. Thanks."

"I would not have called you but for one post."

My curiosity gets the best of me, and I ask, "What was it?"

"Friendship comes in various colors. When it turns green, it's time to move on."

"Did Janice write that?"

"No, Reah."

I jump out of bed.

"Reah?"

The last thing Janice said to me before she hung up the phone that day, was that I thought only of myself. She scolded me for not showing up to book club and said Mark and I had always been jealous of her and John. She was right in one sense, Mark had been green-eyed envious of John, but me? I'd only used Janice to try and win back Natasha and Reah.

Nikki, you never learn.

Barb used to say I couldn't fill in my friendship pit with a bulldozer.

"No worries," Mary insists. "Carolyn gave it to them good."

Carolyn is the quietest, nicest woman you'll ever meet in your life. A kindergarten teacher after college, now she works part-time in the school district with children with disabilities. There is only one line you don't cross with Carolyn, and that's hurting her friends.

"I wanted to warn you before you hear it from someone else. Stay out of this war, Nikki. Fight your important battles. Your friends have your back on this one."

By Sunday night there was surge after surge of combat in the Janice versus Nikki housewives Facebook war. Carolyn let me know later that my real friends kept posting true friendship pictures until it annoyed Natasha so much she mentioned my name, Nikki Grey, in one of her posts.

That did not sit well with my daughters. Delanie stepped in and ended the war. Gianna had called and told her about it. The final post of the evening was Delanie to Natasha, "Don't you ever mention my mother's name again. She was the best friend you ever had, and you threw her friendship away."

Natasha waved her white flag. She removed the post with my name in it, and the war ended.

But great damage had been done between Reah and me. Sometimes words can hurt as horribly as sticks and stones.

I retired Sunday evening proudly. I never opened Facebook once.

But you're still relying on your friends, Nikki.

Monday morning, Mrs. Higgins pats me on the back. "I'm proud of you for staying out of that nasty battle."

I was shocked she'd heard about it. She waved a finger at me, calling me to follow her.

"I called Janice Everglade last night. I don't think she'll be giving you any more problems. I know what she's been doing, buttering me up to get her daughter a job. The superintendent is aware of it," she said after closing the door to her office.

Mrs. Higgins is the quintessential sweet little old lady. She's loved me for years, and I've loved her right back. She feels terrible about the budget cuts. I can see the pain in her eyes. "I'm sorry, Nikki, the school board is going to insist on furloughing part-time people."

This potential layoff is another feather to weigh me down. Another link snapped. I smile and tell her I understand because I don't want her to hurt, too, but my world unravels like a ball of yarn rolling down a mud-slicked hill.

This can't come at a worse time. How can I leave Mark if I don't have a job?

After a long, exhausting week, where I constantly busy myself with insignificant chores rather than grasping my impending job loss, I sit down on a Monday night, search deep inside my soul for anything remotely resembling courage and begin working on my resume.

I've been light-headed for days. The stare-aways and night jerks have returned with a vengeance, so before I go to bed that night, I slip my medication into my mouth and swallow.

I know the exhaustion will begin again, but I'll get through it. I can't worry about seizing. I have to decide what to do about my marriage.

I lie down on my bed, inviting fatigue. For once, I welcome this side effect.

Sleep is my elixir.

But eleven days later, Jody rushes me to the hospital on a Friday night. I've had an allergic reaction to Tegretol. She said I threw up extensively in the emergency room, and people were gagging and running out of the building.

Chapter 21 The medication

"They told me I was drinking too much water. I wasn't, but I didn't want to bother you while you were on vacation," CJ told Doctor Jim from her hospital bed.

It took a war and near death, but I've finally won Evy back.

"Girlfriend," he says when he shows up in the hospital. "I can't believe Mark forged your name. I'm going to cut his fingers off and work my way down if you know what I mean. I should have known you'd never sign that petition."

"You just love me because I'm dying," I respond.

During my hospital holiday, I remained miserably nauseated. Something about my liver skyrocketing from an under thirty-five count to over eight hundred caused the nausea. In the emergency room, Doctor Death—I can't shake this guy—said I should be dead.

Sunday evening, my neurologist, Jim, a running friend, drove directly from the airport to the hospital to chastise me for not calling him. He had given me his cell number when I restarted the medication and instructed me to contact him if I had problems.

"You were on vacation. I didn't want to bother you," I told him.

Dr. Jim was furious. After a long sermon about how he gave me his number for a reason, and I should call him if anything goes wrong again, he prescribed a new medication.

Evy drives me home late Monday morning.

Doctor Death couldn't add more time to my sentence because I never lost consciousness, although I would have knocked myself out with a fire extinguisher if I could have reached up from my gurney and grabbed it. I'll forever pity anyone with hepatitis. That was my diagnosis: drug-induced hepatitis.

"How did you not know it was the medicine?" Evy asks as he settles me on the couch.

"With Jim on vacation, his receptionist and Dr. Felt's nurse tossed me back and forth like two kids with a ball. One said flu, the other, medicine. I didn't know who to believe."

I start the new medication in a week or so. Doctor Jim believes I'll tolerate the next one better; I've taken it before. I recall this prescription lends a soapy taste in my mouth that I loathe, along with the usual fatigue but not many other reactions. The last time I took it, the bad taste disappeared after a month and the fatigue, after a few months.

When people hear you have epilepsy, they assume you'll take the medication and the seizures will stop. What they don't realize is the medication is horrific. That's the reason I fought taking it. I do not pass out from seizures. I have never passed out—except for the marijuana mistake—so electing to swallow pills that cause harsh side effects is a tough decision.

But I can't risk having a grand mal seizure now that Mark is running back and forth between Fairview and Pittsburgh. I get my license back in a few weeks.

So I muster through the fatigue and the stare-aways. Delanie is home, so burdening my friends for rides ends. Delanie and Gianna have struck a new comradery, and Delanie carts her anywhere she wants. They've always gotten along, but this Rosalee thing strengthens the bond between my girls.

Mark sees this, too. They've united against him.

When he comes home for his long weekend, Hux tells him to get his stuff the hell out of his room. Mark retreats to the kids' game room in the basement to sleep. He carves away a space of his own near the couch, shoving old toys to the side so he can work and watch a small television. It's demeaning. He's an outcast in his own home. He can't even coax Furgy down to the basement.

"Do you want him to leave for good, Mom?" Delanie asks me one day.

"I don't know, Delanie. Do you?"

"He's my dad. I can visit him anywhere. But Mom, he left you to die. If Jody hadn't come, I don't know what would have happened."

I had called Mark on the Friday morning of the day Jody took me to the hospital. I explained my temperature was 103 and asked him to come home. He agreed, but later phoned, saying I should pop a few ibuprofens and go to bed. He'd be there tomorrow. He apologized for not being able to come home but wouldn't relent when I begged. He insisted he had work to do.

I did go to bed and, for some odd reason, maybe fate, Gianna checked on me around dinner time. I was trembling. She called Jody, and basically, that call saved my life.

Doctor Death said if I hadn't been in such great physical condition, I might have died.

See! I'm not crazy. Running is good for me.

We continue living like a family of zombies, preparing to experience the worst Christmas of our lives. I manage to purchase a few items the kids want. Mark does his own thing, but the four of us silently wonder the same thing. What's he buying Rosalee? And what about—her—the mother?

A huge fight ensues between Mark and Hux three days before Christmas. I hear them yelling upstairs, so I go and stand at the bottom of the staircase.

"I made a mistake, Hux. I love your mother."

This seems too personal of an argument to engage in with your son. They shout back and forth, then Delanie comes out of her bedroom.

"What are you going to do about the little girl, Dad?" she cuts in. "We realize it's not her fault, but she's ruined our lives. Everyone knows. Gianna is being bullied. Today, Amy Everglade asked her what she was getting her little sister for Christmas."

That got me stomping up the stairs. I shuffle down the hall and send Mark to the basement like he's a child being punished. Then I traipse into Gianna's little pink room with her books and her dolls and her sparkly pom-poms and find her crying in the closet. I rip the comforter off her bed, kick everything on the floor of her closet aside, and I lie down and hold her in my arms until she falls asleep.

Much later, the shouting resumes, but I keep still. Gianna's body hugs mine in our safe little corner of the world. Her breathing is light and even. In my arms, sleep has come to pacify her.

Later, the front door squeaks open and slams shut. Mark starts his car, and the purr of his engine drifting away sends a shiver through me. I cry myself to sleep beside Gianna.

The next day I wake, stiff and aching. Gianna asks if she can stay home with Delanie. I don't think twice about calling her in sick. Then I dress and drive to my last day of work before the Christmas holiday.

At the district building, life proceeds without a glitch. The janitor lights a gigantic evergreen in the front foyer. Parents send cookies and gifts for administrators. Kids from different school choirs arrive to sing carols. The halls glimmer with gold and holly. I can't help but feel encouraged by the warm Christmas spirit.

We will get through this.

Then, later in the morning, I pass by the wall of boxy mail slots and notice there are pink slips everywhere. Apprehensively, I approach and lift mine from my box. We part-timers have been laid off. We need not return after the first of the year. They toss a glimmer of hope at the end, so we don't shred their files on our last day: they may recall some of us next fall.

Merry f'ing Christmas.

Now, I don't even have a job. Nothing. Zilch. I'll earn a piddling of unemployment. The amount won't cover our monthly food bill. I may have to tolerate Mark's cheating for the rest of my life, I think.

Evy stops around five o'clock. He's there to take me to the store to buy Gianna a gift. I want to get her something special this year, so I've picked out a little gold ring with a heart and a small diamond to let her know she will always hold my heart.

Evy doesn't press me when I tell him I'm too tired to go. "Naggy, you need to get a hold of yourself."

When I don't respond, he attempts encouragement. "You're stronger than you think."

He strokes my hair once and leaves me lying on the couch.

I fall into a dead sleep, barely wake when Delanie drops bags of tacos on the counter, and the three kids sit down in the kitchen to eat. They laugh and guffaw at the table, blessing me with sweet comfort.

I am happiest when falling asleep to the sound of my children's laughter. Once your kids go away to college, there's nothing more soothing in life than when they come home, and you know they are safe in the next room.

I fall asleep peacefully and wake much later.

When I go upstairs to climb into bed, I find a wrapped package on my comforter. It's sitting alongside a note from

Evy and the big-girl-pants barrette he bought me last summer.

His note reads:

"Naggy, I bought the ring and wrapped it for Gianna. I found your big-girl-pants barrette in that messy old roll-top desk. (You need to clean that out.) Now put it on. Tomorrow I want you to change your attitude. You're lignum vitae. You can do this. I know you don't think you can, but you can. I love you, but you need to get a grip. This could get much worse."

And then it does. The day after Christmas, Rosalee's mother dies.

Chapter 22 The flashlight

*"How do I turn this stupid light off?" CJ asked
Jeff.*

We continue pretending we're a normal suburban
family as we march through the holidays and bundle up to
prepare for winter.

My sentence served, I retrieve my license, which could
not be better timed since Delanie and Hux return to school
shortly after the first of the year. Because the woman has
died, Mark spends more time in Pittsburgh with Rosalee.
Gianna and I are left to fend for ourselves.

House maintenance chores fall to me. In mid-January
when the snowy weather breaks, I take advantage of the 55-
degree heatwave to clean up our yard. Sun slices through
grey clouds, so I am outside all day, raking leaves and
trimming the bushes that Mark never got to last fall.

I'm hard at work, so I don't notice women arriving in
cars up the street. I've spent five arduous hours working in
the back yard before moving to more carefully groom the
front. My forearms and biceps ache and burn, screaming
from months of not lifting at the gym, but the pain feels
good. I much prefer physical over mental agony.

My mind wanders, and I rake harder, faster, taking
weeks of anguish out on my poor yard. I'm scraping up the
soil with leaves. Gathering dirt and autumn's death together
into mounds to be bagged.

I stop and breathe deeply, wishing I could bag and toss a little of the muck in my life as easily.

When Mark does come home now, he has resumed sleeping in Hux's room. Typically, he arrives late on Thursday night or early evening on Friday. Then, like the faithful father he has become to Rosalee, he leaves Sunday.

He and his partner have begun to split their clients, and this is going better than expected. Mark has enough business on his own to hire another full-time attorney and a part-time marketer. He's garnered extra clients from various cities, but most sit within a six-hour drive of Fairview, including Pittsburgh, where several thriving accounts are located.

I'm still searching for employment.

He's still begging to get back in my bed.

It's Wednesday, and I mull over our sleeping arrangements while I return to my raking. It's not really his nightly snooze he's asking about. It's our marriage. He doesn't want to lose me and the kids, so he apologizes profusely for spending time in Pittsburgh. Rosalee has three more major surgeries to endure.

"The poor little thing," he said when he called earlier today. "She just had a birthday. This is too much for a four-year-old to endure."

He's attempting to sway feeble, frail, feels-sorry-for-everybody Nikki, but this coaxes no empathy from me. Instead, I calculate in my head when he slept with Rosalee's mother. Late March. I grip my rake, scrape the earth vigorously, and think back five years. How were we getting along? When you're married so long, the years run together.

He uses the number of years we've been together as a defense. "We've had a great marriage until now. I know you still love me. I'll make this up to you, Nikki. Once Rosalee is done with her operations."

She's had two corrective surgeries already. In between these extensive hospital stays, she slept at her grandparents' home.

I wonder what they think of Mark. The man with two families.

Maybe they don't know.

I'm deep in thought and don't realize I'm working in the pitch black until a car, headlights ablaze, rides down the street. I quit raking and turn the house and garage lights on. I bag up the last of the leaves and cart them to the street for the garbage. That's when I notice the neighbor four houses down has lit up our neighborhood with her exotic house lights.

I remember today is the date of the book club. I recall the book they're discussing: *Educated*. When Janice invited me back into the inner sanctum, I read the books for November, December, and January. *Crawdads*, *Idaho*, and *Educated*.

I'm embarrassed not to have noticed the women arriving. They probably think I was outside snooping, which I would have been doing if I'd remembered the date.

I hurry inside, turn off my lights, and run upstairs to Hux's room, which sits at the front of our house. I must clear a path to the window in the dark. I nudge his clothes and Mark's boxes aside then peer out into the night from behind his curtains, frightened someone might see me.

I realize the house is too dark to see inside, so I step in front of the window and gaze out brazenly.

Ellie has quit the book club, and Reah says she's quitting, but I don't believe her. She's too enamored by Janice. My eyes scan the street for Reah's SUV, but I don't see it.

I hit the jackpot by stumbling upon an unopened bag of potato chips. I drag a chair to the window, sit down, and chomp away while I gaze down the street. It's quiet in my empty house. My chewing dominates my hearing until—what's that sound? I stop chomping. It's the rattle.

Did Hux forget to remove the bag of balls banging at my soul for months? I specifically told him to get his butt up on that roof and dislodge them.

I open the window and lean my hands on the roof, gaze up at the chimney. I can't see a thing.

I retrieve a flashlight, but still can't see, so I trudge down to the garage and sift through the debris on Mark's workbench and toolbox—I'll be glad to see those monstrosities go if he leaves—until I find his high-powered flashlight.

When I reenter the house, the clock teases me by shining a fluorescent 6:05 at me. Everyone should be at the book club by now. I hurry back to Hux's room and peer down the street.

Thank God, I don't see Reah's car. Of course, she could have ridden with someone else. I sit back on the chair, chomp more chips, and consider waiting through their dinner and discussion until they leave for the night.

Then I hear the rattle again and remember I've retrieved Mark's massive light. I open the window and crawl out onto the lower roof of our house.

The outside of our home has two levels of roofing, one low, one high. The higher roof sports a chimney with a wide metal plate sitting above it. This landing is strong enough for Hux to golf off. Four corner posts hold the metal landing a foot above the top of the chimney, so smoke from our fireplace can escape.

I stand up carefully and direct the light toward the chimney. Sure enough, a bag clumps off to one side.

I inch over the shingles toward the higher roof. I could heave myself up onto it to retrieve the annoyance. I glance down. I hate heights. But at least I never trimmed the front bushes. If I take a tumble, I'll have a cushion. I gaze up again.

I can't do it. I cower as I always do with everything in my life. I become so frightened I squat and crab walk across the shingles back to the window.

I'm about to climb in when I see another car edging down the street. I flip the switch to turn off Mark's light but instead, my flashlight turns into a lantern with a light as bright as the Statue of Liberty's.

I panic. I see the car coming.

OMG, that's Reah's car!

I bounce between anger and embarrassment. Frantically, I hit buttons to turn off the light. The flashlight-turned-lantern has a mind of its own. It begins blinking. I'm a lighthouse. A blinking beacon enlightening the entire neighborhood of how pathetic I am.

The car slows. I twist toward the window but, of course, it has closed. I set the beacon down and use both hands, attempting to heave it open.

It won't budge.

The car slows in front of my house. I can't help myself. I look straight into the driver's window at Reah. I shift my weight as I squat in shame. The tip of my sneaker taps the light, and the blinking beacon rolls over and over, down the roof. It becomes airborne then falls to the bushes, catches on the top of my tallest shrub, and swings back and forth, illuminating our front yard.

Reah watches it fall. Then she ducks her head and glances upward toward me. She's as embarrassed to be caught going to book club as I am to be spying from the roof of my house.

We flash awkward little waves toward one another. She continues down the road, and I lie flat on the roof, pretending I've gone in the window until she gets out of her car and goes into the house. I'd rather freeze to death than have her save me.

And I nearly do.

I sit on the roof for over an hour. I don't say a word when someone drops Gianna off because if I embarrass her, she'll stop talking to me again. I sit another five minutes before Gianna walks down the hall past Hux's room. Then I bang and bang until she hears me. By then the temperature has dipped so low I'm shivering. She opens the window, and I crawl in, my hands and face mottled with shame and frostbite.

"Oh my God, you are embarrassing. Did anyone see you?"

"Oh, no," I say all serious.

"Oh my God, they did! You couldn't lie to save your soul!"

I sigh. She's right. I couldn't. That's her father's talent.

Chapter 23 The question

"The trick is to never ask a question you don't know the answer to," Zak (the attorney) told CJ.

Mounds of snow have fallen over Fairview when Mark asks the question.

I'm calling this month reflective February. By now, I've evaluated my reliance on friendships and realized something about myself. I'm the sort who can't accept losing anyone in my life—no one. I've assessed the years behind me and fathomed the years ahead, and I've had an epiphany: People who move couches and people who move bodies slip into and out of our world at the perfect time.

I've got to let go of those friends who move couches.

Reah moves couches.

I believe in God. I believe he is goodness, a logical being so much smarter than us that he fits life's intricate pieces together finely. Yes, we have free will, but he is all-knowing. He knows us better than we know ourselves. He sees what decisions we will make long before we realize there are decisions to be made. So there was no coincidence that I am held captive on my roof the moment Reah rides by. He was telling us something.

I imagine God up in the clouds sitting in front of His virtual computer—the world. He has the ability to offset our failings and bad choices with kind acts and goodness. He realigns us onto our true path, snapping a weak and a strong puzzle piece firmly into place next to each other.

If Mark forges my signature on a petition causing Evy to break his friendship with me, God, in His infinite logic, fits the pieces together. Evy shows up back in my life when I am too weak to get off the couch, and he produces the best Christmas present for me to give Gianna at the exact time she needs to feel special because of the bullying she's endured over Mark's bad choice.

That's infinite wisdom amalgamating good and evil with precise effectiveness.

Gianna's ring fits her perfectly. It never leaves her finger. She twirls it around and around when she becomes nervous about her parents, her home, her future. Every time I see her twist that ring, I think of Evy, and it reminds me to be stronger for Gianna. And every time she catches me smiling at her while she stands twisting it, she's reminded her mother will forever love her, unconditionally, and she smiles back—at the exact time I need a flicker of love most.

Infinite wisdom.

The little miracles we don't notice in life flutter around us, waiting to be discovered.

So Reah and I catching each other in weak moments is no coincidence.

I haven't always been the best friend to her. I barely remember her father's funeral, yet every year she asks how I'm doing on the anniversary of my mother's death. Reah helped me through many Christmases, helped fill my loneliness for years. Equally, I've done favors for her.

Yet maybe it's time for Reah and me to part ways. Not angrily but naturally.

So as Mark drives up I-79 from Pittsburgh to Fairview in one of the worst snowstorms we've seen in years because he says, "We need to talk," I put my faith in God that I will have the strength to get through whatever Mark has in store for me.

But not in my wildest dreams was I prepared for his question.

We began going to Tracy the counselor together last month and, although I've not agreed to take him back into my bedroom, we've made progress. So while I wait for him, I wonder if he's going to force me to decide between reconciliation or separation. I send Gianna to Ellie's house for the night, and I stare out the big beautiful, bay window of my living room. The weather's turned. I watch thick, heavy snowflakes fall lazily to earth, thinking, I can do this.

Then Mark shows up and asks a question that, even after my soul-searching during reflective February, floors me.

Like a vacuum, he sucks every particle of air out of my lungs when he says, "Will you raise Rosalee with me?"

"Excuse me?"

"I know what I'm asking might seem inconceivable," he says, "but she has no mother. I'm asking you, Nikki, will you be her mother? We can raise her together. I know it will be hard on the kids at first, but they'll accept her. Love her. They're good kids. This was my mistake. Not Rosalee's."

Immediately, my mind races back to God and His big computer screen.

What the fuck?

If I could stretch a hand through the clouds to His keyboard, I'd rip it out from underneath His fingernails.

I stand up, laughing, of all things. My mouth drops so low I think I strained the tendons flanking my jaw. "Are you kidding me?"

"Nikki." He puts his face in his hands and cries.

I pace back and forth, laughing, wordless.

"Please," he pleads. "I know you need time to grasp this. But we are making progress with the counseling. I love you. You know I love you. I've just made such a mess of my life."

I stop pacing and stare at him. Finally, after minutes of watching him cry, I extend my arm, point toward the front door, and scream two words. "Get out."

"Nikki," he begs. "Don't do this to us."

"Me? I'm doing this?"

"No, no," he sobs. "I've done this. But all I ask is that you think about this little girl. She has no one. She's alone."

Alone. Of course! He's playing me.

"Her grandfather is sick. She can't live with them."

"Get out," I say again. "I don't care where you go. Sleep at your office. At a friend's. I don't care if you go to a girlfriend's house. Just get out."

"There's no girlfriend, Nikki. I never loved Rosalee's mother. I've never loved any woman but you. It was a mistake. A bad, horrible mistake."

"I don't care. You drop this on me and expect me to what? Jump up and down and say, 'Oh goodie, here's the fourth child I wanted'."

"No, of course not." He wipes his face and nose. "I'll go. I will. Just promise me one thing."

"I'm not promising you anything, Mark."

"Okay, but please, think about it. We could move to another neighborhood, so no one bothers Gianna. Or you. We can figure out a way to make this work."

"Just leave, Mark. Get out of here."

He goes then. Cries. Begs for forgiveness from the front porch. I slam the door in his face.

I am alone.

I search around me, praying for some tiny miracle to spark in the hopeless night and lead me, lend me a morsel of comfort. But no miracles emerge.

How can I agree to raise this child?

But how do I live without Mark?

How do I survive—alone?

Chapter 24 The ice cream

"I like the vanilla ice cream," Mike Filutze told
CJ when the nurse brought his evening snack.

"You can't be serious." Val responds first. "You're not saying yes, are you?"

I've spent four days wandering around my world aimlessly. If anyone asked what I had done between Friday and Tuesday night, I couldn't tell them. I don't remember.

Jody is winding up and down Seattle's streets, following realtors around in search of a house, so I don't bother her. Honestly, I'm so blindsided, I've hardly spoken to anyone.

When Evy calls Monday and realizes there is something wrong with me, he, Val, and Ellie show up at my house on Tuesday night when Gianna has play practice, so I tell them what Mark has asked me to do.

"What did you say to him?" Evy asks.

"I was shocked. I didn't say anything."

"You can't be considering it," Val rages.

"I don't know, Val. I don't even have a job."

"Well, get one," she shouts, and this shocks me. In the years I've known her, she's never once yelled at me.

"I'm trying, but it's not that easy."

"If you do this," Ellie adds. "If you raise his daughter. You'll be the laughingstock of the neighborhood."

"I'm already the laughingstock. What's the difference?"

"The difference," Evy says. "Is that people will eventually forget Mark had an affair if you take him back, but uprooting that poor little girl? Pretending she's yours? It's like running around with an arrow sticking out of your chest saying 'Honest, he didn't shoot me. I'm fine'."

"Everyone thinks it's easy to leave, but how do I survive with three children on my own when I haven't worked in years?"

"You'll figure it out," Evy retorts. "You're a brilliant woman."

"I don't feel brilliant."

"Nikki, if you're not going to think of yourself, think of the child," Val argues. "People will never treat that little girl right. They'll never forget she's Mark's illegitimate kid."

"They might forget," I say. "Eventually."

"If you send her to an Australian boarding school, maybe." Val stands. She might be madder than anyone. "Have you lost your mind? What purpose does your raising her serve? She'll be branded as an adulterer's mistake."

I've never considered the consequences to Rosalee, only to myself and my three children.

"But how do Gianna, Hux, Delanie, and I survive? I've filled out over fifty job applications. So far, I've not interviewed for one stinking position—even a basic booking-keeping job."

"Fill out fifty more." She flails her arms. "You have to kick his ass out."

Her adamancy confounds me. "Val, if I can't work, I can't leave Mark."

This is such a nightmare. Even my friends are turning on me.

"What do the kids say?" Evy asks. "Because they ought to have some say in this. It's their lives we're talking about, too."

"They don't know."

"You haven't told them?"

"No, Evy, how do I tell them their father wants to bring his illegitimate kid home to share pizza and watch cartoons with them? Where's she going to sleep? With Gianna? What do I say? 'Do you mind moving your stuff over? Rosalee's moving in.' There's just not a good way to broach the subject."

"That should tell you something about the entire situation," Val screeches. "Nikki, you can't seriously be thinking about raising this child. In Fairview? They'll eat you alive. They'll eat her alive. Fairview thrives on rumors and gossip."

"Mark says we can move before Gianna goes back to school in the fall."

"You're not thinking straight," Evy scolds. "You've got to get a hold of yourself. Is that counselor not helping you?"

"I haven't talked to her since Mark asked me to raise Rosalee. Besides, it's hard to tell her everything I'm feeling with Mark right there."

"Wait," he says. "Aren't you going alone anymore?"

"No, just with Mark."

"Why?"

"I don't know. Maybe I'm giving up."

I was struggling before Mark asked me to raise Rosalee. I've lost so much weight that the skin underneath my arms sags and wrinkles. My face is haggard. I ran into Blake the Pro at the grocery store yesterday, and he asked if he could buy me lunch.

How has my life come to this?

Mark's called me every day, proclaiming his love, begging me not to divorce him, to be a mother to Rosalee. He'll do anything.

"Don't give up," Evy says before they leave that evening. "Never give up."

"Thanks, Evy."

"This is your decision, and even though I want you to leave the no-good, worthless, useless lump of a scoundrel, rogue—"

"All right, all right," I say.

"I'll support you either way because I love you." He kisses me and leaves with Ellie and Val.

No little miracles.

I have an hour before Gianna comes home, and I can't bear to be home alone with my thoughts, so I jump in my car and head for Manchester, hoping a little miracle awaits me there.

When I walk through the door, Barb strolls toward me and wraps her arms around me. I appreciate this.

Her embrace warms me. Music from the sixties plays from a large computer in the corner of the main room. People listen from their chairs. Some of the residents stare at us curiously. Others, blankly. A few smile. They recognize my face but aren't sure from where. Their expressions aren't condemning. They don't judge me about Mark.

Is that the miracle?

Barb becomes excited when an old Nancy Sinatra song plays. She wants to dance, so I take her hands, and we swing our arms and hips. Barb sings the words, and we sway awkwardly to the music's tempo like two little girls. The other residents aren't dancing, but I'm not embarrassed. No one cares what we do.

Here in the Alzheimer's unit of Manchester, your worth isn't counted by how you look, what you own, what people say about you, or whether your husband cheated on you or not. Here there are no cliques, bad friendships, neighborhood book clubs. There's only music and people and vacuous time.

I close my eyes and, in my head, Barb and I float back in time to our childhood. We're sifting sand through our toes, building sandcastles on the beach. Mom and Dad are with us, and they're young. Barb and I prance along the water's edge, skipping stones, and shrieking from the water's chilliness. Dad and I use red and yellow plastic buckets to bury Barb up to her neck in the sand. Mom unpacks sandwiches and homemade cookies. When Mom calls us, Barb stands, sand clinging to every inch of her. She grabs my hand. We run to the water, jump in, and swim through cool waves that wash every particle of dirt from us.

I hear someone shout ice cream and suddenly, we've left the beach, heading for Sara's. Sara's is the ice cream shop that sits at the entrance of the beach and plays old music all day long over its loudspeakers, so, in my mind, we dance again, and our sticky ice cream slides down the sides of our cones and drips onto our flip flops and the hot asphalt of the parking lot.

I open my eyes. Barb smiles.

Is she remembering, too?

I think back eight years, to when I first realized something wasn't right with her. Then back seven years, to her diagnosis. Then six, to one of our last long runs together. Carol, Laura, Jan, Heather, and I took her out of Manchester and ran along the path beside the lake.

Barb gasped at birds flying low over the shoreline. We'd all seen the same birds rising and dipping along the lake many times, but none of us recognized their beauty until that day. Barb gazed at me, and I said, "Go on." She ran to the water's edge, flapping her arms, laughing, and yelling, "Fly, birds, fly away!"

To those of us watching, she appeared brilliant in the moment, sadly young and callow yet mindlessly happy in a world that was slipping through her fingers.

Now, I wonder if, deep down in her soul, she doesn't remember those moments in time when she witnessed life's splendor.

Those little miracles.

Has she forgotten the family picnics, Christmas parties, hikes, or our last running trip when we spent a weekend in Niagara Falls? A girls' weekend away spent jogging alongside the river that led to the falls, its water rushing powerfully past us, an unstoppable force.

There were times in our lives when we weren't speaking, but they don't matter now that her hands are in mine and mine are in hers, and we are dancing in a room where no one cares. Only the moment matters.

I open my eyes. We've stopped dancing, and she's smiling radiantly at me.

"I love you," she rejoices.

Little miracles.

"I love you, too." For a moment, happiness settles in my heart.

A nurse hails "ice cream" a second time, and residents shuffle toward the dining hall. I lead Barb to her little table, sit down beside her, and we wait for her ice cream.

When a nurse arrives with a tray, I stand, rub Barb's back, and promise to come next week.

"Come, yes." She smiles warmly.

"I will." I step away, so they can serve her.

"Here you go, Barb." The nurse places her ice cream dish and spoon in front of her.

She picks up her spoon with one hand and lifts the fingers of her other to the nurse's sleeve. She tugs it gingerly.

"Who was that woman?" she asks.

The nurse looks at me and then at Barb. This is a first.

"That's your sister," she responds, surprised.

"I don't have a sister," she tells her.

Chapter 25 The wheel

"Let me make my own mistakes, Mom. I'll learn
from them," Jilly told CJ.

"If we divorce, we'll lose the house." Mark relays over the phone one weekend when he can't make it home.

I take this as a personal affront to both Gianna and me. Is he sacrificing the welfare of one daughter for another? I still haven't found a job, and he's confident I won't. Our town is small.

Plus, something has changed in Mark.

He spends two rather than four long weekends at home in February and announces he's altering his schedule to be in Fairview during the week and in Pittsburgh on weekends.

Rosalee's last surgery is scheduled in March, and he reveals he'll bring her to Fairview in May. At times, he talks as if I've agreed to raise her. He's that sure of himself. He utters her name as if he's speaking of some destitute third-world baby whom I couldn't possibly not fall in love with because she has great medical needs and no family.

While he talks, I think. In my mind, I jump from one bed to another. Alone or with Mark? With Mark or alone?

I picture a life raising Rosalee. Mark working long days, golfing, traveling. He can only be unselfish for so long before he leaves Rosalee alone with me, which he has promised not to do. But he'll eventually have to placate his need to golf, attend business trips, work out at the gym, carouse with the guys.

Sleep with other women.

I'm curled up on the sofa when this deduction slaps me. I straighten. Mark's been faithful until now. He's cheated one time. He won't do it again.

Why would such a thought cross my mind?

My memory speeds back in time to the Christmas after Delanie was born, and the chance encounter I had with a man much like I'd had with the attorney at The Sunset Restaurant.

"Mark," this man said. "Nice to see you. Happy holidays. Tell your wife—" Oddly, I stepped out from behind Mark, and he stopped. The man glances at me then back to Mark. Red-faced, he says, "Oh, this must be—"

Mark quickly introduces me, and when I ask later who he was, Mark nonchalantly says someone he golfed with.

Something had not been right.

Then there was the time Hux talked about the lady with the red hair that walked in the park with him and Daddy. Hux was three. He had been enamored by her hair. Mark sloughed it off.

There were hang-up calls one summer, too. I don't remember the year, but I recall it happening again much later. The second time, Jody had asked, "Hasn't this happened before?" And Ellie had remarked, "Maybe you should change your number."

I swing my legs off the couch. Did they suspect something? Back then?

Immediately, I pick up the phone and call Jody. I ask her flat out.

"Jody, do you think Mark has cheated on me before?" Surprisingly, I never asked this question of anyone. Why? I wonder.

"I don't know, Nikki. I truly don't."

"But if you had to guess, what is your gut telling you?"

She was quiet for a long time. She didn't answer my question, but when she finally spoke, I heard what her gut was saying, loud and clear.

"This is what I'm going to do. I'm going to call Ellie and ask her to take Gianna for a few days. Then I'm going to book a flight for you to come out here and spend some time with me. Don't even think about arguing. I have a free round-trip flight. I love you, Nikki."

OMG, Rosalee's mother wasn't his first.

Jody makes all the arrangements. Ellie keeps Gianna for a few days. Evy takes Furgy because Mark isn't home, and I drive to Cleveland and board a plane headed for Seattle. Jody picks me up at the airport, and I cry in her arms. Still, she says nothing.

We immerse ourselves into her world of bags and boxes and trips to the store. She and Archie have bought a house. I spend the first two days helping her decorate, something I'm good at. Once the majority of the boxes have been unpacked, we sit for a relaxing evening. Jody opens a bottle of wine and thanks me profusely.

"This isn't exactly the vacation I planned for you." She laughs.

"It did me good to keep my mind off myself for a while."

"I think it did. I was going to stop you and talk a few times, but we were having fun. I didn't want to ruin the moment."

"We always have fun together. Thank you for not ruining it. I was having a blast spending your money. Even in the pouring rain. Does it rain here every day?"

"I hope not. But that would be better than snow."

Always the optimist.

"Want another glass of wine?" she asks.

"No, thanks. I stick to one these days. I worry about the effects of alcohol with the epilepsy medication."

"You've tolerated this one well?"

"I have."

"If you feel panicky again, promise you'll call me right away. Archie has thousands of frequent-flyer miles to use, and you know I love having you visit."

"I know. I promise."

Jody misses me as much as I miss her.

"Okay." I set my empty wineglass down. "We've avoided the subject as long as we could."

Jody gazes into her half-full glass and swirls the wine around. "I guess we have."

"Why do you think he's cheated on me before, Jody? Do you know something?"

"Nikki." She sets her glass down. "If I'd had solid proof, I would have said something, but I don't. I've thought long and hard about why I feel the way I do about Mark. I never trusted him. He's dishonest, demeaning, and he plays on your guilt."

"He does that with perfection. He's guilted me into giving him his way for years."

"Do you think he's doing the same now?"

"What do you mean?"

"All this talk about the house and you not getting a job. You'll get a job, Nikki. You're in a tough situation, I agree, but it will change before May. You'll find something."

"I hope so."

Quiet hits us again. I listen to the creaks of Jody's house and chuckle to myself. There's no lonely rattle in her home.

"Do you think he's done this before? Cheated?" I don't look at her when I ask.

"I do. I keep thinking back to his long trips and those hang-up calls. You received those three times."

"Was it three? Or two?"

"Nikki." She puts a hand over mine. "Does it matter how many times it was? If Mark was a great husband who made one mistake, I might encourage you to forgive him."

"Would you encourage me to raise his child?"

"No," she responds quickly. "I'm shocked he's asked you. That wouldn't be good for you and Gianna, nor for the little girl."

I don't respond, and Jody, the person I trust more than anyone in the world, says, "Let him go, Nikki. You can do this on your own. You have lots of friends who can help you."

"I've relied on friends for too long."

"There's that, too. You hang on to friendships far too long. You need to forget Reah. I have. She's grown away from us. You've taken that too hard. You have me and Val and Evy, your running and high school friends. You have to move on. We will always love Reah. We had some wonderful years together, but they're over."

"I've been depending on you and Reah and Ellie since I was little. Now all of a sudden, I feel alone."

"You have to do this alone, but you'll never be completely alone. There's a big difference."

We talk long into the night, so by the time I'm ready to leave, Jody's words have strengthened me.

"Remember," she says, when she drops me off at the airport. "I'm only a phone call away."

Yes, I think, Jody is a true friend, but then I must leave and travel home, alone.

After several hours in flight and driving from Cleveland back to Fairview where mounds of melting snow edge the highway, I'm feeling revived. I turn into my driveway, and Gianna runs out the front door to greet me.

Ellie is inside making dinner. Gianna won an award at school. She excitedly tells me how her stomach fluttered when they announced her name at the school assembly. She says Ellie quit the book club, which I already knew, and how glad she is because she and Olivia, Ellie's daughter, don't want anything to do with Amy Everglade for the rest of their lives.

She chatters on. She's won the award for starting an anti-bullying campaign at school.

Unbeknownst to me, throughout February, every time Gianna stepped into the cafeteria, Amy's lunch table made loud remarks about her sharing a room with her little sister, and that Gianna's father had two families. They told everyone to call her Giannalee to make it clear everyone knew about Rosalee.

But unlike me, Gianna is no patsy. She rallied her own troops and started the anti-bullying club. She set up a "worry-free" zone in the cafeteria where kids sitting alone, or those feeling threatened or demeaned, had a safe place to sit and other kids to eat lunch with.

She shows me her award, and I read the letter the principal has sent home saying how Gianna's act impressed the school board. The administration has considered implementing a "worry-free" cafeteria zone for every school. In the first two days at Gianna's school, fifty-five kids sat in her section.

"I am proud of you," I tell her.

"Mom, do you know some of the students who were bullied have disabilities? I mean, come on. I can see bullying me. I'm strong," she says selflessly. "But how can kids bully someone who is mentally challenged or in a wheelchair?"

I choke back tears. This is a terrible situation Gianna and I are in, but she's inspired good from it.

Later that evening after we eat dinner and everyone leaves, Gianna says to me, "I'm going to be a special education teacher when I grow up."

"I think you would make a great teacher," I encourage. We open the computer and google Pennsylvania educational programs. She wants to know about Mercyhurst, a college in town.

"I want to stay close to home," she reassures me.

"I would like that more than anything in the world," I admit. "But when the time comes, we'll visit other schools, too. We'll look at all your options. I want you to be as happy as Hux and Delanie are with their choices."

She leans back on the couch beside me, her eyes raking my face. I think she's going to say something else about teaching, but she says, "I love you, Mom. We can get through this."

She loops her fingers into mine, and we sit for a long time talking about her life, the future, and how much awaits her. For once, no gloomy overtone haunts us. We relax, enjoyably anticipating the future.

I will remember that lovely hour, holding hands with my daughter on the couch, for the rest of my life.

Hail Mary full of grace, I wish to be as strong as Gianna. Please, I need a miracle.

Then the miracle comes.

At eight o'clock the next morning, I receive a phone call from an old boss. I had worked ten years for this man.

"Mr. Bruno, hello. How are you?"

"I'm well, but retiring soon," he responds. "Jack is taking over the business."

We catch up and out of the blue he asks, "Someone told me you might be interested in going back to work full-time. Is that true?"

He wants to know if I can start in April. I tell him I can, but that I booked a ten-day vacation in England at the end of May and beginning of June. He says that's wonderful and perfectly acceptable. We hang up, both elated.

And just like that. I'm back in the game.

Mark calls later, and when I tell him I've gotten a job, he sounds absolutely panicked. He professes his love for me.

Tells me he can't live without me, and I ask him why he hasn't been coming home as often.

"Because of Rosalee's surgeries," he insists. Then he tells me he's bought me a gift and will be home next week. He can't wait to see me and Gianna. He hopes I had fun in Seattle, but he misses me.

When he hangs up, I toy with my final decision. Divorcing someone is never easy.

For some reason, what Val once said after Mark returned from one of his West Coast conferences comes to mind. "That's a beautiful necklace, Nikki. What crime did Mark commit out in San Fran?"

A crime of the heart.

He's sure I won't leave him. He'll snap a five-hundred-dollar necklace on me and think he's won.

Two clear pictures of my future bloom in my mind. One with Mark and one without.

Tears well up in my eyes.

Am I strong enough to do this?

What did Ellie say I was? Pine. Soft and pliable. I've never been able to live alone. But, is he still cheating?

You know he is.

What if he's always been a cheater?

He has been and always will be.

I start to breathe hard. Panic. I grab my cell phone to call Jody or Ellie or Carol or Carolyn or someone stronger than me to get me through this!

And in the solitude of my house, with my hand clutching my cell, and the noisy, lonely rattle of the roof wailing above me, everything becomes clear. The road ahead materializes in my mind. I'm staring at the dotted white lines of a street. I'm not driving. I'm a pathetic passenger in my own car, never steering. Always, always, always relying on everyone else to goad me forward.

I straighten my back, instantly aware that I must do what I've kept myself from doing all my life.

In my head, the people in my car disappear one by one, and the vehicle takes an abrupt turn.

On the couch, I set down my cell phone. In my head, I grab the wheel.

Chapter 26 The team

"Good for you. You raised two strong women who didn't have to stay in a bad marriage," CJ said to her brother, Mike, when he remarked he and his wife, Barb, had been married over forty years but their children were all divorced.

I pick the Ides of March, March 15th, to call my team together. What better day?

I pound a meat clever on my kitchen table. "Hear, hear, the case of TPN is about to begin."

"TPN?" Val asks.

"Valerie," Evy scolds. "We're about to take down Toilet Paper Nikki."

"Stop." I point the clever at him. "This is the rise of Toilet Paper Nikki, not the fall."

"This is getting exciting." Evy wiggles in his seat.

Ellie and Val lean in, and I announce my plans and swear them to secrecy. I've hardly slept in days. I stand, go to the closet and fetch my Toilet-Paper Nikki storyboard.

"What's that?" Ellie helps me prop it up on the table.

"This is how Evy is going to get back at Janice Everglade, and how I am going to get back at Mark."

Then I make them raise their right hand and swear on the soul of all of the bachelors, bachelorettes, and Vanderpump Rules kids, that they will never breathe a word of this until all is done.

I hold the storyboard, so they can all see it. We stand and gaze at my masterpiece's steps, listed under the categories:

The Team
The Pro
The Bank
The Float
The Party
The Trip

Then I tell them today is the assembling of the team. Next, we are going to get Evy's parade approved. And more than that, we are going to park the gaudiest, most flamboyant float they can design right in front of Janice Everglade's house.

"There's a town meeting next Saturday, and Janice is presenting her petition," Evy informs us. "Rumor has it the supervisors are approving it."

"I've done some homework," I say. "Do you know what all three supervisors love?"

"What?"

"Golf."

"Brilliant." Evy applauds.

"What have I missed?" Val.

"Step two." I point to "the pro." "Blake the Pro is gay. We are going to fill that meeting with everyone Evy can get there. Blake is going to be our featured speaker."

"He'll never do it." Ellie.

"I can be very convincing," I promise.

"And if not." Evy wiggles his head. "Maybe I can do the convincing."

We make plans to meet back at my house on Friday. Evy promises to shepherd Blake the Pro here if he has to tie him up and toss him in the trunk.

We dance on.

"Step three." I point again. "The bank. I have to do this on my own. I'm leaving Marky."

They jump up and scream. Val and Evy lock elbows and do a silly dance. Ellie hugs me.

"You have to do something for me, Ellie."

"I will do anything."

"Mark has been here during the week. He's changed his schedule and leaves on Saturday mornings now. Despite how he insists he has only cheated on me once, I think he's cheating again."

"It wouldn't surprise me." Ellie grimaces. "I never liked him."

"Neither did Evy and I," Val admits.

"Why didn't you guys tell me?"

"We tried, Naggy, but you defended him. We love you. We stopped."

I lean an arm on Evy's shoulder and reel him closer. "I love you, too, but no more pampering wimpy Toilet Paper Nikki."

"You're lignum vitae."

"I am." I wink at him, and we sit down to hammer out my plan. I explain Mark leaves every Saturday and then stops in a town called Zelienople for gas. He began gassing up there on Saturdays a while ago. I checked the credit card bills online for the last three months. He's buying coffee on Sunday mornings in Zelienople rather than closer to the hospital.

"I have to make sure. I suspect he's cheating again. I need pictures. I need someone to follow him. He leaves about ten-ish."

Ellie raises her hand. "Let me do it. I can follow him next week. I'm driving to Grove City."

Of course, I knew this. "Perfect."

Ellie lowers her hand and claps. "This is exciting. I always wanted to be a private detective. Plus, I have the best camera."

"That you do," Evy agrees.

"But wait. Wouldn't checking his phone be easier than following him?" Ellie asks.

"You have the head for this," I compliment, and Ellie smiles proudly. "He has a business phone I can't access. I've checked every drawer in this house. He must keep the records at work."

"Doesn't matter." Ellie shakes her head vigorously. "I'll find out. Grove City is only thirty miles from Zelienople. You can count on me."

I hug her. "I know I can."

"This will be a blast." She claps her hands again.

"Girlfriend." Evy turns to her. "While you're at the Grove City outlets can you pick me up a—"

I interrupt Evy with a pound of my meat-cleaving gavel onto the table in front of him. "No frivolous sidetracking."

"Oh my, you sound authoritative." Evy purses his lips. "Do you mind if I borrow that?"

I slap it in front of him again, harder. He jumps. "Concentrate."

"Don't get all hostile on me. I was kidding. What are my tasks?"

"You just make sure you get Blake the Pro to my house this Friday. Gianna has a sleepover. You'll also need to call all of your friends and make sure they will show up at Saturday's supervisor's meeting."

"What can I do?" Val stands.

"You and that great big lovable bear of a husband of yours can use your artistic skills and build the most vulgar, biggest, flamboyant float you can build. We're going to ride that float right after—"

I wait for effect and everyone complains. "Right after all of Evy's friends attend Janice Everglade's garden party."

"You've lost your mind," Evy sits back, disappointed.

"Hear me out. Every year, the Everglades hire security to park cars in their side lot for the party. Once you get past the security, you're able to meander anywhere across her twenty-acre lake-front grounds."

"We'll never get in." Evy waves his hand.

"Ye of little faith." I slip my fingers into my notebook and pluck out a copy of an invitation to the garden party. "Can you keep a secret?"

They all say yes. I make Ellie promise twice. "The superintendent has run off the invitations for the Everglades ever since their first party five years ago. Guess who's retiring this year?"

"Who?"

"Mrs. Higgins."

"Oh, that woman loves you," Ellie shouts.

"Yes, she does, and she can't stand Janice. Seems Janice has complained to the superintendent, who is John's golf partner, for years about her. She was more than happy to provide us with fifty copies of the invitation."

"You're kidding." Evy stands.

"She only wants one thing in return."

"What's that?"

"She wants to ride on one of the floats."

"I just found my new idol." Evy puts a hand on one hip. "We are going to light up Janice Everglade's house with a rainbow of guests."

We celebrate our potential plots as if we can pull off everything. I explain they must keep everything secret not only for Mrs. Higgins, but because I'm going to surreptitiously ferry Mark's and my money from his name to mine. This may require he sign forms at the bank, but he'll concede if I agree to one of his conditions.

"What's that?" They ask.

"Raising Rosalee."

"What?"

"I'll lie and tell him I'll raise her. He thinks I'm going to, anyway."

"But you're not going to raise her, right?" Val double checks.

"No," I reaffirm.

They ponder my plan.

Evy twists his face. "This is never going to be as easy as it seems."

"Listen. By June first, he'll be the sole proprietor of the new firm. All paperwork complete. His partner gone."

This comes as a gift from God. Timing is everything in life.

"I'll say that's partially why we must transfer the money to my name."

"Will he go for that?" Val.

"He suggested we shift our funds months ago."

"What about the house?" Val, again.

"I've got that planned. I'll promise Mark the world until the house is in my name. I'll tell him he must keep everything quiet and can't bring Rosalee home until Delanie and Hux are home to help Gianna through this."

"He'll believe that," Ellie assures. "He told Jim he's worried about Gianna."

"Mark talked to Jim about Rosalee?"

"He did. I don't think he can talk to too many others. He knows you talk to me, though, so he's cautious."

"What did Jim say?"

Ellie looks at me hurt, afraid to talk.

"Tell me. I'm not Toilet Paper Nikki anymore."

"He said you're crazy if you take him back. He never liked Mark, either. I think he knows more than he's saying."

We've camped and vacationed with Ellie and Jim. Mark often discussed business with Jim. Sports, too. Maybe Mark admitted to a little wrestling under the covers, also. Jim would never tell Ellie. She'd tell me.

"I'm going to find out more," Ellie promises.

"Do you think he'll know if Mark cheated on me before?"

Ellie purses her lips thoughtfully before she responds. "Maybe. Remember the time we took the kids to the amusement park for the weekend, and Mark took off a few hours? Said it was work?"

There were signs. Why had I overlooked them?

"They stayed up late at the campfire that night."

"I remember. Yes. Find out," I say. "Looks like I picked the right person to be the investigator."

Ellie straightens and smiles. There's been mucky book-club tension between us, but Ellie's a good friend. I lean across the table and grab her hand.

"Thanks, El. Knowing he is worried about Gianna is huge when it comes to the money."

"What's your bank plan?" Val thinks ahead.

"I'll say I can't bother Gianna with this until school is over because kids will bully her. They are, too."

"How is Gianna doing?"

"She's wearing her big-girl pants." I tell everyone about her award.

"Yes, she is wearing big-girl pants," Evy agrees. "When this is over, we are celebrating her thirteenth birthday next summer with the biggest coming-of-age party."

"Will Marky agree to put the house in your name?" Val is scatterbrained and absentminded and gifted and brilliant rolled into one. Most people don't know this about her. I do. She'll help me with the planning of everything.

"If he wants me to raise Rosalee, he will. Rosalee's grandparents told Mark they can help him with her but can't raise her. The grandfather is in poor health."

"What's the other condition?"

"That we don't tell a soul about Rosalee coming to live with us until May twenty-first after the kids are home a week."

"That's the day after—" Ellie begins and Evy finishes. "Janice Everglade's spring garden party."

"You got it."

And just like that, my friends, my true friends, begin moving bodies.

Chapter 27 The shirt

"It's only funny until someone gets hurt, then it's hilarious," Jessie's favorite shirt said.

After Gianna leaves on Friday, I jump in the shower then change into jeans. I haven't felt this energized in years. I hurry down the steps to put on a pot of coffee for our planning meeting, a towel around my head and a thrill about me.

The doorbell rings, and I think it's Ellie because the suburban twins are notoriously late. I thrust the door open, and there stands Blake the Pro.

His gaze shoots to my wrapped head, scanty singlet, and bare feet. "Am I early?"

The nice feature of having gay male friends is you don't worry about makeup or clothes. Him standing there in the tight khakis Evy loves on him, immediately widens my lips. I don't care how I look. He can stare at me all day. I'm brazenly happy to see Evy has convinced him to join forces with us against Janice Everglade. I can't hide my excitement. I grab his hand and shake forcefully.

"Oh, hello!"

His gaze falls to my damp grasp.

"Sorry. Shower." I point to my hair.

"I can see that."

Blake the Pro has a smirk forever plastered on his face. I enjoy that feature.

"With this group, seven means seven-thirty. Come on in. I'm just about to put a pot of coffee on." I whip the towel off my head and wipe my hands. My hair falls into a tangled mess. "Or would you prefer tea or a latte?"

"Coffee is fine."

"I'd offer an alcoholic beverage, but I won't allow it until after we conduct our little meeting. The suburban twins become too rowdy."

"The who?"

"Sorry." I fluff my hair with the towel. "Evy and Val. They were born on the same day, so I call them the suburban twins."

"Val Maier?" He asks.

I stop fluffing. "Yes, you know her?"

"I do. My brother mentioned her."

"That's right. You have a brother."

"Yes, he lives here. He's my twin. It's partially the reason I was confused when you mentioned twins."

"A twin! How awesome." The wheels turn in my head. "Evy never mentioned you had a twin. He only said you moved to Fairview to get away from the press."

"Evy seems to know a lot about me." He smiles, and a deep, attractive dimple indents his right cheek. "He caught me up to speed on your parade plans. I'm all for it. I'll do anything I can."

I grab and hug him, thanking God Evy was born with such flamboyant charm. Evy's extremely resourceful when he puts his mind to it. I squeeze Blake the Pro like I'm squeezing Evy, close and personal.

Blake the Pro stands silent, embarrassed-like. I wonder if Evy's asked him for a date.

I lead him to the kitchen, and we exchange small talk. I make a single cup of coffee from one side of my coffeemaker for him while the other half brews a pot. It will be a long night. I decide to let my hair air dry since Blake the Pro has already arrived, so I pin back my tangled locks, and they fall around me, damp and messy.

After he blah blahs about golf, and I refill his coffee cup, the suburban twins walk in.

"You're early," I chirp.

Val sets a dessert she's picked up at a bakery on the counter and heads for the coffee. "You said six-thirty. That's why Evy told Blake seven. We figured we'd never make it on time. We're more than fashionably late."

"We're Coachella tartan tardy," Evy adds, then shakes Blake's hand.

"I said six-thirty?" My mind has been clogged with plans lately.

I whip off my singlet and walk across the kitchen toward the family room, wearing only my bra top. I've set my planning shirt on the handrail between my kitchen and family room. I'm proud of myself for purchasing this t-shirt, which flaunts big block letters that say, "Have plans? Will follow". Some reference to Jesus that sounded perfect for our little covert meetup.

"What are you doing?" Evy asks.

"What?"

"You're walking around half naked."

"It's a running bra, Evy."

"The scantiest one I've ever seen."

I gaze at my chest. "So what?"

"But—" He points at Blake. "You have company."

"It's fine." I wave my hand at Blake. "Did you know he has a brother?"

"I just found that out, happily, I might add." Evy wiggles provocatively. This squirm reveals to me Evy likes Blake's brother, not Blake.

"Oh, good. How great will it be to have them both?" That Blake the Pro is a twin doubles our LGBT support group. "Two for the price of one."

"What?" Val is confused.

"Gay twins. Two supporters," I reveal, enthusiastically.

"Val's gay?" Blake the Pro asks. He tosses a glance at Val.

"Me?" A broken giggle crosses her lips.

"No." I narrow my eyebrows. Give my head a shake. "Val's not gay."

"But you said, the twins." Blake appears as confused as me.

"Not the suburban twins. You and your brother."

The kitchen goes silent—except for that darn roof rattle. I look up.

Darn that Hux.

Blake the Pro draws my thoughts back to the table. "I'm not gay," he announces.

"What?"

"Oh, darling, I told you he wasn't," Evy brags. "But my dreams rallied when he said his brother was."

"Wait." I put a finger in the air. "You had a rainbow chain from last year's parade. The same one Evy has."

"Yes." He smirks. "I support my brother."

"Twins." I muse. "One gay. One not."

"Right." He chuckles.

"This is fun already." Val sits down with a cup of coffee. I hear the front door slam.

"But I thought—"

I stop when Ellie walks in. She glances at me and then at Blake the Pro.

"Nikki? Why aren't you wearing a shirt?"

I feel a hot rush cross my face. I fold my arms over my chest.

"You're not gay." I repeat what I can't digest.

"Nope. Not in the least little bit." He busts out laughing and can barely control himself.

Chapter 28 The choice

"If you can't decide between two items, you won't get either," Jeff's aunt said when they left the store without a toy horse.

After my blunder over the golf twins, we set our plans in motion.

Ellie is following Mark and will talk to Jim. Val and Bruce are drawing plans for floats. Evy's accumulating addresses for invitations, and Blake the Pro, at a standing-room-only township meeting, gives an eloquent speech which convinces all three town supervisors to vote yes and allow the LGBT parade.

Now, it's my turn.

Mark comes home on Sunday, hoping to convince me to turn down my job offer. He's bought a beautiful necklace for me and a smaller rendition for Gianna. He announces he's spending the entire week at home with us.

Not now! He'll be underfoot.

I no sooner think my plan is foiled when he announces Monday morning he must go back to Pittsburgh until Wednesday.

Of course, I think, his girlfriend probably grew angry when he left early over the weekend. Yet this augments my plan. My team stops by on Monday, and I squeeze my butt into brand-new, sexy, ripped jeans and a tight blouse that Val helped me pick out. She says it's sensual. I haven't told

Mark that I'll raise Rosalee yet, and when I do, I want to look sexy. I'm asking my team if I do.

"That's perfect," Ellie, who rarely doles out compliments, says when I try the getup on.

"In that outfit." Blake the Pro makes me blush. "Mark might not hear a word you say. When are you talking to him?"

"Wednesday," I say after gathering myself. For some unclear reason, Blake the Heterosexual's compliments are more frazzling than Blake the Pro's.

On Wednesday evening, I don my garb, practice sex appeal in the mirror upstairs, then lounge in the living room, waiting for Mark. I sprawl lazily on one side of our plush couch. My—hopefully—sumptuous attire is dimmed beneath a soft-glowing lamp that hides the little bulges which have surfaced over time. I hold my best goblet half-filled with wine, my high-heeled feet are crossed on the coffee table at my ankle—an Evy suggestion—and my hair, whippy and messy, hugs my face and falls in wavy blonde tufts about my shoulders.

Mark struts in, hurriedly. He sets his keys on the table near the front door, steps toward the kitchen, then does a double take. His face freezes as if he's seen a ghost.

I choke down the urge to smile. I sip my wine and slowly set my feet on the floor.

"Can we talk?" I swirl my wine a bit; the Sonoma coast Chardonnay brags of alcohol with swooping legs. I've selected only the elegant for this moment. I place my glass onto the table, gingerly.

Maybe I've overdone the ambiance. He appears apprehensive. He glances up the stairs.

"Gianna will be home soon, and I don't want her to hear this." I use my defeated Nikki voice, soft and purry.

"Okay." He sets his briefcase down and strolls uneasily to the chair opposite me as if I'm a seductress and he's a seventeen-year-old.

"I've given this Rosalee question much consideration in the past few months. I've discussed the dilemma with my close friends—in particular, Val." Mark hates Val. But he knows she's smart.

He says nothing.

"With her help, I feel as if I've found a decision I can live with."

Mark and I dated four years before we married. We've been together over twenty-seven. He knows I carry emotional baggage like a big, gaudy purse, close to my gut and out in front of me for everyone to see. "I called Jody and discussed my plan with her, also. She supports my decision."

Mark loves Jody, and if Jody approves of an escapade, you can pretty much validate the act, whether kindness or murder. This is another Val-inspired remark that relaxes the strained muscles in Mark's cheeks a tad.

He sinks into his shoulders, slightly. Self-assurance washes over him, and my blood boils. The Val and Jody pretense is used, at Val's suggestion, so he thinks I'm still dependent on my friends, finding refuge in others, seeking a safe harbor during life's storm. That my reliance on my comrades easily comforts him unleashes an anger in my soul. His belief is written over his face: She's weak. She still loves me. Look at her. She'll never leave.

I stuff anger down my throat as if I'm gagging a victim. *That's what he thinks of me. I am a helpless victim.*

I hear Evy's voice in my head and fall back in time to a recent conversation. "When he pisses you off, and he will, darling, like only an egotistical man with the arrogance of Mark is capable of doing, give him that little pout of your mouth that's so irresistibly cute."

"What pout?"

"Oh, it's wan and pained and set, so delectable that people stop wondering what that boggling brain of yours is thinking and guess your next move."

"Like this?" I try to reproduce it.

"More slack-jawed," Evy says.

"Purse your lips. Use your one front tooth to bite the bottom of your lip," he adds. "There, darling. That's the Naggy allure. I'm surprised you haven't used this little appeal to your advantage."

"She has." Val chimes in. "Unknowingly."

"Really?" I'm dumbstruck.

"Blake?" Evy wiggles a hand under his chin as if he's asking Blake to dance.

Surprisingly, Blake the Pro responds boldly. "It lured me."

A hot sensation spreads across my shoulders and slithers down my arms to my fingertips.

Then everyone at the planning committee agrees. They inform me this is my most endearing expression. They make me practice until I've perfected the sulk.

So, despite the annoyance I'm feeling over Mark, I use it.

Instantly, Mark's lips twitch slightly upward.

I've got him.

"I'm going to do it," I say, sad-like.

This speech I've practiced, too.

"Do?"

"I'm going to raise Rosalee."

"Oh, darl—" He begins to stand, but I jump up first, flash a palm at him and command, "Sit down, Mark, there are several conditions to this agreement."

He sits on the edge of the chair. His plan to keep his happy home inches from his grasp.

"First, we enroll her in day care, so I can work. I'm not giving up this opportunity to get back into the workforce."

"Are you sure? You ma—"

"Stop right there. I'm going back to work."

He looks a bit defeated but agrees.

"Secondly, Rosalee can't move in until Delanie and Hux are home from college. I don't want her here before then."

His eyes shoot to the ceiling as if he's considering the imposition of my condition.

"Gianna has been through a barrage of bullying at school over this. She's relied heavily on Delanie through it, because—well, because I've been rather despondent. I haven't been emotionally here for her."

Quickly he nods as if agreeing—yes, you're a wimp and a loser and a namby-pamby mother who can't hold up for her daughter. But what comes out of his mouth is, "Rosalee's grandparents might allow her to stay there for a few weeks after her last surgery."

"Well, that's a deal breaker, Mark, so you better be one-hundred-percent sure. Amy Everglade has made Gianna's life a living hell, and she will need Delanie's support once Rosalee is living with us. The girls have grown closer over this whole ordeal."

"I know they have. And I'm still friendly with John Everglade. I'll talk to him about Amy. When is Delanie home? End of April?"

"End of May, Mark." Of course, he doesn't know when his children will be home from college. I've had sole responsibility for these kids. I doubt he knows their birthdays.

He must sense my annoyance because he springs fast to answer, "Yes, end of May. That's fine."

"And you'll talk to John Everglade?"

"I will."

"We can't allow Amy to continue bullying Gianna. It's gotten out of control."

"I considered doing that a while ago. I should have. I'll step up. I promise."

I take a deep breath, exhale the past twenty-seven years of cowering in the corner around him and utter, "And I want the house transferred into my name."

His lips spring shut. He squirms in his seat.

"This is a deal breaker, too." I flash the evil eye I've practiced in the mirror. "Maybe I'll feel differently once Rosalee has been with us for a while, but right now? I'm protecting my three kids."

"You mean our kids?"

"I mean my kids." I'm sure this is the first time he's witnessed an uncompassionate rage in me. He leans away, slightly.

"They're my kids, too," he says but it's as timidly stated as anything he's ever said to me. His confidence is ruffled. "But I know I've let them down."

"Exactly, Mark."

"I'll do right by them."

"Then you'll put the house in mine and the kids' names. You travel extensively. If anything happens to you, I don't want Rosalee's grandparents or one of her aunts or uncles showing up for custody and trying to take my kids out of our house. It's happened, you know."

"That will never hap—"

I stand and cut him off. Point a finger. "You're going to do right by your three older children. Our children. You're going to set up a trust fund for Rosalee but leave everything else to our kids or you can get the hell out of this house, and we can battle it out and leave every dime on the courthouse floor."

Mark being an attorney helps. I see his mind churning, adding the court fees and attorney costs and support money. Desperation sweeps him. If there is one thing Mark keeps tucked as a target below his belt, it's his money.

I shoot low and straight.

"I will raise Rosalee but only if you set up our three children financially." I emphasize "our". "You have the assets, Mark. Somewhere. I don't know where, but I'll find them if I have to."

"Nikki, I would never hurt our kids."

"You said you'd never hurt me." I'm so angry I begin crying, which helps plead my case. "You have this entire business deal going on, and you're spending a whole lot of time and money trying to protect your assets. How about you spend some effort on Delanie and Hux and Gianna. Or have you forgotten them?"

"Nikki, I love my—"

"I talked to your accountant, and I don't understand any of his financial jargon. He says I have to sign forms, and you're transferring assets. I don't trust you."

Val and I sat down with Bruce and sorted everything out—right after I visited the best divorce attorney in the tri-state area. Val and Bruce reviewed our finances. Everything is fine. To some degree, because of the business, our personal assets slant in my favor. I only need a few adjustments.

"I would never do anything to make you leave the house."

"You said we couldn't afford to keep the house if we got a divorce."

"We couldn't. Calm down." He walks toward me and puts his hands on my forearms.

Perfectly, I'm shaking. "You expect me to believe you?"

"If we stay together our finances will be fine. Maintaining two households would just be so much harder. I would never allow anything to happen to our kids."

"This is another deal breaker," I say, crying full-out, snot dripping from my nose. "You hurt me, Mark. You had a child with another woman. It will take me a long time to believe you only made one mistake, and you love me. How do I know this won't happen again?"

"It won't. I swear."

"You can't expect me to magically trust you after everything you've done. What you are asking me to do, raise your love child, do you know how degrading that is?"

"She's not a love child, I never—"

"Deal breaker. You put the house in mine and the kid's names, or we get a divorce. I want trust funds for all three kids, too."

"Okay, sh." He pulls me close. Hugs me. Strokes my back. "Calm down. You don't want to have another seizure."

For a moment, I wonder if he still loves me. He sounds sincere. His arms tight around me feel—good.

Oh, no.

He nudges his chin against my head, and I close my eyes and wish this was a bad dream. Wish I did have the strength to raise this blameless little girl, who was born into this mess of a problem through no fault of her own.

With his arms around me, I doubt everything. Am I making a mistake?

He'll cheat again.

Mark feels me crumbling in his arms. He leads me back to the couch and holds me. A paralyzing self-doubt rises deep within me. Somehow, this lack of self-confidence makes me more believable. We talk until Val turns into the driveway. I get up to wash my face before Gianna comes running inside. I'm so despondent that later I'm not sure what he's agreed to and what he hasn't, but I know one thing. He's sure I can't live without him.

Can I?

Before he leaves on Saturday, I ask him if he will give me a few months of counseling before he jumps back in my bed. I tell him I am struggling to forgive him. That I love him. I've never loved anyone but him, and I don't want our marriage to end.

But I need time.

I put on such a good show that I wonder if I am lying or telling the truth.

"Nikki." He hugs me before he leaves. "If you do this for me, I promise. You'll never regret it."

When he's gone, I'm exhausted. I'm confused between the lies and truths I've told. I mix up the feelings I'm having with the feelings I'm supposed to have.

Only one thing I know for sure. Mark is the only man I've ever loved.

Don't cave, Nikki.

All of Saturday I second-guess my decision. Maybe I've been too hasty. Should I call off the entire plan? I consider what life would be like if we moved to another community. How much easier it would be for Gianna and me. Starting anew somewhere else.

Then early Sunday morning, Ellie rings the doorbell. When I open the door, she's crying. She lunges forward and hugs me but says nothing. When she lets go, she removes a picture from her purse. I examine it. The quality is poor, dark and fuzzy, but the subjects are clear.

Mark is having dinner with another woman. The photo shows his hand stretching across the table, his fingers entwined with hers.

"I think he was breaking it off with her," Ellie finally says, wiping her nose with a tissue. "But it doesn't matter. When I showed Jim the pictures, he admitted Mark had other affairs."

"How many?" I ask.

"Jim said at least three besides this woman and Rosalee's mother."

Chapter 29 The bank

"No!" Sharon, Sherry, Kim, and Debbie
screamed when the finance director said she'd give
the $10,000 closing check to CJ for safekeeping.

The picture of Mark and that woman hits me hard. I spend twenty-four hours on the couch with a bag of potato chips and a liter of diet pop, wallowing in self-doubt. I flick from channel to channel. Watch cry-out-loud movies until my tear ducts feel gritty.

He was breaking up with her.

I've regressed.

Ellie and Val show up and force me to shower. Carol, Laura, and Jan knock on my front door and insist I go for a run. Carolyn and Mary come with food. Blake the Pro stops for some odd Nikki-is-desirable speech that I don't have the strength to understand. He's such a sweet guy, and his encouragement does brighten my spirit, but when he leaves, I slip back into a sulk and call Jody for advice. Then Karen. And Nancy. Roselle. Heather. LeAnn. Then I run out of numbers on my speed dial and start over with Evy again. He comes running to my rescue.

I'm a bird flown back to my nest. A chimp who won't leave her troop. I can't shake my dependencies, so Evy slaps me across the face.

"Friends can't live your life for you, Naggy. We can love and support you, but we can't save you from yourself. If you want to spend the rest of your life with a man who cheats on you because the rattling of little balls on the roof scares you at night, well then, you're not the person I thought you were."

He takes out the big-girl barrette, sets it in front of me on the couch, and leaves without another word.

I stare at that pin for three straight hours, listening to the rattle of loneliness on the roof.

I fester. I boil. I cower. I rankle. And finally, I regroup.

Two days later, I'm sitting uneasily in a tall leather chair, my best high heels and skin-tight dress pinching me as I wait for the bank manager. I've decided to proceed with my plan, but I'm so frightened that my stomach flips and flops like a thief in front of a judge. Because that's what I feel like. A thief. I'm moving such a large amount of money around that a teller informs me I must work with the manager. I nearly pee my pants.

I've already completed my tasks at the credit union, tangoed with that teller earlier this morning. I shifted all of the money in our accounts into a single CD in my name. I'm here to do similar work, although I expect more resistance from this financial institution, with which I have less familiarity.

Years ago, when Mark and his best friend opened their practice, we separated most of our assets from his business. I transferred half of our money to my old credit union because they offered a higher interest rate. Occasionally, I purchased higher rates as instructed by Mark. I'd place them in my name, allow them to mature, and transfer them back into Mark's and my account. That practice proved to be a preliminary dream to my absconding with all the funds from our credit union.

"I'll do the same as always," I told Ed, the teller. "Transfer everything back in six months."

Ed had no suspicion whatsoever when I transferred all but twenty-five dollars from our joint account into a CD in my name alone. I'd done it many times before. I listed Mark's name as the successor so as not to stir suspicion, but I'll change that to the three kids once I finalize the divorce.

The "D" word? I said the "D" word?

I shiver.

The bank will not be as easy as the credit union. I take a deep breath, relax my shoulders, and use my pouty face when the manager sits down and asks what he can do for me.

"Mark insists on shifting our monies around. He's buying out his partner."

"I've heard," the stout little man with the glasses perched on the end of his nose says. He picks up the papers in front of him. "Is Mark coming?"

I toss a worried look toward the front door, glance at my watch, and bite my lip with my front tooth as Evy told me to do. "He's supposed to be here."

He studies my worried demeanor. "We can get everything ready for him to sign."

Mark has thrown a tantrum or two at that bank. Once because of a delayed deposit, another because a teller asked him for identification.

"I guess that would be okay." I glance around for effect. "I could get that little card for him to sign. We did that last time." I use the highest, squeakiest, dumbest sounding voice I can muster. "When we purchased those mutual CD thingies."

"Mutual funds."

"Mutual funds." I flutter my eyelashes. Glance around again. "We cash those funds, right? When they mature?"

"No, you cash CDs when they mature. Mark transferred the mutual funds back into your account, let's see." He shuffles through papers. "Eight months ago when the interest rates plummeted."

I knew this. Thank God for the plunge. I bite my lip again. Glance toward the door.

"Mrs. Grey, are you sure you don't want to stop back when Mark can be here?"

"Oh, he'll kill me if I don't take care of this. I was supposed to come last week, but my daughter started her period. And then the dog got worms. It was a bad week."

This trivia comes to me naturally. I'm the queen of drivel. Gianna did start her period, and men hate discussing anything about the female anatomy, so Benjamin the banker becomes flustered.

Disgust walks across his face. "Let's reschedule to when your husband can be here."

"Okay." This isn't exactly how I planned everything. I've set myself up for failure.

"Does he have to come in? He's going to be mad that I messed this up."

"I'll send a copy of everything home with you. Mr. Grey may read it at his leisure and only need sign on the dotted line when he comes in. He can visit tomorrow, or whenever he prefers."

"All right." I can't think of a single excuse to get banker Benjamin to complete the documents in my name and send a signature card home for Mark.

We complete papers for the impending mutual fund. I sign and date my line. Benny Banker marks an x where Mark should sign tomorrow. He draws up withdrawals and deposits to transfer our largest account to a CD. He puts my name first, and I sign. Again, an x where Mark will sign.

I insist Benny cut checks for next year's school bills and taxes and pay in full a running medical bill for my epilepsy stunt last June. Mark has been making payments, but since it is in my name, I want the balance obliterated.

By the time we finish, it's been two hours, and I've acted so dumbly I deserve an Oscar. Still, I go home a failure, fretting how in the world I will finagle Benny the banker to approve the transfers to my name alone without Mark's input.

When I pull into my driveway, oddly, Blake the Pro is at my door. This catches me by surprise. I greet him casually and wave him in after me.

"How did it go?" he asks, once we are inside.

"I think my plan is foiled. They won't transfer the funds unless Mark comes down to the bank tomorrow."

"You're resourceful. You'll think of something."

"I'm not sure about that. How are the parade plans?"

"Val and Bruce designed a masterpiece and are creating a monstrosity of a float. And Evy has all fifty invitations addressed. I told him not to pass them out until closer to the event. Keep anyone from slipping." He laughs. "But he's so excited I don't know if he can hold off."

I smile but am quiet. I'm preoccupied with what I'll say to Mark about the bank meeting, so what Blake tells me next doesn't register immediately.

"He went out with my brother."

"What?"

"Evy. He went on a date with my brother."

"He did?"

Blake nods. His lips turn up. "Bennett's had a crush on Evy for a while."

"That's wonderful!"

At least something good has come from my foiled plan at retribution. A ray of hope fills me. Evy needs a good guy, and if Blake's brother is anything like Blake, this will be a blessing.

We take coffee and go out to the family room where we can sit comfortably. I tuck my legs up underneath me on one side of the couch, and surprisingly, Blake sits down in the middle, unnerving me a bit.

"You're probably wondering why I'm here."

"Sort of," I admit.

"Val asked me to come. She wasn't sure transferring funds at the bank would be easy, and she couldn't come herself. So I'm your moral support."

"Thanks."

"Don't mention it. What's next on your list to do?"

"I have to go to see Mark. He had the papers for the house drawn up, so I want to sign them as quickly as possible."

"For sure."

"The bank manager said we couldn't switch the funds without him coming in, though, so I have to rethink my plan. I hadn't intended on Mark signing the documents where ninety percent of our personal assets are moved into CDs and mutual funds solely in my name. Not leaving the bank with signature cards killed my plan. I don't think I can dance my way out of this."

"Oh, I don't know." He leans back comfortably. "You're a pretty good dancer."

I gaze at him and see his soft expression. It's nice. Honest.

"I'm afraid I'm not a good dancer. I'm rather klutzy."

"True."

"You're supposed to be supporting me, not confirming my clumsiness."

He sets his coffee on a coaster and leans forward. He isn't looking at me. Is that nervousness? His posture slumps slightly.

"Your rather gangly ways are endearing."

"Gangly? Thanks a lot."

"No problem. I'm here to boost your confidence."

"Great start."

"Do you remember your first golf lesson?"

"No, I try and block anything to do with golf out of my head."

He laughs. "The first time I saw you, I thought, my God, I hope she is Rebecca Sunnydale."

"Who?"

"Rebecca Sunnydale. She was my only single in that first group lesson you and Mark took last April. My divorce had just gone through—"

"You were married?"

"Yes."

"Do you have children?"

"Two girls. But what I wanted—"

"That's so sad." I untuck my legs and set my coffee down. "Do you see them?"

"Not as often as I'd like but—"

"You must miss them. How old are they?"

"Nikki," he says, that little smirk edging out of him. "Can I tell my golf story?"

"Your Becca Sunnygirl story?"

"Yes, my Becca Sunnygirl story."

"Go ahead."

"I was hoping you were her."

"Me? Why?"

"I don't think you know the effect you have on people. You exude a—how should I phrase this—a sort of gangly charisma."

"There's that word again. Gangly doesn't exactly sound appealing."

"I assure you it is. You waddled in with that pout Evy talks about plastered over your face. You had not a care in the world about golf or lessons. I couldn't take my eyes off you. I thought, that can't be Becca. I wouldn't be that lucky. Clearly, this woman is golfing because of her husband."

"You knew that right off the bat?"

"Yep."

"How?"

"The way you picked up your bag."

For some reason, I intentionally toss that pouty face at him. "I will never understand men as long as I live. You could tell I hated golf by how I picked up my bag?"

"First of all, you set your expensive bag and clubs on the ground, which no one does. Then, when I called everyone over, you grabbed the handle and picked up your bag backward."

"Oh, wait. I remember this. My golf clubs fell out the back."

"You were sulking. Everyone bounced toward me, and you meandered slowly behind. Your clubs were falling out one by one. You left a trail of them behind you."

"Then Mark got mad and pretended he wasn't yelling."

"And you picked them up and stuffed them into your bag upside down."

"Well, I don't know why the handles don't stick out the top, anyway."

"And Mark said, 'Nikki, these clubs were expensive. What's the matter with you?' And you said, 'I hate golf, that's what's the matter with me. Who chases a little white ball around with a club pretending they like it?' Then you whispered, 'rich people'."

"You heard that?"

"Everyone heard that."

"Ugh. I've got such a temper."

"Then you said, 'I wanted to go rollerblading with Gianna. My kids are more important than any dumb golf lesson'."

"Oh." I tighten my shoulders. "Sorry?"

"No." He laughs. "The thing is, I was standing there thinking. 'Yeah, my girls are more important than any golf lesson, too'."

"Wow, you remember all that?"

"I do."

"Why?

"I don't know why."

"Well, I'm confused. Why are you telling me this?"

"Because Becca Sunnygirl needs to know she deserves better. She shouldn't be treated poorly by an ungrateful husband. And I don't think she would listen to her friends. She had to hear it from a stranger."

I sit silently. He stands.

"If you go back to Mark, if you decide to raise his child, I'll support you. I'll be your friend. But I want you to know that you are better than you believe you are. People are drawn to you."

I stand perplexed and follow him to the front door like a wounded puppy. "I don't know. I always thought I was kind of dull and boring."

He laughs. "There isn't an ounce of dull and boring in you, Nikki Grey. Go talk to Mark. Give him a little of your charm. You'll get your way."

"You think so?"

"I know so."

"How can you be so sure?"

"Because you have a way about you."

"Really?"

"If you didn't, I wouldn't have had a crush on you since that first club fell from your golf bag."

I stand dumbstruck, staring at him.

"And honestly?" he says. "When you tossed my very expensive three wood in the pond? I thought Mark Grey was the luckiest man in the world."

I stand at my threshold, watching his car drive away. I'm so confused my mind spins. He may have been paying me a compliment about a golf club.

Really?

As long as I live, I'll never understand what makes a man run around after and fall in love with frivolous toys.

Chapter 30 The report

"You just had it in your hand. How could you have lost it already? Your office is a black hole,"
Sharon said to CJ.

Blake the Pro's little moral support speech rejuvenates me.

The next morning, I traipse into the lobby of Mark's office, and his secretary, Mary Beth, waves me close.

I approach her, feeling fine and pretty. After all, I caught the eye of a professional golfer; I can win my husband over.

"Hi, Nikki." Mary Beth stands and whispers, "You might want to come back later."

"Why?" I pantomime.

Mary Beth and I have shared a fear of Mark's wrath for the past seven years. She's my confidant more than Mark's. Every year I tell her what to buy me for Christmas, and she tells me what to purchase for her. Our closet relationship has won us dozens of expensive frills, which we wanted but didn't need.

"Someone took over our computers."

"What?"

"Someone in Turkey or Arabia or some third-world country is holding our files hostage. Mark wired them funds, but we won't get our files back until they're holding the money in their hands, and he has a huge patent report due for his major client."

My heart speeds up. "My God! That really happens?"

I'd heard of people's files being held hostage but wasn't sure it was real.

"It does."

"How much did he have to pay?"

This couldn't happen at a better time.

"A thousand, two? I'm not sure. What's worse, he was so upset when he found out, he misplaced the Legler file."

"The what?"

"The file for today's patent meeting. He read it over last night, but now he can't find it."

I wonder where he slept last night.

I swallow the urge to tell Mary Beth to check Mark's girlfriend's apartment. I wonder if he'll blame his new lover for the missing report. Thank God he wasn't home, or I'd be the culprit.

Regardless, I know Mark. He'll take this out on me. When he sees me, he'll flip out about the bank and embarrass me in front of his office staff. Typically, he refrains from yelling around other people—until his mind tangles in gnarly business deals.

My stomach churns. This seesawing of confidence and insecurity sickens me.

I cower to the small kitchen outside Mary Beth's cubicle unsure whether I should talk to Mark or run.

I pour myself a coffee, my hands shaking. When I lift the cup, I knock over the container of sugar packs, jump to catch them, and spill my coffee onto the counter. I grab towels set in the corner, sop up the mess, then quickly toss them into the laundry and attempt to rearrange the cluttered counter to hide my error.

That's when I see the file. Legler Patent stretches across the top.

I stand completely still for a minute. Are there cameras in the lunchroom? I don't think so, but to be safe, I pluck a file out of my bag, gaze at it, then set it on top of the Legler file. I rinse my empty coffee cup in the sink and place it in the dishwasher. Then I lift both files together off the counter.

Can I do this?

He had affairs with three women besides his latest and Rosalee's mother.

I tuck them in my leather bag and zip it shut.

I can do this.

I meander back to Mary Beth's desk. She's in Mark's office now, voices are raised.

I take a deep breath and step toward the door. I hear the franticness in Mary Beth's voice. She's shuffling through the papers on his desk. "I didn't touch it, Mark. Are you sure you brought it with you? Where else have you been? Maybe you should call the Pittsburgh office."

"Check the lunchroom," he suggests.

My knees wobble. My ankles shake in my high heels. I stand completely still, so I don't fall. I attempt a sad-and-worried mien, so he doesn't know I've stolen his file.

"Nikki." He half closes his eyes when Mary Beth leaves and he realizes I'm there. His head sways in a not-now motion. "I can't deal with this now."

"I heard. I'm sorry, Mark."

"What time is our meeting at the bank?" He squats beside a counter to sift through stacked files.

"We can push it back to three o'clock; maybe you'll find your file by then. If not, I can go on my own. I'll agree to anything you say."

"All right."

He's not paying attention to me, and I need him to. If I play this right, I may create an opportunity to handle the bank on my own.

I muster courage and lunge forward when he stands up. I kiss him on the lips and say, "I love you, Mark. I'll say prayers you find your file."

I shake his arm and finally, he glances at me. I use my pout. He freezes. His eyes sweep over me.

"Thanks, Nik."

"I'm so sorry about your computers."

"This has been disastrous."

"I know. Mary Beth explained. If you don't make it to the bank meeting, I'll call. I wrote down your transfer instructions. I can handle the transaction this one time if you can't make it."

"It's not in the lunchroom." Mary Beth returns.

"Want me to check your Jeep on my way out?" I ask. "Sometimes your papers slide forward under the seat from the back."

I've dug files out from underneath Mark's seat countless times. It's funny how we remember the smallest moments in life at just the right time.

"No, but thanks." He hands Mary Beth his keys. "Mary Beth, can you check the Jeep?"

"Okay. I'll get out of your way," I say.

"Oh, Nikki." Mary Beth hollers over her shoulder. "The file Mark completed for you is on my desk."

The transfer of the house into my name!

"I'll grab it. And, Mark. I'll transfer the bank funds just as you explained. You've done right by the kids." I place a hand on his chest, glance into his eyes, and kiss him softly. "Thank you."

I grab the file from Mary Beth's desk and hurry away before I pass out. I drive directly to the little shop that shreds documents and sit outside in the car, wondering what type of person I've become. Can I do this?

Yes, I can.

When I step up to the counter, the young man asks if he can help me, but I can barely speak. My hands are shaking when I finally hand him the file and pay the fee. I stand mutely and watch every last inch of the Legler file being shredded.

I hurry to file the house records at the courthouse and drop a copy off at our attorney's office. Then I stop home to touch up my makeup and head for the 3 p.m. bank meeting.

I play my charades all over with Banker Benny. He calls Mark several times before he gets through. I bite my lip, fidget, ask stupid questions.

Mark insists he can't talk. "Put my wife on," I hear him say.

"Nikki, can you take care of this? I won't make it. We haven't found the file."

"I'm so sorry Mark. Yes, I'll handle everything. I'll bring the little cards to add your name to the accounts. Oh, and Mark?"

"Yeah?"

"I love you."

"I love you, too."

I hand the phone to Banker Benny. Mark tells him to put everything in my name and says he'll sign addendums later. I shed tears of happiness.

Benny the banker misreads this. He stretches across the desk and pats the back of my hand. "Don't worry that pretty little head of yours, Mrs. Grey. I'll take care of everything."

If I hadn't been so happy, I'd have spit in his face. I hand him the instructions Val and Bruce and I devised.

"Thank you so much," I say a half hour later when he finishes. "You have been so kind. I don't know why, but I trust you completely. I know you've done exactly what Mark has asked."

"Yes, I have." He smiles proudly.

I sign the transfers, and he organizes the documents and little cards that Mark must sign into a neat stack on his polished desk.

"These." He taps the papers. "Must contain certified signatures."

I bite my lip. "What's a certified signature?"

He stares at me blankly.

"How about this?" He places eight blue stickies on several documents, making notes to Mark. "Give this to Mark. I'm sure he has a notary in his office who can certify his signature."

"Oh, yes," I say. "He has a secretary, Mary Beth, who writes all his notes."

He dutifully holds back a laugh, slides the forms into the envelope, and smiles. He'll have fun when I leave, laughing over my stupidity. Someday after this is behind me, I'll stop back and have a heart-to-heart discussion with Benny about how he helped me secure my divorce funds.

When we stand, I shake his hand vehemently. I'm so happy I throw my arms around him. "You have been so nice to me. I'm so glad Mark and I have our money here."

"Oh, well." He's flustered. "You're quite welcome, Mrs. Grey. Everything is in your name now, and we will add Mark's name when you return the documents with his signatures."

"And the beneficiaries?"

"All three of your children."

"Thank you." I shake his hand gently, feebly.

I leave the office and drive directly to my favorite document-disappearing shop. I'm so proud of myself, I do a happy dance as copies that need Mark's signature are shredded. The clerk looks at me as if I'm crazy. I can tell she wants to see what's in the file.

"My mortgage," I lie. "I've put my house in order."

By the time Mark gets home that evening, it's late. He's so distressed over his lost file and his computers being hacked that he doesn't ask how the bank visit went. He eats a few bites of the supper I've kept warm for him, retires to

Hux's room, and rises in the wee hours of the morning to make the two-hour drive to Pittsburgh where he's convinced he's left his file.

I take out my TPN board, mark a big black check against bank and tap my marker on the next category: float.

Chapter 31 The float

"I don't want to hurt them, I want to stop
hurting over them," CJ told comfort-friend Carol
during a heart-to-heart discussion about friendship.

Evy hand delivers fifty spring garden party invitations to the most reliable members of the LGBT community. He threatens their lives if they breathe a word about it to anyone.

"Wear your gaudiest outfit but don't get out of your cars until you're all parked. Then parade into Janice Everglade's back yard together in your flashiest manner. Leave the party fifteen minutes before the parade or if the police insist you go, whichever comes first. As long as Janice Everglade's friends see you? Mission accomplished," he's told them.

He also recruited friends to design fifteen floats, five more than they've ever had. Val and Bruce are working on the final grand float of all floats. A six-foot stockade fence surrounds their house, so no one can steal a glimpse. Several float parts peak above the fence, so she's tarped them. Big black mounds of secret artwork clutter her yard.

On a warm Wednesday at the beginning of May, Val invites us over to help her glue rainbow-colored feathers to the base of the float—a hay-ride frame that a tractor will pull. Val convinced a friend to donate an old tractor for the cause. One of Evy's recruits is painting it out on a farm somewhere in the country.

We glue so many feathers on the base of the float our fingers are parched and raw. When we break for lunch, all of us soak our hands in one of Evy's herbal concoctions. I ask Evy what's under the other tarps.

"I'll show you if you promise not to tell."

We promise. Evy grabs the tarp and whips it off the biggest bulge in the yard.

I'm staring at a ten-foot penis.

My mouth drops. "Is this what I think it is?"

"What did you do with that man of yours?" Evy says. "Of course, it is, darling, I want to be upfront and personal. It's for the back of the float, the grand finale. The last thing everyone will remember from this year's parade. We'll park this right in front of Janice's yard."

"Nice." Blake chuckles.

Ellie snaps a picture. "Jody won't believe this."

"I don't believe it," I say.

"Naggy, dear, I have a special surprise for you. A banner to go under this lovely work. We'll nail it on the back panel below this masterpiece Val and Bruce have sculpted so superbly. It's for you."

"For me?"

"Yes, for all the pain and agony you've endured. Would you like to see it?"

"I can hardly wait."

Evy and Val disappear into the house and return holding a banner. They unroll it slowly. "We thought this appropriate."

"This float created in honor of Janice Everglade."

I laugh until I can't breathe. Ellie's bent at the waist, facing her cell at the banner, and Jody's guffawing over miles of airwaves. She wants to come home for the parade.

"Well, maybe it's a tad for me, too," Evy acknowledges. I go up on tiptoes and kiss his cheek.

It takes several minutes and lots of lemonade and laughter to calm ourselves down, but we've got work to do. The parade is in two weeks. We regroup and carry on.

After gluing feathers for five hours, we sit in Val's back yard with lemonade, iced tea, sandwiches, and cookies that Blake the Pro's brother, Bennett, concocts. He's a chef, by the way, nice-looking, kind, quiet, and in awe of Evy's uninhibitedness. He and Evy are a couple now. Everyone loves them together. Evy draws Bennett out, and Bennett reels Evy in. It's a match made in heaven.

"What was it you said to Janice Everglade that made her hate you, Evy?" Blake asks.

"Oh, you wouldn't understand."

"Try me," he says.

"Nope." Evy zips his lips.

But when Blake and his brother leave, Ellie, Val, and I lose our patience. We grab Evy's arms and tackle him onto the ground. Val sits on his stomach, and Ellie and I threaten to stuff the leftover cream-cheese tea sandwiches in his mouth if he doesn't tell. Evy hates cream cheese more than Janice Everglade.

He concedes. Promises a revelation, so we free him. He brushes himself off and calls us vagrants.

"You've been evading this for years." I refuse to let him skirt the issue. "I've asked everyone who was there. No one will tell what you said, so now cough it up."

"Yeah, the snooty country-club girls turn red whenever I ask," Val adds. "People call you undignified and crude, but no one will repeat what you told Janice."

"How could an insult be so degrading?" Ellie asks.

"It wasn't an insult, darling. The comment was aroused by Janice Everglade's coughing spell."

"What?" He sparks my curiosity.

"Oh, for heaven's sake, it wasn't that bad. Hardly offensive at all. I don't know what the fuss was about. Janice Everglade and I found ourselves seated at the same table for the Alzheimer's benefit. You know, the gaudy one where everyone touts fat wallets and attempts to outbid other arrogant swanks for art that resembles kindergarten finger painting. They couldn't spot a good piece if it hit them in the face."

"Who sat you with her?" I ask.

"Someone who has no idea of her shallowness, I'm sure."

"Get on with it," Val groans.

"Janice had this little tickle of a cough she had been trying to suppress. I offered her a cough drop, and she ignored me."

"As if she'd take anything from you."

"Exactly, Naggy. So she kept suppressing her cough in between art exhibits. They parade pictures up onto the stage one by one, and in between, the room becomes quiet as people watch. There are little murmurs of oohhs and aahhs here and there, but the atmosphere is relatively soundless. Right then, Janice Everglade coughs and lets out a fart loud enough to reach over half the little round tables with the white tablecloths and expensive china. Nearly the entire room hears."

"Janice Everglade?" I say. "Farted in public?"

"Two tables over, I hear someone whisper. Was that Janice Everglade?"

"Is this true?" I'm doubting Evy. "I can't believe she'd have the nerve to tell everyone about my toilet-paper escapade if she farted at the Alzheimer's luncheon."

"Oh, it's true." Evy waves a hand. "Lisa, the reporter who was sitting next to her, dizzied from the smell."

"Now, I know you're lying."

"No, darling, all true. The thing was, she had these skin-tight pants on. Remember when she lost all of that weight and was on her pants kick? She didn't wear dresses because she was so proud of her ass that she thought was skinny but was still wide enough to flatten a railroad tie if she sat on it."

"I remember."

"Well, she squeezed those size-sixteen buttocks into a size-ten pair of designer slacks. I looked behind her and said, 'Well, you didn't rip the back of your pants, so it wasn't a fanny flapper. Must have been a 'gina flapper.'"

"A what?"

"That's what Lisa next to her said, and I said, real loud and boisterous, 'Oh, those pants are so tight on her ass you know that fart slithered out the front, girlfriend.' People heard me four tables over."

All of our jaws drop.

"Have you girls never heard of a fanny flapper?"

"No," I choke out.

"When a big, fat guy passes gas, and his cheeks vibrate? I can't believe you women. I had to explain to my table, too."

"Stop." I hold a hand up to him.

We laugh uncontrollably. Evy is appalled at our stupidity and becomes indignant.

When I catch my breath, I say, "You did not say that, Evy."

"Ask anyone who was there. Everyone heard. I haven't seen women so mortified since Hannibal tongue-tied his psychiatrist. People called her Jannie the flapper after that."

Again, uncontrollable guffaws.

"Did anyone say anything?"

"No, but two Janice Everglade haters at the next table wet their pants laughing. They had to leave."

"What did Janice say?"

"Nothing. She simply sat there, red-faced and bothered. Her eyes and mouth were as big as crop circles. She'll never forgive me."

"I'm not sure I'll forgive you." I laugh so hard I nearly pee my own pants.

When we are done, I go home and check float off my list.

Mark doesn't come home that night, but I'm not bothered. I don't care where he's sleeping. I don't even hear the rattle of the roof in bed that night because I laugh myself to sleep.

Chapter 32   The parade

"Bob deserves everything he gets. By the time I explained all he had done to me, the police officer was practically helping us," Debbe told CJ about her midnight prank.

We decide not to park the finale float in front of Janice's house until her guests have arrived. We want to make a grand entrance.

The front of Janice's property brags of two lush green acres that spread across a busy, two-lane road, Route Five. The land behind her eight-thousand-square-foot house stretches four blocks back to the Lake Erie shoreline. The road out front is part of Pennsylvania's Seaway Trail. As drivers pass the lavish homes of the Trail's elite, they catch glimpses of Lake Erie through the trees.

Janice's house sits next to a vacant corner lot on Dorchester Road. On Dorchester, the back lots of six elite houses parallel Janice's property all the way to the lakefront. Three small veins of wealthy-ridden streets jut out the other end of Dorchester, but across from Route Five, Dorchester stretches south toward less wealthy homes.

Fairview's parades, including the LGBT parade, line up south of Route Five on Dorchester, then head south (away from Janice's) toward the little town. Only this year, because Blake the Pro charmed the pants off the township supervisors, Evy's won permission to round Route Five and park his final float on its south berm, smack dab across the street from Janice's party.

This permission is befitting karma for Janice's gay aversion.

A security person will check invitations at her front gate, and a boy with an orange vest will wave a wand, parking cars into straight rows on the impeccable green lawn that Janice's landscaper will rework next week. The guard also welcomes those who come on foot from the Dorchester neighborhood.

We keep our final float one street over from Dorchester, out of view of wealthy eyes. Val and Bruce have cleverly secured the tarps so no one sees the artwork before we line up at Janice's. We don't want Janice getting word of it, waddling her way out front for a gaze, and consequently, turning away the uninvited guests. They must slip in unnoticed.

It's a chilly Saturday afternoon while we wait. I sent Mark on ahead to the party.

He never found his report, of course. He postponed the Legler meeting along with scads of others. Eventually, he retrieved his digital files that had been held hostage by Bin-, Wan-, Kim-, Kan-, or Kumar-somebody across the continent. I've danced and sang and pirouetted around him every hour he's been in my house—yes, my house— regarding the documents that add his name to the new mutual funds and CDs. I lie and swear I've given them to him. His life is so out of control, he believes me.

He asked about the low balance in our checking account, and I showed him the payments for our annual taxes and Delanie's and Hux's tuition.

"I have an accounting degree, Mark. I'm stepping up. I want to be involved."

I thwarted his skepticism with award-winning crying performances over Rosalee. I sprinkled my crying jags with apologies for being insecure and selfish. I lied and said I believed his affair was a one-time mistake.

This morning I told him, "Gianna and I are getting our nails done for the garden party. Can we meet you there?"

Gianna wants nothing to do with Amy Everglade, of course, but I've lied and told Mark they've made amends, so he's not suspicious why I'm not accompanying him to the party. I asked Gianna to play along with me. She agreed. She knows I have something up my sleeve, but a stronger loyalty has blossomed between Gianna and me since we learned of Rosalee.

Not exactly how I wanted to become closer to my kids.

But my three children are coping so well with this life-shattering event that it's baffling. I'm especially enamored with my two girls. How they turned out so strong when they were raised by an emotionally crippled mother is beyond me.

"I must have done something right," I tell Blake the Pro while we sit on the edge of the float, our feet dangling over rainbow-colored feathers. We are patiently awaiting Evy's text to Val and Bruce announcing it's time to haul the float down the street to the Everglade party.

"You've done a lot right," Blake encourages.

"If I did a lot right, I wouldn't be sitting on a float with a big penis, down the street from a house where my cheating husband clangs glasses with his patron."

His face melts into an unusual heaviness.

"My wife cheated on me," he says out of nowhere.

I'm floored. Do wives of famous golf pros cheat on their husbands?

"It wasn't totally her fault," he adds. "I wasn't home much. That's part of the reason I moved to be with my brother. Bennett's good with my girls. He helps me out when they visit."

"Well, I don't care how little you were home. I never cheated on Mark. That's no reason."

"True." He gazes away in contemplation, and I think we are not so different, Blake and me.

"Anyway," I apprise. "Now that you are connected to Evy, trust me, your girls will inherit lots of aunts and uncles. Evy comes with an army of friends. My kids love him, which I appreciate now more than ever. I'll need help with them after today."

"Why?"

"I'm giving Mark the divorce papers as soon as we park this float in front of Janice's house."

"You're leaving him?"

"No. He's leaving me. Our security codes and locks are being changed as we speak. I also hired a friend of Evy's to clean out Mark's closet, desk, and basement corner while the locksmith works on the doors. Evy's friend will deliver a big package to Mark's new girlfriend's house—which Ellie masterfully located."

He gazes at me sadly. "Divorce is tough. Even when you leave for good reason. How are you doing?"

"I don't know." How do you end twenty-three years of a marriage—even a bad marriage—without regret? "I'm treating myself to a trip to England after this is over."

"You are?"

"Yep, booked a trip by myself. Mark thinks I bought two tickets, but I only bought one. I've depended on him and my friends for too long. My parents before them. I've always depended on someone."

He studies me. "You always impressed me as being independent."

"Oh, no. You don't know me. I'm the biggest baby in the world. Afraid of my own shadow. My idea of living dangerously is not wearing my seatbelt."

He laughs. "You can't be that reliant on others if you've gone and booked a European trip alone."

Just him saying the "A" word out loud shakes me up. I'm still not one hundred percent sure I can do this. But it's Mark's money, so I don't care if I go or not.

"We'll see. I haven't boarded the plane yet. I don't know how I'll traipse around England alone."

"You'll do fine."

"I'm not sure how I'll handle being single at all. Evy will be running over every time I need something done or hear a noise in the night."

"I could come help you," he says, sweetly. "Day or night."

When I say nothing he adds, "I'm pretty good with my hands."

"I suggest you not use that as an opening line when you meet a nice girl."

He chuckles. "What I meant was, I can swing a hammer as well as a club."

I laugh, too.

Then he says softly, "And I think I already met a nice girl."

I blush. "That's kind of you to say and a nice offer to help around the house, but I have lots of friends. You're busy. You don't need to be my friend in shining armor come to rescue me."

"Good, because I don't want to be your friend," he blurts out, and his face turns as red as mine. "I'm afraid I'm not good at this. I haven't asked a girl to dinner in over twenty years."

"You're asking me out?"

"I am. Tomorrow evening, maybe?"

I'm floored.

My stomach flutters, and my mouth gushes like a fireplug unloosed. "I have epilepsy."

"I'm pretty sure that's not contagious."

"Well, I'm sort of a klutz."

"You can wear a helmet."

I utter a nervous little laugh and look into his eyes, realizing I do sort of have a crush on him. He's cute in his tailored, golfer way.

Like always, my future flashes in front of me, and my mind whirls and twirls with ways for me to avoid being alone. Could we be a couple? Go to the movies? Dinner? Introduce our children to each other?

I'm regressing. The doors in my world are shutting, and Blake's opened a window, providing an escape route. I'm unattractively trying to squeeze out of this empty, lonely house with the frightening, annoying rattle on the roof.

I can't keep relying on others.

I calm down. Take a breath of fresh reality.

"You know what?" I've surrendered. "I've lived my entire life dependent on other people. So, no, Blake the Pro, I can't have dinner with you. It's not that I don't want to. I just can't. I have to get through this. Go to England on my own before I can think about letting anyone else in my life."

"How about this," he says after thinking. "You go to England on your own. That will be good for you. Help prove to yourself you are independent. Then when you get back—"

"If I get back," I interrupt.

"You'll get back." He chuckles.

"You don't know me that well."

"Maybe not, but I know you're resourceful and even though you might not believe this, you're resilient, too."

This baffles me. Resilience is a characteristic reserved for stronger, more confident women, not Nikki Grey. I've fallen short in the tough and confidence areas. Mark and I both felt he had married down, so when I decided to divorce him, I assumed I'd spend the rest of my life alone.

How I hate that word.

Then here sits Blake the Pro asking me out on a date as if I'm a normal human being and not some friend-bothering chicken of a woman.

After I sit wordlessly for a minute, he says, "How about this? When—I mean if—you get back from England in one piece. We will go for lunch and see how that works. If we have a good time? We'll take it slow afterward, so I don't infringe on your newfound independence."

"Okay," I decide. Then a thought hits me. "But I hate golf."

"That's probably a good thing. I can't afford to keep replacing clubs."

Val jumps out of the tractor and starts removing tarps. She hollers, "Evy texted. His friends are inside the gate, out of their cars, and headed for Janice's back yard. It's showtime, people."

We hurry, expecting Janice will come dashing out front flailing her arms and hollering commands any minute.

Val rips the last of the tarps off hastily. The canvas hooks onto the front of the penis, rips up a few nails, and the penis bobs up and down. We jump off the float. Bruce fires up the engine and takes off up the street, slowly crawling toward the Everglades' house. The bobbing makes the float much more comical.

"Did you see my improvement?" Val nudges me and points to the sign on the back. She's painted GF in front of Janice's name.

"What's the GF for?" Blake asks.

"Oh, girlfriend," I answer, and we jump back on the float and ride to the Everglades'.

By the time we arrive, Janice is screaming at the poor security guard and young boy parking cars. She's chastising them for letting uninvited guests enter.

"But they had invitations, Ms. Everglade," the man says.

People meander from around the side of the house and file out the large front doors. Neighbors from bordering sub-developments mosey up and linger on the berm of Route Five. Traffic slows. People shout from cars. Neighbors and party guests laugh. Janice shrieks loudly and frantically, unintentionally beckoning anyone within hearing distance to investigate the commotion. The crowd on the lawn amalgamated with the mob on the street creates complete pandemonium.

The LGBT community has lavishly graced her party in parade attire. Erotic and exotic costumes, as well as men in drag, draw different reactions from the crowd. Bruce beeps his horn and gives the truck gas occasionally, so that the penis bobs.

Evy and Ellie step up onto the float with Val, Blake, and me.

"You!" Janice Everglade screams. She runs toward us, crossing the street where cars are jammed to a halt now. I think she's going to tug Evy off the float, but she stops at the side, unaware of the bobbing penis. She jabs Evy's leg with a finger for each word.

"You. Are. The. Cause. Of. This. You and your gay brigade."

Evy shoos her away with a wave. "Run off to your little garden party Jannie flapper."

She pounds her fists on the float. "I know the president of your college. I'll have you fired."

"For what? Being gay? I'm sure my attorney will love hearing that one."

"Oh shit," Blake the Pro groans. I look up and see Mark bolting toward me.

"Nikki!" His teeth are clenched. John Everglade has followed him out. "Get the hell down from there. What do you think you're doing?"

"You need to calm down, Mark," Blake says.

I hold a palm up to Blake. "I'm fine."

I turn to Mark. "Sure, I'll get down."

I thrust a hand in my bag, yank out the papers, and jump off the float. I slap the papers at his chest. "Sign on the dotted line."

"What's this?"

"Divorce papers. I'm divorcing you. I'm kicking you out of my house."

"Your house?"

"Yes, the doors are being locked and right now your clothes are in the back seat of a car heading south on I-79 toward your new girlfriend's house."

"I don't—"

"Stop." I hand him the pictures Ellie took. "You didn't think I had the balls did you, Mark? You thought I'd raise your little girl, and you could continue cavorting around like you've done for the past twenty years."

"Twenty-three," Evy corrects.

"Nikki," Mark says, then stops. What could he say? The proof wagged up at him from his fingers.

The float in front of our float takes off. Bruce hollers out his window, "We're rolling."

Blake stretches a hand down, I take hold, and he helps me up and onto the float. We ride away, penis bobbing. I think Janice Everglade passes out when she sees the back sign, but that's hearsay. The overall chaos of the event blots out smaller goings-on. I lose sight of both Mark and Janice.

We have the best parade and after-party ever to grace Fairview township. Evy renamed this year's parade TP Nikki's revenge on GF Janice.

But I don't think it's befitting, so three days later when both Delanie and Hux are home, I have a family meeting of the four of us.

I don't schedule my meeting until eleven o'clock at night. Delanie and Hux are furious because I won't let them go out with their friends before our meeting. Gianna, tickled pink, jumps up and down. She's hoping for some great adventure.

I've insisted they put on black shirts and pants, cover themselves from head to foot. I won't start the meeting until they do, so when they stomp down the steps, they are raving mad.

"I've called you here tonight—" I begin, but Delanie cuts me off.

"Mom, what are we doing? Let's just get it done, so we can go out."

"No," I say. "You kids can't push me around anymore."

"C'mon, Mom," Hux whines.

I grab a black sack and wrench it up onto the kitchen table. Gianna jumps up and down again, clapping. She must have peeked inside.

"I'm not the same mother you used to know."

"Tell them who you are, Mom," Gianna squeals.

I gaze into each of their eyes individually. I want them to remember this day for the rest of their lives, this transition of their mother from cowardly to courageous. I want them to know I'm not some weak little pansy who lets everyone walk over her. For once, I'm a role model—okay, maybe not the best role model.

"I'm TP Nikki." I zip open my bag, and they gaze down at thirty-six rolls of toilet paper. "Who's with me?"

Fifteen minutes later the four of us are decorating Janice Everglade's yard until a police officer comes along to shoo us away.

I give him the long sordid description of all the horrible things Janice Everglade has done to anyone throughout the years. It just so happens; the officer knows Janice.

He's gay.

So instead of arresting us, the officer stands guard out front, watching for cars until we have unrolled a plethora of toilet paper. The squares shine in the light of the moon.

Delanie and Hux don't go out that night. We order pizza and chicken wings and have the first Grey Independence Day party.

Sometimes families rise out of the ashes together—maybe with a smidge of dirt on their wings.

Chapter 33 The rattle

"Are people going to think I cheated on you?"
Jeff asked CJ. "I'll explain that's why Friends Who
Move Couches is almost a memoir, not a memoir
because I'm a lonely soul who didn't marry a Mark
Grey. I married a Blake the Pro," CJ responds. "A
who?" Jeff asks. "Never mind."

Of course, life doesn't continue at a battle-winning pace. I miss my flight in Toronto, and my luggage never shows up in England. I purchase two white shirts, black pants, khaki shorts, a black jacket, and four pairs of underwear, which I wear inside out every other day to make them last.

Delanie yammers about her summer job over WhatsApp, through which we communicate. Hux begs through this same messaging program to use my car while I'm gone. I extinguish those homeland fires from afar. I insist Delanie can't quit her job until she finds another and let Hux know both sets of car keys are tucked safely away in my suitcase—which is somewhere in Turkey. (I don't reveal this.)

Regardless of the mishaps, I survive. I end up having a wondrous time in England, visiting Cambridge and Oxford, Buckingham Palace, Stonehenge, and Big Ben. I ride a train to Paris, visit the Louvre, and sip wine and eat cheese in the evening in front of the Eiffel Tower, alone and joyous.

I arrive home, deliberately, on the last day of the school year for Gianna. What a year this has been, I think, when my Uber driver—my rating improved to three!—turns onto our street.

I see Blake then. He's parked in my driveway, leaning against his car, holding a golf club with a big pink ribbon.

"What's this?" I walk up to him, surprised and happy.

"A reward for your newfound independence. If you can travel to England by yourself, you can certainly swing a three-wood off a fairway without a tee."

"How did you know when I would be home?"

"Evy." He grins. "He should be here soon. Bennett cooked dinner for you and the kids."

"Nice. I'm going to like Evy dating your brother."

"I am, too." He lifts the bag from my arm and hands me the golf club. "Where's the rest of your luggage?"

"Don't ask."

He smirks. "Did you enjoy England?"

"I did. There were some ups and downs, but I survived."

That smirk I've seen a hundred times widens on his face. A light sparks, and I realize, all this time, that smirk signified affection.

I feel my lips turn up.

Several times while gallivanting across Europe, I had to force myself to stop thinking of him—his tall, thin, muscular frame, brown eyes, five o'clock shadow. By the end of my trip, I decided he looked nothing like most golfers. Weren't they typically scrawnier?

I nearly giggle.

"So now that you are independent and have accomplished everything you wanted, will you go to dinner with me?" His eyes twinkle.

My stomach flutters. I stare, smiling. "You're right. I have accomplished everything I wanted. All by myself."

Then the wind picks up, and I hear the clatter of the one thing I haven't rid myself of. That awful, clanging, silence-defying noise that has been the bane of my existence for the last year—the lonely roof rattle.

My face sags into dread. "Except one thing."

Blake glances toward my chimney then back at me.

"Don't do it." He's read my mind.

"I have to."

"Are you sure?"

"I'm sure."

Slowly, he shakes his head. "And everything was going so well."

But I'm determined. I'm going up on that roof and rid myself of those nasty, clanging golf balls.

"Wish me luck." I hand him the golf club, take off for the house, unlock the door, and run upstairs to Hux's bedroom. I climb outside and creep toward those dang balls.

Hux pulls up with a car full of friends right as I inch up to the chimney.

"What are you doing, Mrs. Grey?" someone hollers.

"Mom? Why are you on our roof?"

"Because I can't stand these balls rolling around up here any longer."

I rip the bag open, and three of the four balls roll down off the roof and land in the bushes. One defiant ball rolls around on the chimney landing and settles in a dip in the metal.

"Get off my roof, you nasty little ball," I yell. Then I hear Hux calling out below me.

"Mom, don't."

Carefully, I glance over the edge of the roof and see Hux running up the driveway. He grabs the three wood out of Blake's hand and hurls it onto the top of the roof. The club bounces a few times and lands at my feet. I grab it before it slides away.

"Tee up," he yells. "Hit the ball. There's a little dip on the landing."

"What?" I know what he's saying, but I can't believe it.

"Golf off the rooftop."

Hux's friends begin a barrage of cheers, encouraging me to do something entirely against my nature. Then again, divorcing my husband and traveling to England alone is unlike Needy Nikki, too.

I glance at the last, lonely, little ball. Is it sneering at me? I hate the white of it.

"Okay," I decide. "I'll do it."

People shout and cheer. I climb onto the landing, spread my feet apart, and stare down at the ball.

"Maybe I shouldn't." Indecisiveness stalls me. "What if I break Mr. Gorney's bay window?"

"True," Hux says more to himself than me. "That was an expensive drive."

Hux mowed lawns for a year to pay off that blunder.

For seconds, silence reigns below, then Blake says to Hux, "She could aim for it."

"Mr. Gorney's window?" There's surprise in Hux's voice.

Then surety in Blake's. "She'll never hit it if she aims for it."

"Great point," Hux agrees. "Mom, aim for Mr. Gorney's window."

I let up on my stance. Place a hand on my hip. "You know I heard that conversation."

"It's fine, Mom," Hux yells. "If you break it—" He stops and looks at Blake. Blake sighs and nods. "Blake will pay for it."

Just then, a car screeches to the front of our house. Evy jumps out before it stops.

"Naggy, what are you doing?" he screams.

"She's hitting a golf ball off the roof," Hux responds.

"My God, have you all lost your minds? Naggy, stay where you are. Don't move."

Evy bolts into the house. Val and Ellie arrive. This has become quite the show. "How does everyone know I'm home?"

"Evy," Blake, Hux, and Bennett say in unison.

"Of course."

Evy scoffs at Ellie's slippery tongue when his is every bit as slick.

"And you're on the roof for what reason?" Val looks up.

"The balls. I'm done listening to them rattling around at night."

Another car arrives. Delanie has ferried Gianna home from her last day of school. Gianna jumps from the car. "Momma! You're home."

"Hi, honey!" I wave excitedly, ecstatic to see her.

Delanie gets out. "Mom, why are you on the roof with a golf club?"

"Hi, Delanie," I rejoice. "I have lots to tell you guys. I missed you!"

Hux's window squeaks open and out tiptoes Evy. He sidles over shingles as if he's creeping alongside the Grand Canyon.

"What's he doing?" Blake asks.

"I don't know. No one knows how Evy's mind works," Val answers.

"That's what I love about him." Bennett steps up beside Blake, staring at the roof.

Evy nearly slips three times while scooting over to me.

When he arrives at the chimney, he steps onto the landing, and I say a prayer of thanks for his skinny frame because I fear my metal platform will break. It wobbles but holds firm.

"Here," he says, then he swoops my hair off to one side and clips my big-girl-pants barrette on me. "You can't golf with gnarly hair blocking your aim, girlfriend."

Cautiously, I kiss him on the cheek. "Thanks, Evy, for always watching out for me."

"No more fretting over friends who move couches. They are out of your life—including that husband of yours."

"Ex," I remind him.

"Yes. Ex-husband, ex-friends. You don't need them. You have yourself."

"I do. No more friends who move couches." I hug him tight.

He smiles, then says, "Don't get all soft and mushy on me, girlfriend, just hit that ball as if you're aiming for Janice Everglade's front window."

He steps gingerly off the landing, tiptoes to the side, swirls an arm, and screams ten pitches higher than a Rosanne Barr holler, "I give you lignum vitae."

He squats out of my way and dozens of beady eyes gaze up at me.

I resume my stance. Set my fingers on the grip like Blake taught me, straighten my double-jointed arms, glance at Mr. Gorney's bay window, line the face of my club up with his bay window, then I do something I've never done before. I keep my eye on the ball. I swing the club and watch its face smack the ball.

The ball sails up in the air, arches over the street, and smashes directly through the center of Mr. Gorney's bay window.

My jaw drops. The kids go mad. It's pandemonium below. They shout, laugh, scream. I've done it. I've hit my ball, and for the first time in my life, my execution is perfect. The ball lands exactly where it's supposed to. I nailed it.

I raise the golf club in the air, joyously. Evy tiptoes toward me hollering hurrahs. I jump. Hear a crack. Stop. But it's too late, the landing I'm on splits, and I fall forward. Evy tries to catch my body. I wrap my arms around him, and we crash onto the roof, roll over shingles, and slide down the steep pitch. I grab onto the gutter at the bottom of the roof, but it breaks off, and we tumble into my large, ungroomed front bushes—me, Evy, the gutter, and a mangled golf club.

People rush toward us. Bennett plucks Evy out of the bushes, and Hux drags me. When they realize we are fine, everyone cheers.

We brush ourselves off, and immediately, Evy Facetimes Jody.

"Who's hungry?" Bennett removes two trays of food from the back of his car while Evy explains my perfect swing and our life-threatening tumble off the roof to Jody. Everett and the kids hurry into the house, and Blake takes me by the arm.

"Are you sure you're all right?"

"I'm better than all right. I'm wonderful." I brush myself off.

"That was some swing."

"Wasn't it?" I'm proud of myself.

He bends and lifts the three-wood off the ground. It's bent. "Is this something I should get used to?"

I squint my eyes and grit my teeth. "It might be."

He tosses the club on the ground, steps toward me, tugs me close, and kisses me smack on the lips in front of Val, Ellie, and Evy.

When he lets go, I'm lightheaded.

"You know what?" I open my eyes.

"What?"

"You're only the second man I've kissed in the last twenty-seven years."

"Well, here's hoping you don't kiss another man for the next twenty-seven. Have dinner with me?"

"How about you have dinner with us today? We always spend the last day of the school year at my house."

"Only if you agree to go to dinner and a movie, just the two of us, on Saturday."

I bite my lip with one tooth.

"No, no, you can't use that on me. I already know about that."

"But I just got home and haven't seen the kids much, and I—"

He places one hand on the small of my back, the other higher, and draws me close. I feel every firm muscle of his entire body, and my mind trails off. Do golfers work out? Are there gyms at golf courses? He's way more muscular than expected. Then I lose my concentration when his lips touch mine.

He kisses me deeply and gently. Chills rush through me. Val applauds. Ellie announces it's time to break out the wine. And Evy faces his phone toward me.

"Oh, and this just happened," he tells Jody.

"Yes," I utter when Blake finishes kissing me. "Saturday."

I lean toward him, practically begging for another kiss.

"Deal," he states, after the third-best kiss of my life. All three beat even my first kiss with Neal Kurszieski in seventh grade, during a neighborhood spin-the-bottle game. I shake my wandering mind back to Blake and ask, "Are you sure you want to take me on a date? I'm a bit ditsy, easily distracted."

He gives a side-to-side head shake, squints in contemplation, then nods. "I think I can cope with the inattentiveness."

"I can be inconsiderate, too."

"How so?"

"Sometimes? If I'm in a bad mood or don't like the person paying the bill? I order the most expensive item on the menu."

"We'll do fast food. I've never spent so much money on a girl before the first date in my life."

"Don't worry," I promise. "Everything will be smooth sailing from here on out."

He sighs. "Something tells me you sail like you golf."

"True. I sank a catamaran once."

He closes his eyes. Shakes his head. "I don't want to know."

"You're right. No more disasters. I'm done with the past. The uncoordinated, unlucky Nikki Grey is dead. I'm taking my maiden name back. I'm a new, more-exciting me."

"What's your maiden name?"

"Stone."

He smirks.

"Okay, not exciting, but I promise; I'm luckier now. I just finished the worst year of my life. This is a new year. A new beginning."

Blake slips his fingers into mine. I grip tightly and say, "Nothing can go wrong now."

He arches his eyebrows at the exact moment Val hollers, "I rummaged through Deidra's closet."

Oh, no.

She's holding a knapsack in the air. "Anyone want to have some fun?"

Author's Note

While my life, friends, family, and true-life quotes at the beginning of each chapter inspired much of this almost memoir, many aspects differ.

First, it's true I come from a small family and am frivolously addicted to friendship, but thankfully, I married Jeff Zahner, not Mark Grey. Throughout my thirty-eight-year marriage to Jeff, I often wondered how many men would so easily smirk and shake their heads at my escapades. In other words, I married a Blake the Pro right off the bat. Jeff and I have been faithful to each other since the day we met. (He assures me I can state this. He does not want to end up a character in one of my thrillers.)

Second, I'm not a cute, little blonde like Reese Witherspoon. I did this for your reading enjoyment. Imagine the same story with a frumpy, old, nagging brunette?

Third, I have one sibling, a brother, Mike. He is married to Barb. Mike is eleven years older than me. He began dating Barb when he was thirteen, and I was two, so Barb has been like a sister to me throughout life. This is a girly book, so I made Barb my sister. The hard, tragic, almost unbearable truth is Mike suffers from early-onset dementia, and Barb, from early-onset Alzheimer's.

I do have three children who were rambunctiously mischievous throughout their childhood and teenage years, but I am happy to announce they have surpassed their father's and my wildest expectations, superseding us in education, strength, courage, and character. My oldest daughter earned a master's degree and has a resume grown men would kill for. She worked in the professional sports arena (Phillies, Nationals, Orioles, Capitals, Wizards, and Rams). My son is an attorney. (He is also a poker player and pretty good golfer.) My youngest daughter grew up to challenge her father and I as much (if not more) than her two older siblings. She did become a teacher and is currently completing her doctorate in Special Education. Yes, I remain a royal pain in the butt to them, but no one will ever love them like their mother.

Finally, Jody and Val do not live by me. They were my first friends. Val and I played together in the nursery of St Luke's Church in Erie, Pennsylvania alongside our mothers who attended mass there. Jody moved into my childhood neighborhood when she was two, and I was three. These two women are both brilliant, yet so interestingly opposite in nature that I transplanted them into my adult neighborhood. They remain the greatest of friends from afar. I love them both.

All other friend characters, from Carol and Carolyn to Doctor Jim, are real except for Evy and Ellie (who are the culmination of all my friends), and Janice Everglade (whom I hope I never meet). Reah and Natasha are not the real names of the two friends who broke my heart. Our parting was exaggerated for interest, but I do still struggle over the loss of their friendship. I have come to realize we were friends at a time when we needed each other most. I must trust God's wisdom, wish them the best in life, and carry on.

One final note, I am truly a girl's girl and wonderfully blessed with great friends. The one thing I am sure of in life is that the friends I do have would move bodies for me—and I, for them.

Made in the USA
Monee, IL
02 October 2020

43784104R00150